THE GUN-BRAND

JAMES B. HENDRYX

AF473264

The Gun-Brand

James B. Hendryx

© 1st World Library, 2007
PO Box 2211
Fairfield, IA 52556
www.1stworldlibrary.com
First Edition

LCCN: 2007927835

Softcover ISBN: 978-1-4218-4551-7
Hardcover ISBN: 978-1-4218-4467-1
eBook ISBN: 978-1-4218-4635-4

Purchase *"The Gun-Brand"*
as a traditional bound book at:
www.1stWorldLibrary.com/purchase.asp?ISBN=978-1-4218-4551-7

1st World Library is a literary, educational organization dedicated to:

- Creating a free internet library of downloadable ebooks
- Hosting writing competitions and offering book publishing scholarships.

Interested in more 1st World Library books?
contact: literacy@1stworldlibrary.com
Check us out at: www.1stworldlibrary.com

1st World Library Literary Society

Giving Back to the World

"If you want to work on the core problem, it's early school literacy."

- James Barksdale, former CEO of Netscape

"No skill is more crucial to the future of a child, or to a democratic and prosperous society, than literacy."

- Los Angeles Times

"Literacy... means far more than learning how to read and write... The aim is to transmit... knowledge and promote social participation."

- UNESCO

"Literacy is not a luxury, it is a right and a responsibility. If our world is to meet the challenges of the twenty-first century we must harness the energy and creativity of all our citizens."

- President Bill Clinton

"Parents should be encouraged to read to their children, and teachers should be equipped with all available techniques for teaching literacy, so the varying needs and capacities of individual kids can be taken into account."

- Hugh Mackay

CONTENTS

CHAPTER I

THE CALL OF THE RAW

Seated upon a thick, burlap-covered bale of freight—a "piece," in the parlance of the North—Chloe Elliston idly watched the loading of the scows. The operation was not new to her; a dozen times within the month since the outfit had swung out from Athabasca Landing she had watched from the muddy bank while the half-breeds and Indians unloaded the big scows, ran them light through whirling rock-ribbed rapids, carried the innumerable pieces of freight upon their shoulders across portages made all but impassable by scrub timber, oozy muskeg, and low sand-mountains, loaded the scows again at the foot of the rapid and steered them through devious and dangerous miles of swift-moving white-water, to the head of the next rapid.

They are patient men—these water freighters of the far North. For more than two centuries and a quarter they have sweated the wilderness freight across these same portages. And they are sober men—when civilization is behind them—far behind.

Close beside Chloe Elliston, upon the same piece, Harriet Penny, of vague age, and vaguer purpose, also watched the loading of the scows. Harriet Penny was Chloe Elliston's one concession to convention—excess baggage, beyond the outposts, being a creature of fear. Upon another piece, Big Lena, the gigantic Swedish Amazon who, in the capacity of general factotum, had accompanied Chloe Elliston over half the world, stared stolidly at the river.

Having arrived at Athabasca Landing four days after the departure of the Hudson Bay Company's annual brigade, Chloe had engaged transportation into the North in the scows of an independent. And, when he heard of this, the old factor at the post shook his head dubiously, but when the girl pressed him for the reason, he shrugged and remained silent. Only when the outfit was loaded did the old man whisper one sentence:

"Beware o' Pierre Lapierre."

Again Chloe questioned him, and again he remained silent. So, as the days passed upon the river trail, the name of Pierre Lapierre was all but forgotten in the menace of rapids and the monotony of portages. And now the last of the great rapids had been run—the rapid of the Slave—and the scows were almost loaded.

Vermilion, the boss scowman, stood upon the running-board of the leading scow and directed the stowing of the freight. He was a picturesque figure—Vermilion. A squat, thick half-breed, with eyes set wide apart beneath a low forehead bound tightly around with a handkerchief of flaming silk.

A heavy-eyed Indian, moving ponderously up the rough plank with a piece balanced upon his shoulders, missed his footing and fell with a loud splash into the water. The Indian scrambled clumsily ashore, and the piece was rescued, but not before a perfect torrent of French-English-Indian profanity had poured from the lips of the ever-versatile Vermilion. Harriet Penny shrank against the younger woman and shuddered.

"Oh!" she gasped, "he's swearing!"

"No!" exclaimed Chloe, in feigned surprise. "Why, I believe he is!"

Miss Penny flushed. "But, it is terrible! Just listen!"

"For Heaven's sake, Hat! If you don't like it, why do you listen?"

"But he ought to be stopped. I am sure the poor Indian did not *try* to fall in the river."

Chloe made a gesture of impatience. "Very well, Hat; just look up the ordinance against swearing on Slave River, and report him to Ottawa."

"But I'm afraid! He—the Hudson Bay Company's man—told us not to come."

Chloe straightened up with a jerk. "See here, Hat Penny! Stop your snivelling! What do you expect from rivermen? Haven't the seven hundred miles of water trail taught you *anything*? And, as for being afraid—I don't care *who* told us not to come! I'm an Elliston, and I'll go whereever I want to go! This isn't a pleasure trip. I came up here for a purpose. Do you think I'm going to be scared out by the first old man that wags his head and shrugs his shoulders? Or by any other man! Or by any swearing that I can't understand, or any that I can, either, for that matter! Come on, they're waiting for this bale."

Chloe Elliston's presence in the far outlands was the culmination of an ideal, spurred by dissuasion and antagonism into a determination, and developed by longing into an obsession. Since infancy the girl had been left much to her own devices. Environment, and the prescribed course at an expensive school, should have made her pretty much what other girls are, and an able satellite to her mother, who managed to remain one of the busiest women of the Western metropolis—doing absolutely nothing—but, doing it with *eclat*.

The girl's father, Blair Elliston, from his desk in a luxurious office suite, presided over the destiny of the Elliston fleet of yellow-stack tramps that poked their noses into queer ports and put to sea with queer cargoes—cargoes that smelled sweet and spicy, with the spice of the far South Seas. Office sailor though he was, Blair Elliston commanded the respect of even the roughest of his polyglot crews—a respect not wholly uncommingled with fear.

For this man was the son of old "Tiger" Elliston, founder of the fleet. The man who, shoulder to shoulder with Brooke, the elder, put the fear of God in the hearts of the pirates, and swept wide trade-lanes among the islands of terror-infested Malaysia. And through Chloe Elliston's veins coursed the blood of her world-roving ancestor. Her most treasured possession was a blackened and scarred oil portrait of the old sea-trader and adventurer, which always lay swathed in many wrappings in the bottom of her favourite trunk.

In her heart she loved and admired this grandfather, with a love and admiration that bordered upon idolatry. She loved the lean, hard features, and the cold, rapier-blade eyes. She loved the name men called him; Tiger Elliston, an earned name—that. The name of a man who, by his might and the strength and mastery of him, had won his place in the world of the men who dare.

Since babyhood she had listened with awe to tales of him;

and the red-letter days of her childhood's calendar were the days upon which her father would take her down to the docks, past great windowless warehouses of concrete and sheet-iron, where big glossy horses stood harnessed to high-piled trucks—past great tiers of bales and boxes between which trotted hurrying, sweating men—past the clang and clash of iron truck wheels, the rattle of chains, the shriek of pulleys, and the loud-bawled orders in strange tongues. Until, at last, they would come to the great dingy hulk of the ship and walk up the gangway and onto the deck, where funny yellow and brown men, with their hair braided into curious pigtails, worked with ropes and tackles and called to other funny men with bright-coloured ribbons braided into their beards.

Almost as she learned to walk she learned to pick out the yellow stacks of "papa's boats," learned their names, and the names of their captains, the bronzed, bearded men who would take her in their laps, holding her very awkwardly and very, very carefully, as if she were something that would break, and tell her stories in deep, rumbly voices. And nearly always they were stories of the Tiger—"yer gran'pap, leetle missey," they would say. And then, by palms, and pearls, and the fires of blazing mountains, they would swear "He wor a man!"

To the helpless horror of her mother, the genuine wonder of her many friends, and the ill-veiled amusement and approval of her father, a month after the doors of her *alma mater* closed behind her, she took passage on the *Cora Blair*, the oldest and most disreputable-looking yellow stack of them all, and hied her for a year's sojourn among the spicy lotus-ports of the dreamy Southern Ocean—there to hear at first hand from the men who knew him, further deeds of Tiger Elliston.

To her, on board the battered tramp, came gladly the men

of power—the men whose spoken word in their polyglot domains was more feared and heeded than decrees of emperors or edicts of kings. And there, in the time-blackened cabin that had once been *his* cabin, these men talked and the girl listened while her eyes glowed with pride as they recounted the exploits of Tiger Elliston. And, as they talked, the hearts of these men warmed, and the years rolled backward, and they swore weird oaths, and hammered the thick planks of the chart-table with bangs of approving fists, and invoked the blessings of strange gods upon the soul of the Tiger—and their curses upon the souls of his enemies.

Nor were these men slow to return hospitality, and Chloe Elliston was entertained royally in halls of lavish splendour, and plied with costly gifts and rare. And honoured by the men, and the sons and daughters of men who had fought side by side with the Tiger in the days when the yellow sands ran red, and tall masts and white sails rose like clouds from the blue fog of the cannon-crashing powder-smoke.

So, from the lips of governors and potentates, native princes and rajahs, the girl learned of the deeds of her grandsire, and in their eyes she read approval, and respect, and reverence even greater than her own—for these were the men who knew him. But, not alone from the mighty did she learn. For, over rice-cakes and *poi*, in the thatched hovels of Malays, Kayans, and savage Dyaks, she heard the tale from the lips of the vanquished men—men who still hated, yet always respected, the reddened sword of the Tiger.

The year Chloe Elliston spent among the copra-ports of the South Seas was the shaping year of her destiny. Never again were the standards of her compeers to be her standards—never again the measure of the world of convention to be her measure. For, in her heart the awakened spirit of Tiger Elliston burned and seared like a living flame, calling for other wilds to conquer, other savages to subdue—to crush down, if need be, that it might build up into the very civilization of which the unconquerable spirit is the forerunner, yet which, in realization, palls and deadens it to extinction.

For social triumphs the girl cared nothing. The heart of her felt the irresistible call of the raw. She returned to the land of her birth and deliberately, determinedly, in the face of opposition, ridicule, advice, and command—as Tiger Elliston, himself, would have done—she cast about until she found the raw, upon the rim of the Arctic. And, with the avowed purpose of carrying education and civilization to the Indians of the far North, turned her back upon the world-fashionable, and without fanfare or trumpetry, headed into the land of primal things.

When the three women had taken their places in the head scow, Vermilion gave the order to shove off, and with the swarthy crew straining at the rude sweeps, the heavy scows threaded their way into the North.

Once through the swift water at the tail of Slave Rapids, the four scows drifted lazily down the river. The scowmen distributed themselves among the pieces in more or less comfortable attitudes and slept. In the head scow only the boss and the three women remained awake.

"Who is Pierre Lapierre?" Chloe asked suddenly.

The man darted her a searching glance and shrugged. "Pierre Lapierre, she free-trader," he answered. "Dees scow, she Pierre Lapierre scow."

If Chloe was surprised at this bit of information, she succeeded admirably in disguising her feelings. Not so Harriet Penny, who sank back among the freight pieces to stare fearfully into the face of the younger woman.

"Then you are Pierre Lapierre's man? You work for him?"

The man nodded. "On de reevaire I'm run de scow—me—Vermilion! I'm tak' de reesk. Lapierre, she tak' de money." The man's eyes glinted wickedly.

"Risk? What risk?" asked the girl.

Again the man eyed her shrewdly and laughed. "Das plent' reesk—on de reevaire. De scow—me'be so, she heet de rock in de rapids—bre'k all to hell—*Voila*!" Somehow the words did not ring true.

"You hate Lapierre!" The words flashed swift, taking the man by surprise.

"*Non*! *Non*!" he cried, and Chloe noticed that his glance flashed swiftly over the sprawling forms of the five sleeping scowmen.

"And you are afraid of him," the girl added before he could frame a reply.

A sudden gleam of anger leaped into the eyes of the half-breed. He seemed on the point of speaking, but with an unintelligible muttered imprecation he relapsed into sullen silence. Chloe had purposely baited the man, hoping in his anger he would blurt out some bit of information concerning the mysterious Pierre Lapierre. Instead, the man crouched silent, scowling, with his gaze fixed upon the forms of the scowmen.

Had the girl been more familiar with the French half-breeds of the outlands she would have been suspicious of the man's sudden taciturnity under stress of anger—suspicious, also, of the gradual shifting that had been going on for days among the crews of the scows. A shifting that indicated Vermilion was selecting the crew of his own scow with an eye to a purpose—a purpose that had not altogether to do with the scow's safe conduct through white-water. But Chloe had taken no note of the personnel of the scowmen, nor of the fact that the freight of the head scow consisted only of pieces that obviously contained provisions, together with her own tent and sleeping outfit, and several burlapped pieces marked with the name "MacNair." Idly she wondered who MacNair was, but refrained from asking.

The long-gathering twilight deepened as the scows floated northward. Vermilion's face lost its scowl, and he smoked in silence—a sinister figure, thought the girl, as he crouched in the bow, his dark features set off to advantage by his flaming head-band.

Into the stillness crept a sound—the far-off roar of a rapid. Sullen, and dull, it scarce broke the monotony of the silence—low, yet ever increasing in volume.

"Another portage?" wearily asked the girl.

Vermilion shook his head. "*Non*, eet ees de Chute. Ten miles of de wild, fast wataire, but safe—eef you know de way. Me—Vermilion—I'm tak' de scow t'rough a hondre tam—*bien*!"

"But, you can't make it in the dark!"

Vermilion laughed. "We mak' de camp to-night. To-mor', we run de Chute." He reached for the light pole with which he indicated the channel to the steersman, and beat sharply upon the running-board that formed the gunwale of the scow. Sleepily the five sprawling forms stirred, and awoke to consciousness. Vermilion spoke a guttural jargon of words and the men fumbled the rude sweeps against the tholes. The other three scows drifted lazily in the rear and, standing upon the running-board, Vermilion roared his orders. Figures in the scows stirred, and sweeps thudded against thole-pins. The roar of the Chute was loud, now—hoarse, and portentous of evil.

The high banks on either side of the river drew closer together, the speed of the drifting scows increased, and upon the dark surface of the water tiny whirlpools appeared. Vermilion raised the pole above his head and pointed toward a narrow strip of beach that showed dimly at the foot of the high bank, at a point only a few hundred yards above the dark gap where the river plunged between the upstanding rocks of the Chute.

Looking backward, Chloe watched the three scows with their swarthy crews straining at the great sweeps. Here was action—life! Primitive man battling against the unbending forces of an iron wilderness. The red blood leaped through the girl's veins as she realized that this life was to be her life—this wilderness to be her wilderness. Hers to bring under the book, and its primitive children, hers—to govern by a rule of thumb!

Suddenly she noticed that the following scows were much nearer shore than her own, and also, that they were being rapidly out-distanced. She glanced quickly toward shore. The scow was opposite the strip of beach toward which the others were slowly but surely drawing. The scow seemed motionless, as upon the surface of a mill-pond, but the beach, and the high bank beyond, raced past to disappear in the deepening gloom. The figures in the following scows—the scows themselves—blurred into the shore-line. The beach was gone. Rocks appeared, jagged, and high—close upon either hand.

In a sudden panic, Chloe glanced wildly toward Vermilion, who crouched in the bow, pole in hand, and with set face, stared into the gloom ahead. Swiftly her glance travelled over the crew—their faces, also, were set, and they stood at the sweeps, motionless, but with their eyes fixed upon the pole of the pilot. Beyond Vermilion, in the forefront, appeared wave after wave of wildly tossing water. For just an instant the scow hesitated, trembled through its length, and with the leaping waves battering against its bottom and sides, plunged straight into the maw of the Chute!

CHAPTER II

VERMILION SHOWS HIS HAND

Down, down through the Chute raced the heavily loaded scow, seeming fairly to leap from wave to wave in a series of tremendous shocks, as the flat bottom rose high in the fore and crashed onto the crest of the next wave, sending a spume of stinging spray high into the air. White-water curled over the gunwale and sloshed about in the bottom. The air was chill, and wet—like the dead air of a rock-cavern.

Chloe Elliston knew one moment of swift fear. And then, the mighty roar of the waters; the mad plunging of the scow between the towering walls of rock; the set, tense face of Vermilion as he stared into the gloom; the laboured breathing of the scowmen as they strained at the sweeps, veering the scow to the right, or to the left, as the rod of the pilot indicated; the splendid battle of it; the wild exhilaration of fighting death on death's own stamping ground flung all thought of fear aside, and in the girl's heart surged the wild, fierce joy of living, with life itself at stake.

For just an instant Chloe's glance rested upon her companions; Big Lena sat scowling murderously at Vermilion's broad back. Harriet Penny had fainted and lay with the back of her head awash in the shallow bilge water. A strange *alter ego*—elemental—primordial—had taken possession of Chloe. Her eyes glowed, and her heart thrilled at the sight of the tense, vigilant figure of Vermilion, and the sweating, straining scowmen. For the helpless form of Harriet Penny she felt only contempt—the savage, intolerant contempt of the strong for the weak among firstlings.

The intoxication of a new existence was upon her, or, better, a world-old existence—an existence that was new when the world was new. In that moment, she was a throw-back of a million years, and through her veins fumed the ferine blood of her paleolithic forebears. What is life but proof of the fitness to live? Death, but defeat.

On rushed the scow, leaping, crashing from wave to wave, into the Northern night. And, as it rushed and leaped and crashed, it bore two women, their garments touching, but between whom interposed a whole world of creeds and fabrics.

Suddenly, Chloe sensed a change. The scow no longer leaped and crashed, and the roar of the rapids grew faint. No longer the form of Vermilion appeared couchant, tense; and, among the scowmen, one laughed. Chloe drew a deep breath, and a slight shudder shook her frame. She glanced about her in bewilderment, and, reaching swiftly down, raised the inert form of Harriet Penny and rested it gently against her knees.

The darkness of night had settled upon the river. Stars twinkled overhead. The high, scrub-timbered shore loomed formless and black, and the flat bottom of the scow rasped harshly on gravel. Vermilion leaped ashore, followed by the scowmen, and Chloe assisted Big Lena with the still unconscious form of Harriet Penny. As if by magic, fires flared out upon the shingle, and in an incredibly short time the girl found herself seated upon her bed-roll inside her mosquito-barred tent of balloon silk. The older woman had revived and lay, a dejected heap, upon her blankets, and out in front Big Lena was stooping over a fire. Beyond, upon the gravel, the fires of the scowmen flamed red, and threw wavering reflections upon the black water of the river.

Chloe was seized with a strange unrest. The sight of Harriet Penny irritated her. She stepped from the tent and filled her lungs with great drafts of the spruce-laden night-breeze that wafted gently out of the mysterious dark, and rippled the surface of the river until little waves slapped softly against the shore in tiny whisperings of the unknown—whisperings that called, and were understood by the new awakened self within her.

She glanced toward the fires of the rivermen where the dark-skinned, long-haired sons of the wild squatted close about the flames over which pots boiled, grease fried, and chunks of red meat browned upon the ends of long toasting-sticks. The girl's heart leaped with the wild freedom of it. A sense of might and of power surged through her veins. These men were her men—hers to command. Savages and half-savages whose work it was to do her bidding—and who performed their work well. The night was calling her—the vague, portentous night of the land beyond outposts. Slowly she passed the fires, and on along the margin of the river whose waters, black and forbidding, reached into the North.

"The unconquered North," she breathed, as she stood upon a water-lapped boulder and gazed into the impenetrable dark. And, as she gazed, before her mind's eye rose a vision. The scattered teepees of the Northland, smoke-blackened, filthy, stinking with the reek of ill-tanned skins, resolved themselves into a village beside a broad, smooth-flowing river.

The teepees faded, and in their place appeared rows of

substantial log cabins, each with its door-yard of neatly trimmed grass, and its beds of gay flowers. Broad streets separated the rows. The white spire of a church loomed proudly at the end of a street. From the doorways dark, full-bodied women smiled happily—their faces clean, and their long, black hair caught back with artistic bands of quill embroidery, as they called to the clean brown children who played light-heartedly in the grassed dooryards. Tall, lean-shouldered men, whose swarthy faces glowed with the love of their labour, toiled gladly in fields of yellow grain, or sang and called to one another in the forest where the ring of their axes was drowned in the crash of falling trees.

Her vision of the North—the conquered North—her North!

As Sir James Brooke and Tiger Elliston overthrew barbarism and established in its place an island empire of civilization, so would she supersede savagery with culture. But, her empire of the North should be an empire founded not upon blood, but upon humanity and brotherly love.

The girl started nervously. Her brain-picture resolved into the formless dark. From the black waters, almost at her feet, sounded, raucous and loud, the voice of the great loon. Frenzied, maniacal, hideous, rang the night-shattering laughter. The uncouth mockery of the raw—the defiance of the unconquerable North!

With a shudder, Chloe turned and fled toward the red-flaring fires. In that moment a feeling of defeat surged over her—of heart-sickening hopelessness. The figures at the fires were unkempt, dirty, revolting, as they gouged and tore at the half-cooked meat into which their yellow fangs drove deep, as the red blood squirted and trickled from the corners of their mouths to drip unheeded upon the sweat-stiffened cotton of their shirts. Savages! And she, Chloe Elliston, at the very gateway of her empire, fled incontinently to the protection of their fires!

Wide awake upon her blankets, in the smudge-pungent tent where her two companions slept heavily, Chloe sat late into the night staring through the mosquito-barred entrance toward the narrow strip of beach where the dying fires of the scowmen glowed sullenly in the darkness, pierced now and again by the fitful flare of a wind-whipped brand. Two still forms wrapped in ragged blankets, lay like logs where sleep had overcome them.

A short distance removed from the others, the fire of Vermilion burned brightly. Between this fire and a heavily smoking smudge, four men played cards upon a blanket spread upon the ground. Silently, save for an occasional grunt or mumbled word, they played—dealing, tossing into the centre the amount of their bets, leaning forward to rake in a pot, or throwing down their cards in disgust, to await the next deal.

The scene was intrinsically savage. At the end of the day's work, primitive man followed primitive instinct. Gorged to repletion, they slept, or wasted their substance with the improvidence of jungle-beasts. And these were the men Chloe Elliston had pictured labouring joyously in the upbuilding of homes! Once more the feeling of hopelessness came over her—seemed smothering, stifling her. And a great wave of longing carried her back to the land of her own people—the land of convention and sophistry.

Could it be that they were right? They who had scoffed, and ridiculed, and forbade her? What could *she* do in the refashioning of a world-old wild—one woman against the established creeds of an iron wilderness? Where, now, were her dreams of empire, her ideals, and her castles in Spain? Was she to return, broken on the wheel? Crushed between the adamantine millstones of things as they ought not to be?

The resolute lips drooped, a hot salt tear blurred Vermilion's camp-fire and distorted the figures of the gambling scowmen. She closed her eyes tightly. The writhing green shadow-shapes lost form, dimmed, and resolved themselves into an image—a lean, lined face with rapier-blade eyes gazed upon her from the blackness—the face of Tiger Elliston!

Instantly, the full force and determination of her surged through the girl's veins anew. The drooping lips stiffened. Her heart sang with the joy of conquest. The tight-pressed lids flew open, and for a long time she watched the shadow-dance of the flames on her tent wall. Dim, and elusive, and far away faded the dancing shadow-shapes—and she slept.

Not so Vermilion, who, when his companions tired of their game and sought their blankets, sat and stared into the embers of his dying fire. The half-breed was troubled. As boss of Pierre Lapierre's scowmen, a tool of a master mind, a unit of a system, he had prospered. But, no longer was he a unit of a system. From the moment Chloe Elliston had bargained with him for the transportation of her outfit into the wilderness, the man's brain had been active in formulating a plan.

This woman was rich. One who is not rich cannot afford to transport thirty-odd tons of outfit into the heart of the wilderness, at the tariff of fifteen cents the pound. So, throughout the days of the journey, the man gazed with avarice upon the piles of burlapped pieces, while his brain devised the scheme. Thereafter, in the dead of night occurred many whispered consultations, as Vermilion won over his men. He chose shrewdly, for these men knew Pierre Lapierre, and well they knew what portion would be theirs should the scheme of Vermilion miscarry.

At last, the selection had been made, and five of the most desperate and daring of all the rivermen had, by the lure of much gold, consented to cast loose from the system and "go it alone." The first daring move in the undertaking had succeeded—a move that, in itself, bespoke the desperate character of its perpetrators, for it was no accident that sent the head scow plunging down through the Chute in the darkness.

But, in the breast of Vermilion, as he sat alone beside his camp-fire, was no sense of elation—and in the heart of him was a great fear. For, despite the utmost secrecy among the conspirators, the half-breed knew that even at that moment, somewhere to the northward, Pierre Lapierre had learned of his plot.

Eight days had elapsed since the mysterious disappearance of Chenoine—and Chenoine, it was whispered, was half-brother to Pierre Lapierre. Therefore, Vermilion crouched beside his camp-fire and cursed the slowness of the coming of the day. For well he knew that when a man double-crossed Pierre Lapierre, he must get away with it—or die. Many had died. The black eyes flashed dangerously. He—Vermilion—would get away with it! He glanced toward the sleeping forms of the five scowmen and shuddered. He, Vermilion, knew that he was afraid to sleep!

For an instant he thought of abandoning the plan. It was not too late. The other scows could be run through in the morning, and, if Pierre Lapierre came, would it not be plain that Chenoine had lied? But, even with the thought, the avaricious gleam leaped into the man's eyes, and with a muttered imprecation, he greeted the first faint light of dawn.

Chloe Elliston opened her eyes sleepily in answer to a gruff call from without her tent. A few minutes later she stepped out into the grey of the morning, followed by her two companions. Vermilion was waiting for her as he watched the scowmen breaking open the freight pieces and making up hurried trail-packs of provisions.

"Tam to mush!" sad the man tersely.

"But where are the other scows?" asked Chloe, glancing toward the bank where the scow was being rapidly unloaded. "And what is the meaning of this? Here, you!" she cried, as a half-breed ripped the burlap from a bale. "Stop that! That's mine!" By her side, Vermilion laughed, a short, harsh laugh, and the girl turned.

"De scow, she not com'. We leave de rivaire. We tak' 'long de grub, eh?" The man's tone was truculent—insulting.

Chloe flushed with anger. "I am not going to leave the river! Why should I leave the river?"

Again the man laughed; there was no need for concealment now. "Me, Vermilion, I'm know de good plac' back in de hills. We go for stay dere till you pay de money."

"Money? What money?"

"Un hondre t'ousan' dollaire—cash! You pay, Vermilion—he tak' you back. You no pay—" The man shrugged significantly.

The girl stared, dumbfounded. "What do you mean? One hundred thousand dollars! Are you crazy?"

The man stepped close, his eyes gleaming wickedly. "You reech. You pay un hondre t'ousan' dollaire, or, ba gar, you nevaire com' out de bush!"

Chloe laughed in derision. "Oh! I am kidnapped! Is that it? How romantic!" The man scowled. "Don't be a fool, Vermilion! Do you suppose I came into this country with a hundred thousand dollars in cash—or even a tenth of that amount?"

The man shrugged indifferently. "*Non*, but you mak' de write on de papaire, an' Menard, he tak' heem to de bank—Edmonton—Preence Albert. He git de money. By-m-by, two mont', me'be, he com' back. Den, Vermilion, he tak' you close to de H.B. post—*bien*! You kin go hom', an' Vermilion, he go ver' far away."

Chloe suddenly realized that the man was in earnest. Her eyes flashed over the swarthy, villainous faces of the scowmen, and the seriousness of the situation dawned upon her. She knew, now, that the separating of the scows was the first move in a deep-laid scheme. Her brain worked rapidly. It was evident that the men on the other scows were not party to the plot, or Vermilion would not have risked running the Chute in the darkness. She glanced up the river. Would the other scows come on? It was her one hope. She must play for time. Harriet Penny sobbed aloud, and Big Lena glowered. Again Chloe laughed into the scowling face of the half-breed. "What about the Mounted? When they find I am missing there will be an investigation."

For answer, Vermilion pointed toward the river-bank, where the men were working with long poles in the overturning of the scow. "We shove heem out in de rivaire. Wen dey fin', dey t'ink she mak' for teep ovaire in de Chute. *Voila*! Dey say: 'Een de dark she run on de rock'—*pouf*!" he signified eloquently the instantaneous snuffing out of lives. Even as he spoke the scow overturned with a splash, and the scowmen pushed it out into the river, where it floated bottom upward, turning lazily in the grip of an eddy. The girl's heart sank as her eyes rested upon the overturned scow. Vermilion had plotted cunningly. He drew closer now—leering horribly.

"You mak' write on de papaire—*non*?"

A swift anger surged in the girl's heart. "No!" she cried. "I will not write! I have no such amount in any bank this side of San Francisco! But if I had a million dollars, you would not get a cent! You can't bluff me!"

Vermilion sprang toward her with a snarl; but before he could lay hands upon her Big Lena, with a roar of rage, leaped past the girl and drove a heavy stick of firewood straight at the half-breed's head. The man ducked swiftly, and the billet thudded against his shoulder, staggering him. Instantly two of the scowmen threw themselves upon the woman and bore her to the ground, where she fought, tooth and nail, while they pinioned her arms. Vermilion, his face livid, seized Chloe roughly. The girl shrank in terror from the grip of the thick, grimy fingers and the glare of the envenomed eyes that blazed from the distorted, brutish features.

"Stand back!"

The command came sharp and quick in a low, hard voice—the voice of authority. Vermilion whirled with a snarl. Uttering a loud cry of fear, one of the scowmen dashed into the bush, closely followed by two of his companions. Two men advanced swiftly and noiselessly from the cover of the scrub. Like a flash, the half-breed jerked a revolver from his belt and fired. Chenoine fell dead. Before Vermilion could fire again the other man, with the slightest perceptible movement of his right hand, fired from the hip. The revolver dropped from the half-breed's hand. He swayed unsteadily for a few seconds, his eyes widening into a foolish, surprised stare. He half-turned and opened his lips to speak. Pink foam reddened the corners of his mouth and spattered in tiny drops upon his chin. He gasped for breath with a spasmodic heave of the shoulders. A wheezing, gurgling sound issued from his throat, and a torrent of blood burst from his lips and splashed upon the ground. With eyes wildly rolling, he clutched frantically at the breast of his cotton shirt and pitched heavily into the smouldering ashes of the fire at the feet of the stranger.

But few seconds had elapsed since Chloe felt the hand of Vermilion close about her wrist—tense, frenzied seconds, to the mind of the girl, who gazed in bewilderment upon the bodies of the two dead men which lay almost touching each other.

The man who had ordered Vermilion to release her, and who had fired the shot that had killed him, stood calmly watching four lithe-bodied canoemen securely bind the arms of the two scowmen who had attacked Big Lena.

So sudden had been the transition from terror to relief in her heart that the scene held nothing of repugnance to the girl, who was conscious only of a feeling of peace and security. She even smiled into the eyes of her deliverer, who had turned his attention from his canoemen and stood before her, his soft-brimmed Stetson in his hand.

"Oh! I—I thank you!" exclaimed the girl, at a loss for words.

The man bowed low. "It is nothing. I am glad to have been of some slight service." Something in the tone of the well-modulated voice, the correct speech, the courtly manner, thrilled the girl strangely. It was all so unexpected—so out of place, here in the wild. She felt the warm colour mount to her face.

"Who are you?" she asked abruptly.

"I am Pierre Lapierre," answered the man in the same low voice.

In spite of herself, Chloe started slightly, and instantly she knew that the man had noticed. He smiled, with just an appreciable tightening at the corners of the mouth, and his eyes narrowed almost imperceptibly. He continued:

"And now, Miss Elliston, if you will retire to your tent for a few moments, I will have these removed." He indicated the bodies. "You see, I know your name. The good Chenoine told me. He it was who warned me of Vermilion's plot in time for me to frustrate it. Of course, I should have rescued you later. I hold myself responsible for the safe conduct of all who travel in my scows. But it would have been at the expense of much time and labour, and, very possibly, of human life as well—an incident regrettable always, but not always avoidable."

Chloe nodded, and, with her thoughts in a whirl of confusion, turned and entered her tent, where Harriet Penny lay sobbing hysterically, with her blankets drawn over her head.

CHAPTER III

PIERRE LAPIERRE

A half-hour later, when Chloe again ventured from the tent, all evidence of the struggle had disappeared. The bodies of the two dead men had been removed, and the canoemen were busily engaged in gathering together and restoring the freight pieces that had been ripped open by the scowmen.

Lapierre advanced to meet her, his carefully creased Stetson in hand.

"I have sent word for the other scows to come on at once, and in the meantime, while my men attend to the freight, may we not talk?"

Chloe assented, and the two seated themselves upon a log. It was then, for the first time that the girl noticed that one side of Lapierre's face—the side he had managed to keep turned from her—was battered and disfigured by some recent misadventure. Noticed, too, the really fine features of him—the dark, deep-set eyes that seemed to smoulder in their depths, the thin, aquiline nose, the shapely lips, the clean-cut lines of cheek and jaw.

"You have been hurt!" she cried. "You have met with an accident!"

The man smiled, a smile in which cynicism blended with amusement.

"Hardly an accident, I think, Miss Elliston, and, in any event, of small consequence." He shrugged a dismissal of the subject, and his voice assumed a light gaiety of tone.

"May we not become better acquainted, we two, who meet in this far place, where travellers are few and worth the knowing?" There was no cynicism in his smile now, and without waiting for a reply he continued: "My name you already know. I have only to add that I am an adventurer in the wilds—explorer of *hinterlands*, free-trader, freighter, sometime prospector—casual cavalier." He rose, swept the Stetson from his head, and bowed with mock solemnity.

"And now, fair lady, may I presume to inquire your mission in this land of magnificent wastes?" Chloe's laughter was genuine as it was spontaneous.

Lapierre's light banter acted as a tonic to the girl's nerves, harassed as they were by a month's travel through the fly-bitten wilderness. More—he interested her. He was different. As different from the half-breeds and Indian canoemen with whom she had been thrown as his speech was from the throaty guttural by means of which they exchanged their primitive ideas.

"Pray pause, Sir Cavalier," she smiled, falling easily into the gaiety of the man's mood. "I have ventured into your wilderness upon a most unpoetic mission. Merely the establishment of a school for the education and betterment of the Indians of the North."

A moment of silence followed the girl's words—a moment in which she was sure a hard, hostile gleam leaped into the man's eyes. A trick of fancy doubtless, she thought, for the next instant it had vanished. When he spoke, his air of light raillery was gone, but his lips smiled—a smile that seemed to the girl a trifle forced.

"Ah, yes, Miss Elliston. May I ask at whose instigation this school is to be established—and where?" He was not looking at her now, his eyes sought the river, and his face showed only a rather finely moulded chin, smooth-shaven—and the lips, with their smile that almost sneered.

Instantly Chloe felt that a barrier had sprung up between herself and this mysterious stranger who had appeared so opportunely out of the Northern bush. Who was he? What was the meaning of the old factor's whispered warning? And why should the mention of her school awake disapproval, or arouse his antagonism? Vaguely she realized that the sudden change in this man's attitude hurt. The displeasure, and opposition, and ridicule of her own people, and the surly indifference of the rivermen, she had overridden or ignored. This man she could not ignore. Like herself, he was an adventurer of untrodden ways. A man of fancy, of education and light-hearted raillery, and yet, a strong man, withal—a man of moment, evidently.

She remembered the sharp, quick words of authority—the words that caused the villainous Vermilion to whirl with a snarl of fear. Remembered also, the swift sure shot that had ended Vermilion's career, his absolute mastery of the situation, his lack of excitement or braggadocio, and the expressed regret over the necessity for killing the man. Remembered the abject terror in the eyes of those who fled into the bush at his appearance, and the servility of the canoemen.

As she glanced into the half-turned face of the man, Chloe saw that the sneering smile had faded from the thin lips as he waited her answer.

"At *my own* instigation." There was an underlying hardness of defiance in her words, and the firm, sun-reddened chin unconsciously thrust forward beneath the encircling mosquito net. She paused, but the man, expressionless, continued to gaze out over the surface of the river.

"I do not know exactly *where*," she continued, "but it will be *somewhere*. Wherever it will do the most good. Upon the bank of some river, or lake, perhaps, where the people of the wilderness may come and receive that which is theirs of right—"

"Theirs of right?" The man looked into her face, and Chloe saw that the thin lips again smiled—this time with a quizzical smile that hinted at tolerant amusement. The smile stung.

"Yes, theirs of right!" she flashed. "The education that was freely offered to me, and to you—and of which we availed ourselves."

For a long time the man continued to gaze in silence, and, when at length he spoke, it was to ask an entirely irrelevant question.

"Miss Elliston, you have heard my name before?"

The question came as a surprise, and for a moment Chloe hesitated. Then frankly, and looking straight into his eyes she answered:

"Yes, I have."

The man nodded, "I knew you had." He turned his injured eye quickly from the dazzle of the sunlight that flashed from the surface of the river, and Chloe saw that it was discoloured and bloodshot. She arose, and stepping to his side laid her hand upon his arm.

"You *are* hurt," she said earnestly, "your eye gives you pain."

Beneath her fingers the girl felt the play of strong muscles as the arm pressed against her hand. Their eyes met, and her heart quickened with a strange new thrill. Hastily she averted her glance and then—The man's arm suddenly was withdrawn and Chloe saw that his fist had clinched. With a rush the words brought back to him the scene in the trading-room of the post at Fort Rae. The low, log-room, piled high with the goods of barter. The great cannon stove. The two groups of dark-visaged Indians—his own Chippewayans, and MacNair's Yellow Knives, who stared in stolid indifference. The trembling, excited clerk. The grim chief trader, and the stern-faced factor who watched with approving eyes while two men fought in the wide cleared space between the rough counter and the high-piled bales of woollens and strouds.

Chloe Elliston drew back aghast. The thin lips of the man had twisted into a snarl of rage, and a living, bestial hate seemed fairly to blaze from the smouldering eyes, as Lapierre's thoughts dwelt upon the closing moments of that fight, when he felt himself giving ground before the hammering, smashing blows of Bob MacNair's big fists. Felt the tightening of the huge arms like steel bands about his body when he rushed to a clinch—bands that crushed and burned so that each sobbing breath seemed a blade, white-hot from the furnace, stabbing and searing into his tortured lungs. Felt the vital force and strength of him ebb and weaken so that the lean, slender fingers that groped for MacNair's throat closed feebly and dropped limp to dangle impotently from his nerveless arms. Felt the sudden release of the torturing bands of steel, the life-giving inrush of cool air, the dull pain as his dizzy body rocked to the shock of a crashing blow upon the jaw, the blazing flash of the blow that closed his eye, and, then—more soul-searing, and of deeper hurt than the blows that battered and marred—the feel of thick fingers twisted into the collar of his soft shirt. Felt himself shaken with an incredible ferocity that whipped his ankles against floor and counter edge. And, the crowning indignity of all—felt himself dragged like a flayed carcass the full length of the room, out of the door, and jerked to his feet upon the verge of the steep descent to the lake. Felt the propelling impact of the heavy boot that sent him crashing headlong into the underbrush through which he rolled and tumbled like a mealbag, to bring up suddenly in the cold water.

The whole scene passed through his brain as dreams flash—almost within the batting of an eye. Half-consciously, he saw the girl's sudden start, and the look of alarm upon her face as she drew back from the glare of his hate-flashing eyes and the bestial snarl of his lips. With an effort he composed himself:

"Pardon, Miss Elliston, I have frightened you with an uncouth show of savagery. It is a rough, hard country—this land of the wolf and the caribou. Primal instincts and brutish passions here are unrestrained—a fact responsible for my present battered appearance. For, as I said, it was no accident that marred me thus, unless, perchance, the prowling of the brute across my path may be attributed to accident—rather, I believe it was timed."

"The brute! Who, or what is the brute? And why should he harm you?"

"MacNair is his name—Bob MacNair." There was a certain tense hardness in the man's tone, and Chloe was conscious that the smouldering eyes were regarding her searchingly.

"MacNair," said the girl, "why, that is the name on

those bales!"

"What bales?"

"The bales in the scow—they are on the river-bank now."

"My scows carrying MacNair's freight!" cried the man, and motioning her to accompany him he walked rapidly to the bank where lay the four or five pieces, upon which Chloe had read the name. Lapierre dropped to his knees and regarded the pieces intently, suddenly he leaped to his feet with a laugh and called in the Indian tongue to one of his canoemen. The man brought him an ax, and raising it high, Lapierre brought it crashing upon the innocent-looking freight piece. There was a sound of smashing staves, a gurgle of liquid, and the strong odour of whiskey assailed their nostrils.

The piece was a keg, cunningly disguised as to shape, and covered with burlap. One by one the man attacked the other pieces marked with the name of MacNair, and as each cask was smashed, the whiskey gurgled and splashed and seeped into the ground. Chloe watched breathlessly until Lapierre finished, and with a smile of grim satisfaction, tossed the ax upon the ground.

"There is one consignment of firewater that will never be delivered," he said.

"What does it mean?" asked Chloe, and Lapierre noticed that her eyes were alight with interest. "Who is this MacNair, and—"

For answer Lapierre took her gently by the arm and led her back to the log.

"MacNair," he began, "is the most atrocious tyrant that ever breathed. Like myself, he is a free-trader—that is, he is not in the employ of the Hudson Bay Company. He is rich, and owns a permanent post of his own, to the northward, on Snare Lake, while I vend my wares under God's own canopy, here and there upon the banks of lakes and rivers."

"But why should he attack you?"

The man shrugged. "Why? Because he hates me. He hates any one who deals fairly with the Indians. His own Indians, a band of the Yellow Knives, together with an onscouring of Tantsawhoots, Beavers, Dog-ribs, Strongbows, Hares, Brushwoods, Sheep, and Huskies, he holds in abject peonage. Year in and year out he forces them to dig in his mines for their bare existence. Over on the Athabasca they call him Brute MacNair, and among the Loucheaux and Huskies he is known as The-Bad-Man-of-the-North.

"He pays no cash for labour, nor for fur, and he sees to it that his Indians are always hopelessly in his debt. He trades them whiskey. They are his. His to work, and to cheat, and to debauch, and to vent his rage upon—for his passions are the wild, unbridled passions of the fighting wolf. He kills! He maims! Or he allows to live! The Indians are his, body and soul. Their wives and their children are his. He owns them. *He* is the law!

"He warned me out of the North. I ignored that warning. The land is broad and free. There is room for all, therefore I brought in my goods and traded. And, because I refused to grind the poor savages under the iron heel of oppression, because I offer a meagre trifle over and above what is necessary for their bare existence, the brute hates me. He came upon me at Fort Rae, and there, in the presence of the factor, his clerk, and his chief trader, he fell upon me and beat me so that for three days I lay unable to travel."

"But the others!" interrupted the girl, "the factor and his men! Why did they allow it?"

Again the gleam of hate flashed in the man's eyes. "They allowed it because they are in league with him. They fear him. They fear his hold upon the Indians. So long as he maintains a permanent post a hundred and seventy-five miles to the northward—more than two hundred and fifty by the water trail—they know that he will not seriously injure the trade at Fort Rae. With me it is different. I trade here, and there, wherever the children of the wilderness are to be found. Therefore I am hated by the men of the Hudson Bay Company who would have been only too glad had MacNair killed me."

Chloe, who had listened eagerly to every word, leaped to her feet and looked at Lapierre with shining eyes. "Oh! I think it is splendid! You are brave, and you stand for the right of things! For the welfare of the Indians! I see now why the factor warned me against you! He wanted to discredit you."

Lapierre smiled. "The factor? What factor? And what did he tell you?"

"The factor at the Landing. 'Beware of Pierre Lapierre,' he said; and when I asked him who Pierre Lapierre was, and why I should beware of him, he shrugged his shoulders and would say nothing."

Lapierre nodded. "Ah yes—the company men—the factors and traders have no love for the free-trader. We cannot blame them. It is tradition. For nearly two and one-half centuries the company has stood for power and authority in the outlands—and has reaped the profits of the wild places. Let us be generous. It is an old and respectable institution. It deals fairly enough with the Indians—by its own measure of fairness, it is true—but fairly enough. With the company I have no quarrel.

"But with MacNair—" he stopped abruptly and shrugged. The gleam of hate that flashed in his eyes always at the mention of the name faded. "But why speak of him—surely there are more pleasant subjects," he smiled, "for instance your school—it interests me greatly."

"Interests you! I thought it displeased you! Surely a look of annoyance or suspicion leaped from your eyes when I mentioned my mission."

The man laughed lightly. "Yes? And can you blame me—when I thought you were in league with Brute MacNair? For, since his post was established, no independent save myself has dared to encroach upon even the borders of his empire."

Chloe Elliston flushed deeply. "And you thought I would league myself with a man like *that*?"

"Only for a moment. Stop and think. All my life I have lived in the North, and, except for a few scattered priests and missionaries, no one has pushed beyond the outposts for any purpose other than for gain. And the trader's gain is the Indian's loss—for, few deal fairly. Therefore, when I came upon your big outfit upon the very threshold of MacNair's domain, I thought, of course, this was some new machination of the brute. Even now I do not understand—the expense, and all. The Indians cannot afford to pay for education."

It was the girl's turn to laugh. A rippling, light-hearted laugh—the laughter of courage and youth. The barrier that had suddenly loomed between herself and this man of the North vanished in a breath. He had shown her her work, had pointed out to her a foeman worthy of her steel. She darted a swift glance toward Lapierre who sat staring into the fire. Would not this man prove an invaluable ally in her war of deliverance?

"Do not trouble yourself about the expense," she smiled. "I have money—'oodles of it,' as we used to say in school—millions, if I need them! And I'm going to fight this Brute MacNair until I drive him out of the North! And you? Will you help me to rid the country of this scourge and free the people from his tyranny? Together we could work wonders. For your heart is with the Indians, as mine is."

Again the girl glanced into the man's face and saw that the deep-set black eyes fairly glittered with enthusiasm and eagerness—an eagerness and enthusiasm that a keener observer than Chloe Elliston might have noticed, sprang into being suspiciously coincident with her mention of the millions. Lapierre did not answer at once, but deftly rolled a cigarette. The end of the cigarette glowed brightly as he filled his lungs and blew a plume of grey smoke into the air.

"Allow me a little time to think. For this is a move of importance, and to be undertaken not lightly. It is no easy task you have set yourself. It is possible you will not win—highly probable, in fact, for—"

"But I *shall* win! I am *right*—and upon my winning depends the future of a people! Think it over until tomorrow, if you will, but—" She paused abruptly, and her soft, hazel eyes peered searchingly into the depths of the restless black ones. "Your sympathies *are* with the Indians, aren't they?"

Lapierre tossed the half-smoked cigarette onto the ground. "Can you doubt it?" The man's eyes were not gleaming now, and into their depths had crept a look of ineffable sadness.

"They are my people," he said softly. "Miss Elliston, *I am an Indian*!"

CHAPTER IV

CHLOE SECURES AN ALLY

A shout from the bank heralded the appearance of the first scow, which was closely followed by the two others. When they had landed, Lapierre issued a few terse orders, and the scowmen leaped to his bidding. The overturned scow was righted and loaded, and the remains of the demolished whiskey-kegs burned. Lapierre himself assisted the three women to their places, and as Chloe seated herself near the bow, he smiled into her eyes.

"Vermilion was a good riverman, but so am I. Do you think you can trust your new pilot?"

Somehow, the words seemed to imply more than the mere steering of a scow. Chloe flushed slightly, hesitated a moment, and then returned the man's smile frankly.

"Yes," she answered gravely, "I know I can."

Their eyes met in a long look. Lapierre gave the command to shove off, and when the scows were well in the grip of the current, he turned again to the girl at his side. Their hands touched, and again Chloe was conscious of the strange, new thrill that quickened her heart-beats. She did not withdraw her hand, and the fingers of Lapierre closed about her palm.

He leaned toward her. "Only quarter Indian," he said softly. "My grandmother was the daughter of a great chief."

The girl felt the hot blood mount to her face and gently withdrew her hand. Somehow, she could not tell why, the words seemed good to hear. She smiled, and Lapierre, who was watching her intently, smiled in return.

"We are approaching quick water; we will cover many miles today, and tonight beside the camp-fire we will talk further."

Chloe's eyes searched the scows. "Where are the two who attacked Lena? Your men captured them."

Lapierre's smile hardened. "Those who deserted me for Vermilion? Oh, I—dismissed them from my service."

Hour after hour, as the scows rushed northward, Chloe watched the shores glide past; watched the swirling, boiling water of the river; watched the solemn-faced scowmen, and the silent, vigilant pilot; but most of all she watched the pilot, whose quick eye picked out the devious channel, and whose clear, alert brain directed, with a movement of the lancelike pole, the labours of the men at the sweeps.

She contrasted his manner—quiet, graceful, sure—with that of Vermilion, the very swing of whose pole proclaimed the vaunting, arrogant braggart. And she noted the difference in the attitude of the scowmen toward these two leaders. Their obedience to Vermilion's orders had been a surly, protesting obedience; while their obedience to Lapierre's slightest motion was the quiet, alert obedience that proclaimed him master of men, as his own silent vigilance proclaimed him master of the roaring waters.

When the sun finally dipped behind the barren scrub-topped hills, the scows were beached at the mouth of a deep ravine, from whose depths sounded the trickle of a tiny cascade. Lapierre assisted the women from the scow, issued a few short commands, and, as if by magic, a dozen fires flashed upon the beach, and in an incredibly short space of time Chloe found herself seated upon her blankets inside her mosquito-barred tent.

Supper over, Harriet Penny immediately sought her bed, and Lapierre led Chloe to a brightly burning camp-fire.

Nearby other fires burned, surrounded by dark, savage figures that showed indistinct in the half-light. The girl's eyes rested for a moment upon Lapierre, whose thin, handsome features, richly tanned by long exposure to the Northern winds and sun, presented a pleasing contrast to the swart flat faces of the rivermen, who sat in groups about their fires, or lay wrapped in their blankets upon the gravel.

"You have decided?" abruptly asked Chloe, in a voice of ill-concealed eagerness. Lapierre's face became at once grave, and he gazed sombrely into the fire.

"I have pondered deeply. Through the long hours, while the scow rushed into the North, there came to me a vision of my people. In the rocks, in the bush, and the ragged hills I saw it; and in the swirl of the mighty river. And the vision was good!"

The voice of the man's Indian grandmother spoke from his lips, and the soul of her glowed in his deep-set eyes.

"Even now *Sakhalee Tyee* speaks from the stars of the night sky. My people shall learn the wisdom of the white man. The power of the oppressor shall be broken, and the children of the far places shall come into their own."

The man's voice had dropped into the rhythmic intonation of the Indian orator, and his eyes were fixed upon the names that curled, lean and red, among the dry sticks of the camp-fire. Chloe gazed in fascination into the rapt face of this man of many moods. The soul of the girl caught the enthusiasm of his words, and she, too, saw the vision—saw it as she had seen it upon the wave-lapped rock of the river-bank.

"You will help me?" she cried; "will join forces with me in a war against the ruthless exploitation of a people who should be as free and unfettered as the air they breathe?"

Lapierre bent his gaze upon her face slowly, like one emerging from a trance.

"Yes," he answered deliberately; "it is of that I wish to speak. Let us consider the obstacles in our path—the matter of official interference. The government will soon learn of your activities, and the government is prone to look askance at any tampering with the Indians by an institution not connected with the Church or the State."

"I have my permit," Chloe answered, "and many commendatory letters from Ottawa. The men who rule were inclined to think I would accomplish nothing; but they were willing to let me try."

"That, then, disposes of our most serious difficulty. Will you tell me now where you intended to locate?"

"There is too much traffic upon the river," answered the girl. "The scow brigades pass and repass; and, at least until my little colony is fairly established, it must be located in some place uncontaminated by the presence of so rough, lawless, and drunken an element. As I told you before, I do not know where my ideal site is to be found. I had intended to talk the matter over with the factor at Fort Rae."

"What! That devil of a Haldane? The man who is hand-in-glove with Brute MacNair!"

"You forget," smiled the girl, "that until this day I never even heard of Brute MacNair."

The man smiled. "Very true. I had forgotten. But it is fortunate indeed that chance threw us together. I tremble to think what would have been your fate should you have acted upon the advice of Colin Haldane."

"But surely you know the country. You will advise me."

"Yes, I will advise you. I am with you in this venture; with you to the last gasp; with you heart and soul, until that devil MacNair is dead or driven out of the North, and his Indians scattered to the four winds."

"Scattered! Why scattered? Why not held together for their education and betterment? And you say you will be with me until MacNair is either dead or driven out of the North. What then—will you desert me then? This MacNair is only an obstacle in our path—an obstacle to be brushed aside that the real work may begin. Yet you spoke as though he were the main issue."

Lapierre interrupted her, speaking rapidly: "Yes, of course. Bear with me, I pray you. I spoke hastily, and without thinking. My feelings for the moment carried me away. As you see, the marks of the Brute's hands are still too fresh upon me to regard him impersonally—an obstacle, as it were. To me he is a brute! A fiend! A demon! I *hate* him!"

Lapierre shook a clenched fist toward the North, and the words fairly snarled between his lips. With an effort he controlled himself. "I have in mind the very place for your school, a spot accessible from all directions—the mouth of the Yellow Knife River, upon the north arm of Great Slave Lake. There you will be unmolested by the debauching rivermen, and yet within easy reach of any who may desire to take advantage of your school. The very place above all places! In the whole North you could not have chosen a better! And I shall accompany you, and direct the building of your houses and stockade.

"MacNair will learn shortly of your fort—everything is a 'fort' up here—and he will descend upon you like a ramping lion. When he finds you are a woman, he will do you no violence. He will scent at once a rival trading-post and will hurt your cause in every way possible; will use every means to discredit you among the Indians, and to discourage you. But even he will do a woman no physical harm.

"And right here let me caution you—do not temporize with him. He stands in the North for oppression; gain at any cost; for debauchery—everything that you do not. Between you and Brute MacNair there can be no truce. He is powerful. Do not for a moment underrate either his strength or his sagacity. He is a man of wealth, and his hold upon the Indians is absolute. I cannot remain with you, but through my Indians I shall keep in touch with you, work with you; and together we will accomplish the downfall of this brute of the North."

For a long time the two figures sat by the fire while the camp slept, and talked of many things. And when, well toward midnight, Chloe Elliston retired to her tent, she felt that she had known this man always. For it is the way of life that stress of events, and not duration of time, marks the measure of acquaintance and intimacy. Pierre Lapierre, Chloe Elliston had known but one day, and yet she believed that among all her acquaintances this man she knew best.

By the fire Lapierre's eyes followed the girl until she disappeared within the tent, and as he looked a huge figure arose from the deep shadows of the scrub, and with a hand grasping the flap of the tent, turned and stared, silent and grim and forbidding, straight into Lapierre's eyes.

The man turned away with a frown. The figure was Big Lena.

CHAPTER V

PLANS AND SPECIFICATIONS

At the mouth of the Slave River the outfit was transferred to twelve large freight canoes, each carrying three tons, and manned by six lean-shouldered canoemen, in charge of one Louis LeFroy, Lapierre's boss canoeman. Straight across the vast expanse of Great Slave Lake they headed, and skirting the shore of the north arm, upon the evening of the second day, entered the Yellow Knife River.

The site selected by Pierre Lapierre for Chloe Elliston's school was, in point of location, as the quarter-breed had said, an excellent one. Upon a level plateau at the top of the high bank that slants steeply to the water of the Yellow Knife River, a short distance above its mouth, Lapierre set the canoemen to cutting the timber and brush from a wide area. The girl had come into the North fully prepared for a long sojourn, and in her thirty-odd tons of outfit were found all tools necessary for the clearing of land and the erection of buildings. Brushwood and trees fell before the axes of the half-breeds and Indians, who worked in a sort of frenzy under the lashing drive of Lapierre's tongue; and the night skies glowed red in the flare of the flames where the brush and tree-tops burned in the clearing.

Two days later a rectangular clearing, three hundred by five hundred feet, was completed, and early in the morning of the third day Chloe stood beside Lapierre and looked over the cleared oblong with its piles of smoking grey ashes, and its groups of logs that lay ready to be rolled into place to form the walls of her buildings.

Lapierre seemed ill at ease. Immediately upon the arrival of the outfit he had dispatched two of his own Indians northward to spy upon the movements of MacNair, for the man made no secret of his desire to be well upon his way before the trader should learn of the building of the fort on the river.

It had been Chloe's idea to lay out her "village," as she called it, upon a rather elaborate scheme, the plans for which had been drawn by an architect whose clients' tastes ran to million-dollar "summer cottages" at Seashore-by-the-Sea.

First, there was to be the school itself, an ornate building of crossed rafters and overhanging eaves. Then the dormitories, two long, parallel buildings with halls, individual rooms, and baths—one for the women and one for men—the two to be connected by a common dining-hall in such a manner as to form three sides of a hollow square. Connected to the dining-hall was to be a commodious kitchen, and back of that a fully equipped carpenter-shop and a laundry.

There were also to be a trading-post, where the Indians could purchase supplies at cost; a six-room cottage for the accommodation of Big Lena, Miss Penny, and Chloe; and numerous three-room cabins for the housing of whole families of Indians, which the girl fondly pictured as flocking in from the wilderness to have the errors of their heathenish religion pointed out to them upon a brand-new blackboard, and the discomforts of their nomadic lives assuaged by an introduction to collapsible bath-tubs and the multiplication table. For hers was to be a mission as well as a school. Truly the souls north of sixty were destined to owe her much. For they borrow cheerfully, and repay—never.

So much for Chloe Elliston's plan. Lapierre, however, had his own eminently more practical, if less Utopian, ideas concerning the erection of a trading-post; for in the quarter-breed's mind the planting of an independent trading-post upon the very threshold of MacNair's wilderness empire was of far greater importance than the establishment of a school, or mission, or any other institution—especially when the post was one which he himself had set about to control. The man's eyes gleamed and the thin lips smiled as his glance rested momentarily upon the figure of the girl—the unwitting, and therefore the more powerful, weapon that chance had placed in his hands in his battle against MacNair.

His idea of a post was simplicity itself: One long, log trading-room with an ell for a storehouse, and a room—two at the most—in the rear for the accommodation of the three women. The whole to be erected in the centre of the clearing, and surrounded by a fifteen-foot log stockade.

Boldly he broached his plan.

"But this is *not* a trading-post!" objected the girl. "The store is a side issue and is to be conducted merely to permit those who take advantage of my school to obtain the necessities of life at a fair and reasonable price."

"Your words were well chosen, Miss Elliston. For if you begin to undersell the H.B.C., and more especially the independents, every Indian in the North will proceed to 'take advantage' of your school and of you also."

"But they are being robbed!"

Lapierre smiled. "They do not know it; they are used to it. Let me warn you that to tamper with existing trade schedules, except by one experienced in the commerce of the North, is to invite disaster. You will lose money!"

"But you told me that you yourself gave the Indians better bargains than either the Hudson Bay Company or MacNair."

"I know the North! And you may be assured the concessions are more nominal than real."

"Very well, then," flashed the girl. "My concessions will be more real than nominal, and of that you may be assured. If my store pays expenses, well and good!" And by the tone of the girl's voice, and the slight, unconscious out-thrust of her chin, Pierre Lapierre knew that the time was unpropitious for a further discussion of trade principles.

Chloe was speaking again: "But to return to the buildings—"

Lapierre interrupted her, speaking earnestly: "My dear Miss Elliston, consider the circumstances, the limitations." He tapped lightly the roll of blue-prints the girl held in her hand. "Those plans were made by a man who had not the slightest knowledge of conditions as they exist here."

"The buildings are to be very simple."

"Undoubtedly. But simplicity is relative. A building that would be considered simplicity itself in the States, might well be intricate beyond the possibility of construction here in the wilderness. Do you realize that among our men is not one who can read a blue-print, or has ever seen one? Do you realize that to erect buildings in accordance with these plans would require a force of skilled mechanics under the supervision of a master builder? And do you realize that time is a most important factor in our present undertaking? Who can tell at what moment Brute MacNair may swoop down, upon us like Attila of old, and strike a fatal blow to our little outpost of civilization? And if he finds *me* here—" His voice trailed into silence and his eyes swept gloomily the northern reach of the river.

Chloe appeared unimpressed. "I hardly think he will resort to violence. There is the law—even here in the wilderness. Slow to act, perhaps, because of the inaccessibility of the wild country; but once its machinery is in motion, as unbending and as indomitable as justice itself. You see, I have read of your Mounted Police."

"The Mounted!" Lapierre laughed. "Yes—I see you have *read* of them! Had you derived your information in a more direct manner—had you lived among them—if you *knew* them—your childlike trust in them would seem as absurd, perhaps, as it does to me!"

"What do you mean?" cried the girl, regarding the quarter-breed with a searching glance. "That the men of the Mounted are—that they may be—influenced?"

Again Lapierre laughed—harshly. "Just that, Miss Elliston! They are—crooked. They may be influenced!"

"I cannot believe that!"

"You will—later."

"You mean that MacNair has—"

The man interrupted with a wave of his hand. "What I have told you of MacNair is the truth. I shall prove this to your own satisfaction, at the proper time. Until then, I ask you to believe me. Admitting, then, that I have spoken the truth, do you suppose for an instant that these facts are not known to the Mounted? If not, then the officers are inefficient fools. If they are known, why don't the Mounted remedy matters? Because MacNair is rich! Because he buys them, body and soul! Because he owns them, like he owns the Indians! That's why!

"Just stop and consider what is ahead of a dollar-a-day policeman. When his five-year term of enlistment has expired, he has his choice of enlisting for another term, or making his living some other way. At the end of the five years he has learned to hate the service with a hatred that is soul-searing. It is the hardest, strictest, most exacting, and most ill-paid service in the world; and the five years of the man's enlistment have practically rendered him unfit for earning a living.

"He has lived in the wild country. He knows the wild country. And civilization, with its rapid advance, has left him five years behind the times. Our ex-man of the Mounted is fit for only the commonest labour. And, because there are almost no employers in the North, he cannot turn his knowledge of the wilds to profitable account, unless he turns smuggler, whiskey-runner, or fur-poisoner. The men know this. Therefore, when an officer whose patrol takes him into the far 'back blocks' is approached by a man like MacNair, with his pockets bulging with gold, what report goes down to Regina, and on to Ottawa?

"Yes, Miss Elliston, in the Northland there is law. But the law is a fundamental law—the primitive law of savage might. The strong devour the weak. Only the fit survive—survive to be ruled, to be trampled, to be *owned* by the strongest. And the law is the measure of might! Primal instincts—pristine passions—primordial brutishness permeate the whole North—rule it.

"The wolf and savage *carcajo* drag down the hunger-weakened caribou and the deer, and rip the warm, red flesh from their bones before their eyes have glazed. And, in turn, the wolf and the *carcajo*, the unoffending beaver and musquash, the mink, the fisher, the fox, and the otter are trapped by savage man and the pelts ripped from their twitching bodies while life and sensibility remain. They are harder to skin when cold. And with the thermometer at forty or sixty below zero, the little bodies chill almost instantly if mercifully killed—therefore, they are not killed, but flayed alive and their bleeding bodies tossed upon the snow. They die quickly—then. But—they have lived through the skinning! And that is the North!"

Chloe Elliston shuddered and drew away in horror. "Is—is this possible?" she faltered. "Do they—"

"They do. The fur business is not a pretty business, Miss Elliston. But neither is the North pretty—nor are its inhabitants. But the traffic in fur is inherently the business of the North—and its history is written in blood—the blood and the suffering of thousands of men and millions of animals. But the profits are great. Fashion has decreed that My Lady shall be swathed in fur—therefore, men go mad and die in the barrens, and the quivering red bodies of small animals bleed, and curl up, and stiffen upon the hard crust of the snow! No, the North is not gentle, Miss Elliston—"

"Don't! Don't!" faltered the girl. "It is all too—too horrible —too sickeningly brutal—too—too unbelievable!" She covered her eyes with her hand.

Lapierre answered, dryly. "Yes. The North is that way. It has always been so—and it always will—"

Chloe's hand dropped from her eyes and, she faced him in a sudden burst of passion. Her sensitive lips quivered and her eyes narrowed to the rapier-blade eyes that were the eyes of Tiger Elliston. She tore the roll of blue-prints to bits and ground them into the mould with the heel of her boot.

"*It will not!*" Her voice cut sharply, and hard. "What do you know of what the North *will* be? You know it only as it has been—as it is, perhaps. But, of its future you know nothing. I tell you the North will change! It is a hard land—cruel—elemental—raw! But it is *big*! And, when it awakens, its very bigness, the virile force and strength of it, will turn against its savagery, its cruelty, its brutishness; and above all other lands it will stand for the protection of the weak and for the right of things to live!"

The quarter-breed gazed into her face with a look of undisguised admiration. "Ah, Miss Elliston, you are beautiful, now—beautiful always—but, at this moment—radiant—divine—" Chloe seemed not to hear him.

"And that is to be *my* work—to awaken the North! To bring to its people the comforts—the advantages of civilization!"

"The North is too big for you, Miss Elliston. It is too big for *men*. Pardon, but it is not a woman's land."

The girl's eyes flashed. "Suppose we leave sex out of it, Mr. Lapierre. They said of my grandfather that 'the harder they fought him, the better he liked 'em,' and that 'he never knew when he was licked.' Maybe that is the reason he never was licked, but lived to carry civilization into a land that was a thousand years deeper in savagery than this land is. And today civilization—education—Christianity exist where seventy-five years ago the chance visitor was tortured first and eaten afterward."

Lapierre shrugged. "It is useless to argue. I am in sympathy with your undertaking. I admire your courage, and the high ideals of your mission. But, permit me to remind you that your grandfather, whoever he was, was *not* a woman. Also, that here, in the North, Christianity and education have failed to civilize—the educated ones and the converts are worse than the others."

The girl's eyes darkened and the man noticed the peculiar out-thrust of the chin. He hastened to change the subject.

"I am glad you have abandoned those plans. They were useless. May I now proceed with the building?"

Chloe smiled. "Yes," she answered, "by all means. But, as this is to be *my* undertaking, I think I shall have it *my* way. Build the store first, if you please—"

"And the stockade?"

"There will be no stockade."

"No stockade! Are you crazy? If MacNair—"

"I will attend to MacNair, Mr. Lapierre."

"Do you imagine MacNair will stand quietly by and allow you to build a trading-post here on the Yellow Knife? Do you think he will listen to our explanation that this is a school and that the store is merely a plaything? I tell you he will countenance neither the school nor the post. Education for the natives is the last thing MacNair will stand for."

"As I told you, I will attend to MacNair. My people will not be armed. The stockade would be silly."

Lapierre smiled; drew closer, and dropped his voice to a confidential whisper. "I can put one hundred rifles and ten thousand cartridges in the hands of your people in ten days' time."

"Thank you, Mr. Lapierre. I don't need your guns."

The man made a gesture of impatience. "If you choose to ignore MacNair, you must, at least, be prepared to handle the Indians who will crowd your counter like wolves when they hear you are underselling the H.B.C. When you explain that only those who are members of your school may trade at your post, you will be swamped with enrolments. You cannot teach the whole North.

"Those that you will be forced to turn away—what will they do? They will not understand. Instead of returning to their teepees, their nets, and their traplines, they will hang about your post, growing gaunter and hungrier with the passing of the days. And the hunger that gnaws at their bellies will arouse the latent lawlessness of their hearts, and then—if MacNair has not already struck, he will strike then. For MacNair knows Indians and the workings of the Indian mind. He knows how the sullen hatred of their souls may be fanned into a mighty flame. His Indians will circulate among the hungry horde, and the banks of the Yellow Knife will be swept bare. MacNair will have struck. And with such consummate skill will his hand be disguised, that not the faintest breath of suspicion will point toward himself."

"I shall sell to all alike, while my goods last, whether they are members of my school or not—"

"That will be even worse than—"

"It seems you always think of the worst thing that could possibly happen," smiled the girl.

"'To fear the worst, oft cures the worst,'" quoted Lapierre.

"'Don't cross a bridge 'til you get to it' is not so classic, perhaps, but it saves a lot of needless worry."

"'Foresight is better than hindsight' is equally unclassic, and infinitely better generalship. Bridges crossed at the last moment are generally crossed from the wrong end, I have noticed." The man leaned toward her and looked straight into her eyes. "Oh, Miss Elliston—can't you see—I am thinking of your welfare—of your safety; I have known you but a short time, as acquaintance is reckoned, but already you have become more to me than—"

Chloe interrupted him with a gesture.

"Don't—please—I—"

Lapierre ignored the protest, and, seizing her hand in both his own, spoke rapidly. "I will say it! I have known it from the moment of our first meeting. I love you! And I shall win you—and together we will—"

"Oh, don't—don't—not—now—please!"

The man bowed and released the hand. "I can wait," he said gravely. "But please—for your own good—take my advice. I know the North. I was born in the North, and am of the North. I have sought only to help you. Why do you refuse to profit by my experience? Must you endure what I have endured to learn what I offer freely to tell you? I shudder to think of It. The knowledge gleaned by experience may be the most lasting, but it is dearly purchased, and at a great loss—always." The man's voice was very earnest, and Chloe detected a note of mild reproach. She hastened to reply.

"I *have* profited by your advice—have learned much from what you have told me. I am under obligation to you. I appreciate your interest in—in my work, and am indeed grateful for what you have done to further it. But there are some things, I suppose, one *must* learn by experience. I may be silly and headstrong. I may be wrong. But I stand ready to pay the price. The loss will be mine. See!" she cried excitedly, "they are rolling up the logs for the store."

"Yes," answered the man gravely, "I bow to your wishes in the matter of your buildings. If you refuse to build a stockade we may erect a few more buildings—but as few as you can possibly manage with, Miss Elliston. I must hasten southward."

Chloe studied for some moments. "The store"—she checked them off upon her fingers—"the schoolhouse, two bunkhouses, we can leave off the bathrooms, the river and the lake will serve until winter."

Lapierre nodded, and the girl continued. "We can do without the laundry and the carpenter-shop, and the individual cabins. The Indians can set up their teepees in the clearing, and build the cabins and the other buildings later. But I *would* like a little cottage for myself, and Miss Penny, and Lena. We *could* make three rooms do. Can we have three rooms?"

Lapierre bowed low. "It shall be as you say," he replied. "And now, if you will excuse me, I shall see to it that these *canaille* work. LeFroy they do not fear."

He turned to go, and at that moment Chloe Elliston saw a look of terror flash into his eyes. Saw his fingers clutch and grope uncertainly at the gay scarf at his throat. Saw the muscles of his face work painfully. Saw his colour fade from rich tan to sickly yellow. An inarticulate, gurgling sound escaped his lips, and his eyes stared in horror toward a point beyond and behind her.

She turned swiftly and gazed into the face of a man who had approached unnoticed from the direction of the river, and stood a few paces distant with his eyes fixed upon her. As their glances met the man's gaze continued unflinching, and the soft-brimmed Stetson remained on his head. Her slender fingers clenched into her palms and, unconsciously, her chin thrust forward—for she knew intuitively that the man was "Brute" MacNair.

CHAPTER VI

BRUTE MACNAIR

Estimates are formed, in a far greater measure than most of us care to admit, upon first impressions. Manifestly shallow and embryonic though we admit them to be, our first impressions crystallize, in nine cases out of ten, into our fixed or permanent opinions. And, after all, the reason for this absurdity is simple—egotism.

Our opinions, based upon first impressions—and we rarely pause to analyse first impressions—have become *our opinions*, the result, as we fondly imagine, of our judgment. Our judgment must be right—because it is our judgment. Therefore, unconsciously or consciously, every subsequent impression is bent to bolster up and sustain that judgment. We hate to be wrong. We hate to admit, even to ourselves, that we are wrong.

Strange, isn't it? How often we are right (permit the smile) in our estimate of people?

When Chloe Elliston turned to face MacNair among the stumps of the sunlit clearing, her opinion of the man had already been formed. He was Brute MacNair, one to be hated, despised. To be fought, conquered, and driven out of the North—for the good of the North. His influence was a malignant ulcer—a cancerous plague-spot, whose evil tentacles, reaching hidden and unseen, would slowly but surely fasten themselves upon the civilization of the North—sap its vitality—poison its blood.

In the flash of her first glance the girl's eyes took in every particular and detail of him. She noted the huge frame, broad, yet lean with the gaunt leanness of health, and endurance, and physical strength. The sinew-corded, bronzed hands that clenched slowly as his glance rested for a moment upon the face of Lapierre. The weather-tanned neck that rose, columnlike, from the open shirt-throat. The well-poised head. The prominent, high-bridged nose. The lantern jaw, whose rugged outline was but half-concealed by the roughly trimmed beard of inky blackness. And, the most dominant feature of all, the compelling magnetism of the steel-grey eyes of him—eyes, deep-set beneath heavy black brows that curved and met—eyes that stabbed, and bored, and probed, as if to penetrate to the ultimate motive. Hard eyes they were, whose directness of gaze spoke at once fearlessness and intolerance of opposition; spoke, also, of combat, rather than diplomacy; of the honest smashing of foes, rather than dissimulation.

Ail this the girl saw in the first moments of their meeting. She saw, too, that the eyes held a hostile gleam, and that she need expect from their owner no sympathy—no deference of sex. If war were to be between them, it would be a man's war, waged upon man's terms, in a man's country. No quarter would be given—Chloe's lips pressed tight—nor would any be asked.

The moments lengthened into an appreciable space of time and the man remained motionless, regarding her with that probing, searching stare. Lapierre he ignored after the first swift glance. Instinctively the girl knew that the man had no intention of being deliberately or studiously rude in standing thus in her presence with head covered, and eyeing her with those steel-grey, steel-hard eyes. Nevertheless, his attitude angered her, the more because she knew he did not intend to. And in this she was right—MacNair stared because he was silently taking her measure, and his hat remained upon his head because he knew of no reason why it should not remain upon his head.

Chloe was the first to speak, and in her voice was more than a trace of annoyance.

"Well, Mr. Mind-Reader, have you figured me out—why I am here, and—"

"No." The word boomed deeply from the man's throat, smashing the question that was intended to carry the sting of sarcasm. "Except that it is for no good—though you doubtless think it is for great good."

"Indeed!" The girl laughed a trifle sharply. "And who, then, is the judge?"

"I am." The calm assurance of the man fanned her rising anger, and, when she answered, her voice was low and steady, with the tonelessness of forced control.

"And your name, you Oligarch of the Far Outland? May I presume to ask your name?"

"Why ask? My name you already know. And upon the word of yon scum, you have judged. By the glint o' hate, as you looked into my eyes, I know—for one does not so welcome a stranger beyond the outposts. But, since you have asked, I will tell you; my name is MacNair—Robert MacNair, by my christening—Bob MacNair, in the speech of the country—"

"And, *Brute* MacNair, upon the Athabasca?"

"Yes. Brute MacNair—upon the Athabasca—and the Slave, and Mackenzie—and in the haunts of the whiskey-runners, and 'Fool' MacNair—in Winnipeg."

"And among the oppressed and the down-trodden? Among those whose heritage of freedom you have torn from them? What do they call you—those whom you have forced into serfdom?" For a fleeting instant the girl caught the faintest flicker, a tiny twinkle of amusement, in the steely eyes. But, when the man answered, his eyes were steady.

"*They* call me friend."

"Is their ignorance so abysmal?"

"They have scant time to learn from books—my Indians. They work."

"But, a year from now, when they have begun to learn, what will they call you then—*your* Indians?"

"A year from now—two years—ten years—my Indians will call me—friend."

Chloe was about to speak, but MacNair interrupted her. "I have scant time for parley. I was starting for Mackay Lake, but when Old Elk reported two of yon scum's satellites hanging about, I dropped down the river. By your words it's a school you will be building. If it were a post I would have to take you more seriously—"

"There will be a—" Chloe felt the warning touch of Lapierre's finger at her back and ceased abruptly. MacNair continued, as if unmindful of the interruption.

"Build your school, by all means. 'Tis a spot well chosen by yon devil's spawn, and for his own ends. By your eyes you are honest in purpose—a fool's purpose—and a hare-brained carrying out of it. You are being used as a tool by Lapierre. You will not believe this—not yet. Later—perhaps, when it is too late—but, that is your affair—not mine. At the proper time I will crush Lapierre, and if you go down in the crash you will have yourself to thank. I have warned you. Yon snake has poisoned your mind against me. In your eyes I am foredamned—and well damned—which causes me no concern, and you, no doubt, much satisfaction.

"Build your school, but heed well my words. You'll not tamper, one way or another, with my Indians. One hundred and seventy miles north of here, upon Snare Lake, is my post. My Indians pass up and down the Yellow Knife. They are to pass unquestioned, unmolested, unproselyted. Confine your foolishness to the southward and I shall not interfere—carry it northward, and you shall hear from me.

"Should you find yourself in danger from your enemies—or, your *friends*"—he shot a swift glance toward Lapierre, who had remained a pace behind the girl—"send for me. Good day."

Chloe Elliston was furious. She had listened in a sort of dumb rage as the man's words stung, and stung again. MacNair's uncouth manner, his blunt brutality of speech, his scornful, even contemptuous reference to her work, and, most of all, his utter disregard of her, struck her to the very depths. As MacNair turned to go, she stayed him with a voice trembling with fury.

"Do you imagine, for an instant, I would stoop to seek *your* protection? I would die first! You have had things your own way too long, Mr. Brute MacNair! You think yourself secure, in your smug egotism. But the end is in sight. Your petty despotism is doomed. You have hoodwinked the authorities, bribed the police, connived with the Hudson Bay Company, bullied and browbeaten the Indians, cheated them out of their birthright of land and liberty, and have forced them into a peonage that has filled your pockets with gold."

She paused in her vehement outburst and glared defiantly at MacNair, as if to challenge a denial. But the man remained silent, and Chloe felt her face flush as the shadow of a twinkle played for a fleeting instant in the depths of the hard eyes. She fancied, even, that the lips behind the black beard smiled—ever so slightly,

"Oh, you needn't laugh! You think because I'm a woman you will be able to do as you please with me—"

"I did not laugh," answered the man gravely. "Why should I laugh? You take yourself seriously. You believe, even, that the things you have just spoken are true. They *must* be true. Has not Pierre Lapierre *told* you they are true? And, why should the fact that you are a woman cause me to believe I could influence you? If an issue is at stake, as you believe, what has sex to do with it? I have known no women, except the squaws and the *kloochmen* of the natives.

"You said, 'you think, because I am a woman, you will be able to do as you please with me.' Are women, then, less honest than men? I do not believe that. In my life I have known no women, but I have read of them in books. I have not been to any school, but was taught by my father, who, I think, was a very wise man. I learned from him, and from the books, of which he left a great number. I have always believed women to be uncommonly like men—very good, or very bad, or very commonplace because they were afraid to be either. But, I have not read that they are less honest than men."

"Thank you! Being a woman, I suppose I should consider myself flattered. A year from this time you will know more about women—at least, about *me*. You will have learned that I will not be hoodwinked. I cannot be bribed. Nor can my silence, or acquiescence in your villainy be bought. I will not connive with you. And you cannot browbeat, nor bully, nor cheat me."

"Yes?"

"Yes. And of one thing I am glad. I shall expect no consideration at your hands because I am a woman. You will fight me as you would fight a man."

"Fight you? Why should I fight you? I have no quarrel with you. If you choose to build a school here, or even a trading-post, I have no disposition—no right to gainsay you. You will soon tire of your experiment, and no harm will be done—the North will be unchanged. You are nothing to me. I care nothing for your opinion of me—considering its source, I am surprised it is not even worse."

"Impossible! And do not think that I have not had corroborative evidence. Ocular evidence of your brutal treatment of Mr. Lapierre—and did I not see with my own eyes the destruction of your whiskey?"

"What nonsense are you speaking now? My whiskey! Woman—never yet have I owned any whiskey."

Chloe sneered—"And the Indians—do they not hate you?"

"Yes, those Indians do—and well they may. Most of them have crossed my path at some time or other. And most of them will cross it again—at Lapierre's instigation. Some of them I shall have to kill."

"You speak lightly of murder."

"Murder?"

"Yes, murder! The murder of poor, ignorant savages. It is an ugly word, isn't it? But why dissimulate? At least, we can call a spade a spade. These men are human beings. Their right to life and happiness is as good as yours or mine, and their souls are as—"

"Black as hell! Woman, from LeFroy down, you have collected about you as pretty a gang of cut-throats and outlaws as could have been found in all the North. Lapierre has seen to that. I do not envy you your school. But as long as you can be turned to their profit your personal safety will be assured. They are too cunning, by far, to kill the goose that lays the golden egg."

"What a pretty speech! Your polish—your *savoir vivre*, does you credit, I am sure."

"I do not understand what you are saying, but—"

"There are many things you do not understand now that perhaps you will later. For instance, in the matter of the Indians—*your* Indians, I believe you call them—you have warned, or commanded, possibly, would be the better word—"

"Yes," interrupted the man, "that is the better word—"

"Have commanded me not to—what was it you said—molest, question, or proselyte them."

MacNair nodded. "I said that."

"And I say *this*!" flashed the girl. "I shall use every means in my power to induce your Indians to attend my school. I shall teach them that they are free. That they owe allegiance and servitude to no man. That the land they inhabit is their land. That they are their own masters. I shall offer them education, that they may be able to compete on equal terms with the white men when this land ceases to lie beyond the outposts. I shall show them that they are being robbed and cheated and forced into ignominious serfdom. And mark you this: if I can't reach them upon the river, I shall go to your village, or post, or fort, or whatever you call your Snare Lake rendezvous, and I shall point out to them their wrongs. I shall appeal to their better natures—to their manhood, and womanhood. That's what I think of your command! I do not fear you! I *despise* you!"

MacNair nodded, gravely.

"I have already learned that women are as honest as men—more so, even, than most men. You are honest, and you are earnest. You believe in yourself, too. But you are more of a fool than I thought—more of a fool than I thought any one could be. Lapierre is a great fool—but he is neither honest nor earnest. He is just a fool—a wise fool, with the cunning and vices of the wolf, but with none of the wolf's lean virtues. You are an honest fool. You are like a young moose-calf, who, because he happens to be born into the world, thinks the world was made for him to be born into.

"Let us say the moose-calf was born upon a great mountain—a mountain whose sides are crossed and recrossed by moose-trails—paths that wind in and out among the trees, stamped by the hoofs of older and wiser moose. Upon these paths the moose-calf tries his wobbly legs, and one day finds himself gazing out upon a plain where grass is. He has no use for grass—does not even know what grass is for. Only he sees no paths out there. The grass covers a quagmire, but of quagmires the moose-calf knows nothing, having been born upon a mountain.

"Being a fool, the moose-calf soon tires of the beaten paths. He ventures downward toward the plain. A wolf, skulking through the scrub at the foot of the mountain, encounters, by chance, the moose-calf. The calf is fat. But, the wolf is cunning. He dares not harm the moose-calf hard by the trails of the mountain. He becomes friendly, and the fool moose-calf tells the wolf where he is bound. The wolf offers to accompany him, and the moose-calf is glad—here is a friend—one who is wiser than the moose-kind, for he fears not to venture into the country of no trails.

"Between the mountain and the plain stands a tree. This tree the wolf hates. Many squirrels work about its roots, and these squirrels are fatter than the squirrels of the scrub, for the tree feeds them. But, when the wolf would pounce upon them, they seek safety in the tree. The moose-calf—the poor fool moose-calf—comes to this tree, and, finding no paths curving around its base, becomes enraged because the tree does not step aside and yield the right of way. He will charge the tree! He does not know that the tree has been growing for many years, and has become deeply rooted—immovable. The wolf looks on and smiles. If the moose-calf butts the tree down, the wolf will get the squirrels—and the calf. If the calf does not, the wolf will get the calf."

MacNair ceased speaking and turned abruptly toward the river.

"My!" Chloe Elliston exclaimed. "Really, you are delightful, Mr. Brute MacNair. During the half-hour or more of our acquaintance you have called me, among other things, a fool, a goose, and a moose-calf. I repeat that you are delightful, and honest, shall I say? No; candid—for I know that you are not honest. But do tell me the rest of the story.

Don't leave it like The Lady or the Tiger. How will it end? Are you a prophet, or merely an allegorist?"

MacNair, who was again facing her, answered without a smile. "I do not know about the lady or the tiger, nor of what happened to either. If they were pitted against each other, my bet would be laid on the tiger, though my sympathy might be with the lady. I am not a prophet. I cannot tell you the end of the story. Maybe the fool moose-calf will butt its brains out against the trunk of the tree. That would be no fault of the tree. The tree was there first, and was minding its own business. Maybe the calf will butt and get hurt, and scamper for home. Maybe it will succeed in eluding the fangs of the wolf, and reach its mountain in safety. In such case it will have learned something.

"Maybe it will butt and butt against the tree until it dislodges a limb from high among the branches, and the limb will fall to the ground and crush, shall we say—the waiting wolf? And, maybe the calf will butt, learn that the tree is immovable, swallow its hurt, and pass on, giving the tree a wide berth—pass on into the quagmire, with the wolf licking his chops, as grinning, he points out the way."

Chloe, in spite of herself, was intensely interested.

"But," she asked, "you are quite sure the tree is immovable?"

"Quite sure."

"Suppose, however, that this particular tree is rotten—rotten to the heart? That the very roots that hold it in place are rotten? And that the moose-calf butts 'til he butts it down—what then?"

There was a gleam of admiration in MacNair's eyes as he answered:

"If the tree is rotten it will fall. But it will fall to the mighty push o' the winds o' God—and not to the puny butt of a moose-calf!" Chloe Elliston was silent. The man was speaking again. "Good day to you, madam, or miss, or whatever one respectfully calls a woman. As I told you, I have known no women. I have lived always in the North. Death robbed me of my mother before I was old enough to remember her. The North, you see, is hard and relentless, even with those who know her—and love her."

The girl felt a sudden surge of sympathy for this strange, outspoken man of the Northland. She knew that the man had spoken, with no thought of arousing sympathy, of the dead mother he had never known. And in his voice was a note, not merely of deep regret, but of sadness.

"I am sorry," she managed to murmur.

"What?"

"About your mother, I mean."

The man nodded. "Yes. She was a good woman. My father told me of her often. He loved her."

The simplicity of the man puzzled Chloe. She was at a loss to reply.

"I think—I believe—a moment ago, you asked my name."

"No."

"Oh!" The lines about the girl's mouth tightened. "Then I'll tell you. I am Chloe Elliston—*Miss* Chloe Elliston. The name means nothing to you—now. A year hence it will mean much."

"Aye, maybe. I'll not say it won't. More like, though, it will be forgot in half the time. The North has scant use for the passing whims o' women!"

CHAPTER VII

THE MASTER MIND

After the visit of MacNair, Chloe noticed a marked diminution in the anxiety of Lapierre to resume his interrupted journey. True, he drove the Indians mercilessly from daylight till dark in the erection of the buildings, but his air of tense expectancy was gone, and he ceased to dart short, quick glances into the North, and to scan the upper reach of the river.

The Indians, too, had changed. They toiled more stolidly now with apathetic ears for Lapierre's urging, where before they had worked in feverish haste, with their eyes upon the edges of the clearing. It was obviously patent that the canoemen shared Lapierre's fear and hatred of MacNair.

In the late afternoon of the twelfth day after the rolling of the first log into place, Chloe accompanied Lapierre upon a tour of inspection of the completed buildings. The man had done his work well. The school-house and the barracks with the dining-room and kitchen were comfortably and solidly built; entirely sufficient for present needs and requirements. But the girl wondered at the trading-post and its appendant store-house they were fully twice the size she would have considered necessary, and constructed as to withstand a siege. Lapierre had built a fort.

"Excellent buildings; and solid as the Rock of Gibraltar, Miss Elliston," smiled the quarter-breed, as with a wave of his hand he indicated the interior of the trading-room.

"But, they are so big!" exclaimed the girl, as her glance swept the spacious fur lofts, and the ample areas for the storing of supplies. She was concerned only with the size of the buildings. But her wonder would have increased could she have seen the rows of loopholes that pierced the thick walls—loopholes crammed with moss against the cold, and with their openings concealed by cleverly fitted pieces of bark. Lapierre's smile deepened.

"Remember, you told me you intend to sell to all alike, while your goods last. I know what that will mean. It will mean that you will find yourself called upon to furnish the supplies for the inhabitants of several thousand square miles of territory. Indians will travel far to obtain a bargain. They look only at the price—never at the quality of the goods. That fact enables us free-traders to live. We sell cheaper than the H.B.C.; but, frankly, our goods are cheaper. The bargains are much more apparent than real. But, if I understand your position, you intend to sell goods that are up to H.B.C. standard at actual cost?"

Chloe nodded: "Certainly."

"Very well, then you will find that these buildings which look so large and commodious to you now, must be crowded to the ceiling with your goods, while the walls of your fur lofts will fairly bulge with their weight of riches. Fur is the 'cash' of the North, and the trader must make ample provision for its storage. There are no banks in the wilderness; and the fur lofts are the vaults of the traders."

"But, I don't want to deal in fur!" objected the girl. "I—since you have told me of the terrible cruelty of the trappers,

I *hate fur*! I want nothing to do with it. In fact, I shall do everything in my power to discountenance and discourage the trapping." Lapierre cleared his throat sharply—coughed—cleared it again. Discourage trapping—north of sixty! Had he heard aright? He swallowed hard, mumbled an apology anent the inhalation of a gnat, and answered in all seriousness.

"A worthy object, Miss Elliston—a very worthy object; but one that will require time to consummate. At present the taking of fur is the business of the North. I may say, the only business of thousands of savages whose very existence depends upon their skill with the traps. Fur is their one source of livelihood. Therefore, you must accept the condition as it exists. Think, if you refused to accept fur in exchange for your goods, what it would mean—the certain and absolute failure of your school from the moment of its inception. The Indians could not grasp your point of view. You would be shunned for one demented. Your goods would rot upon your shelves; for the simple reason that the natives would have no means of buying them. No, Miss Elliston, you must take their fur until such time as you succeed in devising some other means by which these people may earn their living."

"You are right," agreed Chloe. "Of course, I must deal in fur—for the present. Reform is the result of years of labour. I must be patient. I was thinking only of the cruelty of it."

"They have never been taught," said Lapierre with a touch of sadness in his tone. "And, while we are on the subject, allow me to advise you to retain LeFroy as your chief trader. He is an excellent man, is Louis LeFroy, and has had no little experience."

"Do you think he will stay?" eagerly asked the girl. "I should like to retain, not only LeFroy but a half-dozen others."

"It shall be as you wish. I shall speak to LeFroy and select also the pick of the crew. They will be glad of a steady job. The others I shall take with me. I must gather my fur from its various *caches* and freight it to the railway."

"You are going to the railway! To civilization?"

"Yes, but it will take me three weeks to make ready my outfit. And in this connection I may be of further service to you. I must depart from here tonight. Instruct LeFroy to make out his list of supplies for the winter. Give him a free hand and tell him to fill the store-rooms. The goods you have brought with you are by no means sufficient. Three weeks from today, if I do not visit you in the meantime, have him meet me at Fort Resolution, and I shall be glad to make your purchases for you, at Athabasca Landing and Edmonton."

"You have been very good to me. How can I ever thank you?" cried the girl, impulsively extending her hand. Lapierre took the hand, bowed over it, and—was it fancy, or did his lips brush her finger-tips? Chloe withdrew the hand, laughing in slight confusion. To her surprise she realized she was not in the least annoyed. "How can I thank you," she repeated, "for—for throwing aside your own work to attend to mine?"

"Do not speak of thanking me." Once more the man's eyes seemed to burn into her soul, "I love you! And one day my work will be your work and your work will be mine. It is I who am indebted to you for bringing a touch of heaven into this drab hell of Northern brutishness. For bringing to me a breath of the bright world I have not known since Montreal—and the student days, long past. And—ah—more than that—something I have never known—love. And, it is you who are bringing a ray of pure light to lighten the darkness of my people."

Chloe was deeply touched. "But I—I thought," she faltered, "when we were discussing the buildings that day, you spoke as if you did not really care for the Indians. And—and you made them work so hard—"

"To learn to work would be their salvation!" exclaimed the man. "And I beg you to forget what I said then. I feared for your safety. When you refused to allow me to build the stockade, I could think only of your being at the mercy of Brute MacNair. I tried to frighten you into allowing me to build it. Even now, if you say the word—"

Chloe interrupted him with a laugh. "No, I am not afraid of MacNair—really I am not. And you have already neglected your own affairs too long."

The man assented. "If I am to get my furs to the railway, do my own trading, and yours, and return before the lake freezes, I must, indeed, be on my way."

"You will wait while I write some letters? And you will post them for me?"

Lapierre bowed. "As many as you wish," he said, and together they walked to the girl's cabin whose quaint, rustic veranda overlooked the river. The veranda was an addition of Lapierre's, and the cabin had five rooms, instead of three.

The quarter-breed waited, whistling softly a light French air, while Chloe wrote her letters. He breathed deeply of the warm spruce-laden breeze, slapped lazily at mosquitoes, and gazed at the setting sun between half-closed lids. Pierre Lapierre was happy.

"Things are coming my way," he muttered. "With a year's stock in that warehouse—and LeFroy to handle it—I guess the Indians won't pick up many bargains—my people!—damn them! How I hate them. And as for MacNair—lucky Vermilion thought of painting *his* name on that booze—I hated to smash it—but it paid. It was the one thing needed to make me solid with *her*. And I've got time to run in another batch if I hurry—got to get those rifles into the loft, too. When MacNair hits, he hits hard."

Chloe appeared at the door with her letters. Lapierre took them, and again bowed low over her hand. This time the girl was sure his lips touched her finger-tips. He released the hand and stepped to the ground.

"Good-bye," he said, "I shall try my utmost to pay you a visit before I depart for the southward, but if I fail, remember to send LeFroy to me at Fort Resolution."

"I will remember. Good-bye—*bon voyage*—"

"*Et prompt retour?*" The man's lips smiled, and his eyes flashed the question.

"*Et prompt retour—certainement!*" answered the girl as, with a wide sweep of his hat, the quarter-breed turned and made his way toward the camp of the Indians, which was located in a spruce thicket a short distance above the clearing. As he disappeared in the timber, Chloe felt a sudden sinking of the heart; a strange sense of desertion, of loneliness possessed her as she gazed into the deepening shadows of the wall of the clearing. She fumed impatiently.

"Why should I care?" she muttered, "I never laid eyes on him until two weeks ago, and besides, he's—he's an *Indian*! And yet—he's a gentleman. He has been very kind to me—very considerate. He is only a quarter-Indian. Many of the very best families have Indian blood in their veins—even boast of it. I—I'm a *fool*!" she exclaimed, and passed quickly into the house.

Pierre Lapierre was a man, able, shrewd, unscrupulous. The son of a French factor of the Hudson Bay Company and his half-breed wife, he was sent early to school, where he remained to complete his college course; for it was the desire of his father that the son should engage in some profession for which his education fitted him.

But the blood of the North was in his veins. The call of the North lured him into the North, and he returned to the trading-post of his father, where he was given a position as clerk and later appointed trader and assigned to a post of his own far to the northward.

While the wilderness captivated and entranced him, the humdrum life of a trader wearied him. He longed for excitement—action.

During the several years of his service with the great fur company he assiduously studied conditions, storing up in his mind a fund of information that later was to stand him in good stead. He studied the trade, the Indians, the country. He studied the men of the Mounted, and smugglers, and whiskey-runners, and free-traders. And it was in a brush with these latter that he overstepped the bounds which, under the changed conditions, even the agents of the great Company might not go.

Chafing under the loss of trade by reason of an independent post that had been built upon the shore of his lake some ten miles to the southward, his wild Metis blood called for action and, hastily summoning a small band of Indians, he attacked the independents. Incidentally, the free-traders' post was burned, one of the traders killed, and the other captured and sent upon the *longue traverse*. In some unaccountable manner, after suffering untold hardships, the man won through to civilization and promptly had Pierre Lapierre brought to book.

The Company stood loyally between its trader and the prison bars; but the old order had changed in the Northland. Young Lapierre's action was condemned and he was dismissed from the Company's service with a payment of three years' unearned salary whereupon, he promptly turned free-trader, and his knowledge of the methods of the H.B.C., the Indians, and the country, made largely for success.

The life of the free-trader satisfied his longing for travel and adventure, which his life as a post-trader had not. But it did not satisfy his innate craving for excitement. Therefore, he cast about to enlarge his field of activity. He became a whiskey-runner. His profits increased enormously, and he gradually included smuggling in his *repertoire*, and even timber thieving, and cattle-rustling upon the ranges along the international boundary.

At the time of his meeting with Chloe Elliston he was at the head of an organized band of criminals whose range of endeavour extended over hundreds of thousands of square miles, and the diversity of whose crimes was limited only by the index of the penal code.

Pierre Lapierre was a Napoleon of organization—a born leader of men. He chose his liegemen shrewdly—outlaws, renegades, Indians, breeds, trappers, canoemen, scowmen, packers, claim-jumpers, gamblers, smugglers, cattle-rustlers, timber thieves—and these he dominated and ruled absolutely.

Without exception, these men feared him—his authority over them was unquestioned. Because they had confidence in his judgment and cunning, and because under his direction they made more money, and made it easier, and at infinitely less risk, than they ever made by playing a lone hand, they accepted his domination cheerfully. And such was his disposition of the men who were the component parts of his system of criminal efficiency, that few, if any, were there among them who could, even if he so desired, have furnished evidence that would have seriously incriminated the leader.

The men who ran whiskey across the line, *cached* it. Other men, unknown to them, disguised it as innocent freight and delivered it to the scowmen. The scowmen turned it over to others who, for all they knew, were bona fide settlers or free-traders; and from their *cache*, the canoemen carried it far into the wilderness and either stored it in some inaccessible rendezvous or *cached* it where still others would come and distribute it among the Indians.

Each division undoubtedly suspected the others, but none but the leader *knew*. And, as it was with the whiskey-running, so was it with each of his various undertakings. Religiously, Pierre Lapierre followed the scriptural injunction; "Let not thy left hand know what thy right hand doeth." He confided in no man. And few, indeed, were the defections among his retainers. A few had rebelled, as Vermilion had rebelled—and with like result. The man dismissed from Lapierre's service entered no other.

Moreover, he invariably contrived to implicate one whom he intended to use, in some crime of a graver nature than he would be called upon to commit in the general run of his duties. This crime he would stage in some fastness where its detection by an officer of the Mounted was exceedingly unlikely; and most commonly consisted in the murder of an Indian, whose weighted body would be lowered to the bottom of a convenient lake or river. Lapierre witnesses would appear and the man was irrevocably within the toil. Had he chosen, Pierre Lapierre could have lowered a grappling hook unerringly upon a dozen weighted skeletons.

Over the head of the recruit now hung an easily proven charge of murder. If during his future activities as whiskey-runner, smuggler, or in whatever particular field of endeavour he was assigned, plans should miscarry—an arrest be made—this man would take his prison sentence in silence rather than seek to implicate Lapierre, who with a word could summon the witnesses that would swear the hemp about his neck.

The system worked. Now and again plans did miscarry—arrests were made by the Mounted, men were caught "with the goods," or arrested upon evidence that even Lapierre's intricate alibi scheme could not refute. But, upon conviction, the unlucky prisoner always accepted his sentence—for at his shoulder stalked a spectre, and in his heart was the fear lest the thin lips of Pierre Lapierre would speak.

With such consummate skill and finesse *did* Lapierre plot, however, and with such Machiavelian cunning and *eclat* were his plans carried out, that few failed. And those that did were credited by the authorities to individual or sporadic acts, rather than to the work of an intricate organization presided over by a master mind.

The gang numbered, all told, upward of two hundred of the hardest characters upon the frontier. Only Lapierre knew its exact strength, but each member knew that if he did not "run straight"—if he, by word or act or deed, sought to implicate an accomplice—his life would be worth just exactly the price of "the powder to blow him to hell."

A few there were outside the organization who suspected Pierre Lapierre—but only a few: an officer or two of the Mounted and a few factors of the H.B.C. But these could prove nothing. They bided their time. One man *knew* him for what he was. One, in all the North, as powerful in his way as Lapierre was in his. The one man who had spies in

Lapierre's employ, and who did not fear him. The one man Pierre Lapierre feared—Bob MacNair. And he, too, bided his time.

CHAPTER VIII

A SHOT IN THE NIGHT

As Lapierre made his way to the camp of the Indians he pondered deeply. For Lapierre was troubled. The fact that MacNair had twice come upon him unexpectedly within the space of a month caused him grave concern. He did not know that it was entirely by chance that MacNair had found him, an unwelcome sojourner at Fort Rae. Accusations and recriminations had passed between them, with the result that MacNair, rough, bluff, and ready to fight at any time, had pounded the quarter-breed to within an inch of his life, and then, to the undisguised delight of the men of the H.B.C., had dragged him out and pitched him ignominiously into the lake.

Either could have killed the other then and there. But each knew that to have done so, as the result of a personal quarrel, would have been the worst move he could possibly have made. And the forebearance with which MacNair fought and Lapierre suffered was each man's measure of greatness. MacNair went about his business, and to Lapierre came Chenoine with his story of the girl and the plot of Vermilion, and Lapierre, forgetting MacNair for the moment, made a dash for the Slave River.

For years Lapierre and MacNair had been at loggerheads.

Each recognized in the other a foe of no mean ability. Each had sworn to drive the other out of the North. And each stood at the head of a powerful organization which could be depended upon to fight to the last gasp when the time came to "lock horns" in the final issue. Both leaders realized that the show-down could not be long delayed—a year, perhaps—two years—it would make no difference. The clash was inevitable. Neither sought to dodge the crisis, nor did either seek to hasten it. But each knew that events were shaping themselves, the stage was set, and the drama of the wilds was wearing to its final scene.

From the moment of his meeting with Chloe Elliston, Lapierre had realized the value of an alliance with her against MacNair. And being a man whose creed it was to turn every possible circumstance to his own account, he set about to win her co-operation. When, during the course of their first conversation, she casually mentioned that she could command millions if she wanted them, his immediate interest in MacNair cooled appreciably—not that MacNair was to be forgotten—merely that his undoing was to be deferred for a season, while he, the Pierre Lapierre once more of student days, played an old game—a game long forgot in the press of sterner life, but one at which he once excelled.

"A game of hearts," the man had smiled to himself—"a game in which the risk is nothing and the stakes—With millions one may accomplish much in the wilderness, or retire into smug respectability—who knows? Or, losing, if worse comes to worst, a lady who can command millions, held prisoner, should be worth dickering for. Ah, yes, dear lady! By all means, you shall be helped to Christianize the North! To educate the Indians—how did she say it? 'So that they may come and receive that which is theirs of right'—fah! These women!"

While the scows rushed northward his plans had been laid—plans that included a masterstroke against MacNair and the placing of the girl absolutely within his power in one move. And so Pierre Lapierre had accompanied Chloe to the mouth of the Yellow Knife, selected the site for her school, and generously remained upon the ground to direct the erection of her buildings.

Up to that point his plans had carried with but two minor frustrations: he was disappointed in not having been allowed to build a stockade, and he had been forced prematurely to show his hand to MacNair. The first was the mere accident of a woman's whim, and had been offset to a great extent in the construction of the trading-post and store-house.

The second, however, was of graver importance and deeper significance. While the girl's faith in him had, apparently, remained unshaken by her interview with MacNair, MacNair himself would be on his guard. Lapierre ground his teeth with rage at the Scotchman's accurate comprehension of the situation, and he feared that the man's words might raise a suspicion in Chloe's mind; a fear that was in a great measure allayed by her eager acceptance of his offer of assistance in the matter of supplies, and—had he not already sown the seeds of a deeper regard? Once she had become his wife! The black eyes glittered as the man threaded the trail toward the camp, where his own tent showed white amid the smoke-blackened teepees of the Indians.

The thing, however, that caused him the greatest uneasiness was the suspicion that there was a leak in his system. How had MacNair known that he would be at Fort Rae? Why had he come down the Yellow Knife? And why had the two Indian scouts failed to report the man's coming? Only one of the Indians had returned at all, and his report that the other had been killed by one of MacNair's retainers had seemed unconvincing. However, Lapierre had accepted the story, but all through the days of the building he had secretly watched him. The man was one of his trusted Indians—so was the one he reported killed.

Upon the outskirts of the camp Lapierre halted—thinking. LeFroy had also watched—he must see LeFroy. Picking his way among the teepees, he advanced to his own tent. Groups of Indians and half-breeds, hunched about their fires, were eating supper. They eyed him respectfully as he passed, and in response to a signal, LeFroy arose and followed him to the tent.

Once inside, Lapierre fixed his eyes upon the boss canoeman.

"Well—you have watched Apaw—what have you found out?"

"Apaw—I'm t'ink she spik de trut'."

"Speak the truth—*hell*! Why didn't he get down here ahead of MacNair, then? What have I got spies for—to drag in after MacNair's gone and tell me he's been here?"

LeFroy shrugged. "MacNair Injuns—dey com' pret' near catch Apaw—dey keel Stamix. Apaw, she got 'way by com' roun' by de Black Fox."

Lapierre nodded, scowling. He trusted LeFroy; and having recognized in him one as unscrupulous and nearly as resourceful and penetrating as himself, had placed him in charge of the canoemen, the men who, in the words of the leader, "kept cases on the North," and to whose lot fell the final distribution of the whiskey to the Indians. But so, also, had he trusted the boasting, flaunting Vermilion.

"All right; but keep your eye on him," he said, smiling

sardonically, "and you may learn a lesson. Now you listen to me. You are to stay here. Miss Elliston wants you for her chief trader. Make out your list of supplies—fill that storehouse up with stuff. She wants you to undersell the H.B.C.—and you do it. Get the trade in here—see? Keep your prices down to just below Company prices, and then skin 'em on the fur—and—well, I don't need to tell you how. Give 'em plenty of debt and we'll fix the books. Pick put a half-dozen of your best men and keep 'em here. Tell 'em to obey Miss Elliston's orders; and whatever you do, keep cases on MacNair. But don't start anything. Pass the word out and fill up her school. Give her plenty to do, and keep 'em orderly. I'll handle the canoemen and pick up the fur, and then I've got to drop down the river and run in the supplies. I'll run in some rifles, and some of the *stuff*, too."

LeFroy looked at his chief in surprise.

"Vermilion—she got ten keg on de scow—" he began.

Lapierre laughed.

"Vermilion, eh? Do you know where Vermilion is?"

LeFroy shook his head.

"He's in hell—that's where *he* is—I dismissed him from my service. He didn't run straight. Some others went along with him—and there are more to follow. Vermilion thought he could double-cross me and get away with it." And again he laughed.

LeFroy shuddered and made no comment. Lapierre continued:

"Make out your list of supplies, and if I don't show up in the mean time, meet me at the mouth of the Slave three weeks from today. I've got to count days if I get back before the freeze-up. And remember this—you are working for Miss Elliston; we've got a big thing if we work it right; we've got MacNair where we want him at last. She thinks he's running in whiskey and raising hell with the Indians north of here. Keep her thinking so; and later, when it comes to a show-down—well, she is not only rich, but she's in good at Ottawa—see?"

LeFroy nodded. He was a man of few words, was LeFroy; dour and taciturn, but a man of brains and one who stood in wholesome fear of his master.

"And now," continued Lapierre, "break camp and load the canoes. I must pull out tonight. Pick out your men and move 'em at once into the barracks. You understand everything now?"

"*Oui*," answered LeFroy, and stepping from the tent, passed swiftly from fire to fire, issuing commands in low guttural. Lapierre rolled a cigarette, and taking a guitar from its case, seated himself upon his blankets and played with the hand of a master as he sang a love-song of old France. All about him sounded the clatter of lodge-poles, the thud of packs, and the splashing of water as the big canoes were pushed into the river and loaded.

Presently LeFroy's head thrust in at the entrance. He spoke no word; Lapierre sang on, and the head was withdrawn. When the song was finished the sounds from the outside had ceased. Lapierre carefully replaced his guitar in its case, drew a heavy revolver from its holster, threw it open, and twirled the cylinder with his thumb, examining carefully its chambers. His brows drew together and his lips twisted into a diabolical smile.

Lapierre was a man who took no chances. What was one

Indian, more or less, beside the absolute integrity of his organization? He stepped outside, and instantly the guy-ropes of the tent were loosened; the canvas slouched to the ground and was folded into a neat pack. The blankets were made into a compact roll, with the precious guitar in the centre and deposited in the head canoe. Lapierre glanced swiftly about him; nothing but the dying fires and the abandoned lodge-poles indicated the existence of the camp. On the shore the canoemen, leaning on their paddles, awaited the word of command.

He stepped to the water's edge, where, Apaw the Indian, stood with the others. For just a moment the baleful eyes of Lapierre fixed the silent figure; then his words cut sharply upon the silence.

"Apaw—*Chahco yahkwa*!" The Indian advanced, evidently proud of having been singled out by the chief, and stood before him, paddle in hand. Lapierre spoke no word; seconds passed, the silence grew intense. The hand that gripped the paddle shook suddenly; and then, looking straight into the man's eyes, Lapierre drew his revolver and fired. There was a quick spurt of red flame—the sound of the shot rang sharp, and rang again as the opposite bank of the river hurled back the sound. The Indian pitched heavily forward and fell across his paddle, snapping it in two.

Lapierre glanced over the impassive faces of the canoemen.

"This man was a traitor," he said in their own language. "I have dismissed him from my service. Weight him and shove off!"

The quarter-breed stepped into his canoe. The canoemen bound heavy stones to the legs of the dead Indian, laid the body upon the camp equipage amidship, and silently took their places.

During the evening meal, Chloe was unusually silent, answering Miss Penny's observations and queries in short, detached monosyllables. Later she stole out alone to a high, rocky headland that commanded a sweeping view of the river, and sat with her back against the broad trunk of a twisted banskian.

The long Northern twilight hung about her like a pall—seemed enveloping, smothering her. No faintest breath of air stirred the piny needles above her, nor ruffled the surface of the river, whose black waters, far below, flowed broad and deep and silent—smoothly—like a river of oil. Ominously hushed, secretive, it slipped out of the motionless dark. Silently portentous, it faded again into the dark, the mysterious half-dark, where the gradually deepening twilight blended the distance into the enshrouding pall of gloom. Involuntarily the girl shuddered and started nervously at the splash of an otter. A billion mosquitoes droned their unceasing monotone. The low sound was everywhere—among the branches of the gnarled banskian, above the surface of the river, and on and on and on, to whine thinly between the little stars.

It was not at all the woman who would conquer a wilderness, that huddled in a dejected little heap at the foot of the banskian; but a very miserable and depressed girl, who swallowed hard to keep down the growing lump in her throat, and bit her lip, and stared with wide eyes toward the southward. Hot tears—tears of bitter, heart-sickening loneliness—filled her eyes and trickled unheeded down her cheeks beneath the tightly drawn mosquito-net.

Darkness deepened, imperceptibly, surely, fore-shortening the horizon, and by just so much increasing the distance that separated her from her people.

"Poor fool moose-calf," she murmured, "you weren't

satisfied to follow the beaten trails. You had to find a land of your own—a land that—"

The whispered words trailed into silence, and to her mind's eye appeared the face of the man who had spoken those words—the face of Brute MacNair. She saw him as he stood that day and faced her among the freshly chopped stumps of the clearing.

"He is rough and bearlike—boorish," she thought, as she remembered that the man had not removed his hat in her presence. "He called me names. He is uncouth, cynical, egotistical. He thinks he can scare me into leaving his Indians alone." Her lips trembled and tightened. "I am a woman, and I'll show him what a woman can do. He has lived among the Indians until he thinks he owns them. He is hard, and domineering, and uncompromising, and skeptical. And yet—" What gave her pause was so intangible, so chaotic, in her own mind as to form itself into no definite idea.

"He is brutish and brutal and bad!" she muttered aloud at the memory of Lapierre's battered face, and immediately fell to comparing the two men.

Each seemed exactly what the other was not. Lapierre was handsome, debonair, easy of speech, and graceful of movement; deferential, earnest, at times even pensive, and the possessor of ideals; generous and accommodating to a fault, if a trifle cynical; maligned, hated, discredited by the men who ruled the North, yet brave and infinitely capable—she remembered the swift fate of Vermilion.

His was nothing of the rugged candour of MacNair—the bluff straightforwardness that overrides opposition; ignores criticism. MacNair fitted the North—the big, brutal, insatiate North—the North of storms, of cold and fighting things; of foaming, roaring white-water and seething, blinding blizzards.

Chloe's glance strayed out over the river, where the farther bank showed only the serried sky-line of a wall of jet.

Lapierre was also of the North—the North as it is tonight; soft air, balmy with the incense of growing things; illusive dark, half concealing, half revealing, blurring distant outlines. A placid North, whose black waters flowed silent, smooth, deep. A benign and harmless North, upon its surface; and yet, withal, portentous of things unknown.

The girl shuddered and arose to her feet, and, as she did so, from up the river—from the direction of the Indian camp—came the sharp, quick sound of a shot. Then silence—a silence that seemed unending to the girl who waited breathlessly, one hand grasping the rough bark of the gnarled tree, and the other shading her eyes as thought to aid them in their effort to pierce the gloom.

A long time she stood thus, peering into the dark, and then, an indistinct form clove the black water of the river, and a long body slipped noiselessly toward her, followed by another, and another.

"The canoes!" she cried, as she watched the sparkling starlight play upon the long Y-shaped ripples that rolled back from their bows.

Once more the sense of loneliness almost overcame her. Pierre Lapierre was going out of the North.

She could see the figures of the paddlers, now—blurred, and indistinct, and unrecognizable—distinguishable more by the spaces that showed between them, than by their own outlines.

They were almost beneath her. Should she call out? One last *bon voyage*? The sound of a voice floated upward; a hard, rasping voice, unfamiliar, yet strangely familiar. In the leading canoe the Indians ceased paddling. The canoe lost momentum and drifted broadside to the current. The men were lifting something; something long and dark. There was a muffled splash, and the dark object disappeared. The canoemen picked up their paddles, and the canoe swung into its course and disappeared around a point. The other canoes followed; and the river rolled on as before—black—oily—sinister.

A broad cloud, pall-like, threatening, which had mounted unnoticed by the girl, blotted out the light of the stars, as if to hide from alien eyes some unlovely secret of the wilds.

The darkness was real, now; and Chloe, in a sudden panic of terror, dashed wildly for the clearing—stumbling—crashing through the bush as she ran; her way lighted at intervals by flashes of distant lightning. She paused upon the verge of the bank at the point where it entered the clearing; at the point where the wilderness crowded menacingly her little outpost of civilization. Panting, she stood and stared out over the smooth flowing, immutable river.

A lightning flash, nearer and more vivid than any preceding, lighted for an instant the whole landscape. Then, the mighty crash of thunder, and the long, hoarse moan of wind, and in the midst of it, that other sound—the horrible sound that once before had sent her dashing breathless from the night—the demoniacal, mocking laugh of the great loon.

With a low, choking sob, the girl fled toward the little square of light that glowed from the window of her cabin.

CHAPTER IX

ON SNARE LAKE

When Bob MacNair left Chloe Elliston's camp, he swung around by the way of Mackay Lake, a detour that required two weeks' time and added immeasurably to the discomfort of the journey. Day by day, upon lake, river, and portage, Old Elk and Wee Johnnie Tamarack wondered much at his silence and the unwonted hardness of his features.

These two Indians knew MacNair. For ten years, day and night, they had stood at his beck and call; had followed him through all the vast wilderness that lies between the railways and the frozen sea. They had slept with him, had feasted and starved with him, at his shoulder faced death in a hundred guises, and they loved him as men love their God. They had followed him during the lean years when, contrary to the wishes of his father, the stern-eyed factor at Fort Norman, he had refused the offers of the company and devoted his time, winter and summer, to the exploration of rivers and lakes, rock ridges and mountains, and the tundra that lay between, in search of the lost copper mines of the Indians; the mines that lured Hearne into the North in 1771, and which Hearne forgot in the discovery of a fur empire so vast as to stagger belief.

But, as the canoe forged northward, Old Elk and Wee

Johnnie Tamarack held their peace, and when they arrived at the fort, MacNair growled an order, and sought his cabin beside the wall of the stockade.

A half hour later, when the Indians had gathered in response to the hurried word of Old Elk and Wee Johnnie Tamarack, MacNair stepped from his cabin and addressed them in their own language, or rather in the jargon—the compromise language of the North—by means of which the minds of white men and Indians meet on common ground. He warned them against Pierre Lapierre, the *kultus* breed of whom most of them already knew, and he told them of the girl and her school at the mouth of the Yellow Knife. And then, in no uncertain terms, he commanded them to have nothing whatever to do with the school, nor with Lapierre. Whereupon, Sotenah, a leader among the young men, arose, and after a long and flowery harangue in which he lauded and extolled the wisdom of MacNair and the benefits and advantages that accrued to the Indians by reason of his patronage, vociferously counselled a summary descent upon the fort of the *Mesahchee Kloochman.*

The proclamation was received with loud acclaim, and it was with no little difficulty that MacNair succeeded in quieting the turbulence and restoring order. After which he rebuked Sotenah severely and laid threat upon the Indians that if so much as a hair of the white *kloochman* was harmed he would kill, with his own hand, the man who wrought the harm.

As for Pierre Lapierre and his band, they must be crushed and driven out of the land of the lakes and the rivers, but the time was not yet. He, MacNair, would tell them when to strike, and only if Lapierre's Indians were found prowling about the vicinity of Snare Lake were they to be molested.

The Indians dispersed and, slinging a rifle over his shoulder,

MacNair swung off alone into the bush.

Bob MacNair knew the North; knew its lakes and its rivers, its forests and its treeless barrens. He knew its hardships, dangers and limitations, and he knew its gentler moods, its compensations, and its possibilities. Also, he knew its people, its savage primitive children who call it home, and its invaders—good and bad, and worse than bad. The men who infest the last frontier, pushing always northward for barter, or for the saving of souls.

He understood Pierre Lapierre, his motives and his methods. But the girl he did not understand, and her presence on the Yellow Knife disturbed him not a little. Had chance thrown her into the clutches of Lapierre? And had the man set about deliberately to use her school as an excuse for the establishment of a trading-post within easy reach of his Indians? MacNair was inclined to believe so—and the matter caused him grave concern. He foresaw trouble ahead, and a trouble that might easily involve the girl who, he felt, was entirely innocent of wrongdoing.

His jaw clamped hard as he swung on and on through the scrub. He had no particular objective, a problem faced him and, where other men would have sat down to work its solution, he walked.

In many things was Bob MacNair different from other men. Just and stern beyond his years, with a sternness that was firmness rather than severity; slow to anger, but once his anger was fairly aroused terrible in meting out his vengeance. Yet, withal, possessed of an understanding and a depth of sympathy, entirely unsuspected by himself, but which enshrined him in the hearts of his Indians, who, in all the world were the men and women who knew him.

Even his own father had not understood this son, who

devoured books as ravenously as his dogs devoured salmon. Again and again he remonstrated with him for wasting his time when he might be working for the company. Always the younger man listened respectfully, and continued to read his books and to search for the lost mines with a determination and singleness of purpose that aroused the secret approbation of the old Scotchman, and the covert sneers and scoffings of others.

And then, after four years of fruitless search, at the base of a ridge that skirted the shore of an unmapped lake, he uncovered the mouth of an ancient tunnel with rough-hewn sides and a floor that sloped from the entrance. Imbedded in the slime on the bottom of a pool of stinking water, he found curious implements, rudely chipped from flint and slate, and a few of bone and walrus ivory. Odd-shaped, half-finished tools of hammered copper were strewn about the floor, and the walls were thickly coated with verdigris. Instead of the sharp ring of steel on stone, a dull thud followed the stroke of his pick, and its scars glowed with a red lustre in the flare of the smoking torches.

Old Elk and Wee Johnnie Tamarack looked on in stolid silence, while the young man, with wildly beating heart, crammed a pack-sack with samples. He had found the ancient mine—the lost mine of the Indians, which men said existed only in the fancy of Bob MacNair's brain! Carefully sealing the tunnel, the young man headed for Fort Norman; and never did Old Elk and Wee Johnnie Tamarack face such a trail. Down the raging torrent of the Coppermine, across the long portage to the Dismal Lakes, and then by portage and river to Dease Bay, across the two hundred miles of Great Bear Lake, and down the Bear River to their destination.

Seven hundred long miles they covered, at a man-killing pace that brought them into the fort, hollow-eyed and gaunt, and with their bodies swollen and raw from the sting of black flies and mosquitoes that swarmed through the holes in their tattered garments.

The men wolfed down the food that was set before them by an Indian woman, and then, while Old Elk and Wee Johnnie Tamarack slept, the chief trader led Bob MacNair to the grave of his father.

"'Twas his heart, lad, or somethin' busted inside him," explained the old man. "After supper it was, two weeks agone. He was sittin' i' his chair wi' his book an' his pipe, an' me in anither beside him. He gi' a deep sigh, like, an' his book fell to the ground and his pipe. When I got to him his head was leant back ag'in his chair—and he was dead."

Bob MacNair nodded, and the chief trader returned to the store, leaving the young man standing silent beside the fresh-turned mound with its rudely fashioned wooden cross, that stood among the other grass-grown mounds whose wooden crosses, with their burned inscriptions, were weather-grey and old. For a long time he stood beside the little crosses that lent a solemn dignity to the rugged heights of Fort Norman.

It cannot be said that Bob MacNair had loved his father, in the generally accepted sense of the word. But he had admired and respected him above all other men, and his first thought upon the discovery of the lost mine was to vindicate his course in the eyes of this stern, just man who had so strongly advised against it.

For the opinion of others he cared not the snap of his fingers. But, to read approval in the deep-set eyes of his father, and to hear the deep, rich voice of him raised, at last, in approbation, rather than reproach, he had defied death and pushed himself and his Indians to the limit of human endurance. And he had arrived too late. The bitterness of the young man's soul found expression only in a hardening of the jaw and a clenching of the mighty fists. For, in the heart of him, he knew that in the future, no matter what the measure of the world might be, always, deep within him would rankle the bitter disappointment—the realization that this old man had gone to his grave believing that his son was a fool and a wastrel.

Slowly he turned from the spot and, with heavy steps, entered the post-store. He raised the pack that contained the samples from the floor, and, walking to the verge of the high cliff that overlooked the river, hurled it far out over the water, where it fell with a dull splash that was drowned in the roar of the rapids.

"Ye'll tak' charge here the noo, laddie?" asked McTurk, the grizzled chief trader, the following day when MacNair had concluded the inspection of his father's papers. "'Twad be what *he'd* ha' counselled!"

"No," answered the young man shortly, and, without a word as to the finding of the lost mine, hurried Old Elk and Wee Johnnie Tamarack into a canoe and headed southward.

A month later the officers of the Hudson Bay Company in Winnipeg gasped in surprise at the offer of young MacNair to trade the broad acres to which his father had acquired title in the wheat belt of Saskatchewan and Alberta for a vast tract of barren ground in the subarctic. They traded gladly, and when the young man heard that his dicker had earned for him the name of Fool MacNair in the conclave of the mighty, he smiled—and bought more barrens.

All of which had happened eight years before Chloe Elliston defied him among the stumps of her clearing, and in the interim much had transpired. In the heart of his barrens he built a post and collected about him a band of Indians who soon learned that those who worked in the mines had a far greater number of brass tokens of "made beaver" to their credit than those who trapped fur.

Those were hard years for Bob MacNair; years in which he worked day and night with his Indians, and paid them, for the most part, in promises. But always he fed them and clothed them and their women and children, although to do so stretched his credit to the limit—raised the limit—and raised it again.

He uncovered vast deposits of copper, only to realize that, until he could devise a cheaper method of transportation, the metal might as well have remained where the forgotten miners had left it. And it was while he was at work upon his transportation problem that the shovels of his Indians began to throw out golden grains from the bed of a buried creek.

When the news of gold reached the river, there was a stampede. But MacNair owned the land and his Indians were armed. There was a short, sharp battle, and the stampeders returned to the rivers to nurse their grievance and curse Brute MacNair.

He paid his debt to the Company and settled with his Indians, who suddenly found themselves rich. And then Bob MacNair learned a lesson which he never forgot—his Indians could not stand prosperity. Most of those who had stood by him all through the lean years when he had provided them only a bare existence, took their newly acquired wealth and departed for the white man's country. Some returned—broken husks of the men who departed. Many would never return, and for their undoing MacNair reproached himself unsparingly, the while he devised an economic system of his own, and mined his gold and worked out his transportation problem upon a more elaborate scale. The harm had been done, however; his Indians were known to be rich, and MacNair found his colony had become the cynosure of the eyes of the whiskey-runners, the chiefest among whom was Pierre Lapierre. It was among these men that the name of Brute, first used by the beaten stampeders, came into general use—a fitting name, from their viewpoint—for when one of them chanced to fall into his hands, his moments became at once fraught with tribulation.

And so MacNair had become a power in the Northland, respected by the officers of the Hudson Bay Company, a friend of the Indians, and a terror to those who looked upon the red man as their natural prey.

Step by step, the events that had been the milestones of this man's life recurred to his mind as he tramped tirelessly through the scrub growth of the barrens toward a spot upon the shore of the lake—the only grass plot within a radius of five hundred miles. Throwing himself down beside a low, sodded mound in the centre of the plot, he idly watched the great flocks of water fowls disport themselves upon the surface of the lake.

How long he lay there, he had no means of knowing, when suddenly his ears detected the soft swish of paddles. He leaped to his feet and, peering toward the water, saw, close to the shore, a canoe manned by four stalwart paddlers. He looked closer, scarcely able to credit his eyes. And at the same moment, in response to a low-voiced order, the canoe swung abruptly shoreward and grated upon the shingle of the beach. Two figures stepped out, and Chloe Elliston, followed by Big Lena, advanced boldly toward him. MacNair's jaw closed with a snap as the girl approached smiling. For in the smile was no hint of friendliness—only defiance, not unmingled with contempt.

"You see, Mr. Brute MacNair," she said, "I have kept my word. I told you I would invade your kingdom—and here I am."

MacNair did not reply, but stood leaning upon his rifle. His attitude angered her.

"Well," she said, "what are you going to do about it?" Still the man did not answer, and, stooping, plucked a tiny weed from among the blades of grass. The girl's eyes followed his movements. She started and looked searchingly into his face. For the first time she noticed that the mound was a grave.

CHAPTER X

AN INTERVIEW

"Oh, forgive me!" Chloe cried, "I—I did not know that I was intruding upon—sacred ground!" There was real concern in her voice, and the lines of Bob MacNair's face softened.

"It is no matter," he said. "She who sleeps here will not be disturbed."

The unlooked for gentleness of the man's tone, the simple dignity of his words, went straight to Chloe Elliston's heart. She felt suddenly ashamed of her air of flippant defiance, felt mean, and small, and self-conscious. She forgot for the moment that this big, quiet man who stood before her was rough, even boorish in his manner, and that he was the oppressor and debaucher of Indians.

"A—a woman's grave?" faltered the girl.

"My mother's."

"Did *she* live here, on Snare Lake?" Chloe asked in surprise, as her glance swept the barren cliffs of its shore.

MacNair answered with the same softness of tone that

somehow dispelled all thought of his uncouthness. "No. She lived at Fort Norman, over on the Mackenzie—that is, she died there. Her home, I think, was in the Southland. My father used to tell me how she feared the North—its snows and bitter cold, its roaring, foaming rivers, its wild, fierce storms, and its wind-lashed lakes. She hated its rugged cliffs and hills, its treeless barrens and its mean, scrubby timber. She loved the warm, long summers, and the cities and people, and—" he paused, knitting his brows—"and whatever there is to love in your land of civilization. But she loved my father more than these—more than she feared the North. My father was the factor at Fort Norman, so she stayed in the North—and the North killed her. To live in the North, one must love the North. She died calling for the green grass of her Southland."

He ceased speaking and unconsciously stooped and plucked a few spears of grass which he held in his palm and examined intently.

"Why should one die calling for the sight of grass?" he asked abruptly, gazing into Chloe's eyes with a puzzled look.

The girl gazed directly, searchingly into MacNair's eyes. The naive frankness of him—his utter simplicity—astounded her.

"Oh!" she cried, impulsively stepping forward. "It wasn't the *grass*—it was—oh! *can't* you *see*?" The man regarded her wonderingly and shook his head.

"No," he answered gravely. "I can not see."

"It was—everything! Life—friends—home! The grass was only the symbol—the tangible emblem that stood for life!" MacNair nodded, but, by the look in his eye, Chloe knew that he did not understand and that pride and a certain natural reserve sealed his lips from further questioning.

"It is far to the Mackenzie," ventured the girl.

"Aye, far. After my father died I brought her here."

"You! Brought her here!" she exclaimed, staring in surprise into the strong emotionless face.

The man nodded slowly. "In the winter it was—and I came alone—dragging her body upon a sled—"

"But why—"

"Because I think she would have wished it so. If one hated the wild, rugged cliffs and the rock-tossed rapids, would one wish to lie upon a cliff with the rapids roaring, for ever and ever? I do not think that, so I brought her here—away from the grey hills and the ceaseless roar of the rapids."

"But the grass?"

"I brought that from the Southland. I failed many times before I found a kind that would grow. It is little I can do for her, and she does not know, but, somehow, it has made me feel—easier—I cannot tell you exactly. I come here often."

"I think she *does* know," said Chloe softly, and brushed hot tears from her eyes. Could *this* be the man whose crimes against the poor, ignorant savages were the common knowledge of the North? Could this be he whom men called Brute—this simple-spoken, straightforward, boyish man who had endured hardships and spared no effort, that the mother he had never known might lie in her eternal rest beneath the green sod of her native land, far from the sights, and sounds that, in life, had become a torture to her soul, and worn her, at last, to the grave?

"Mr.—MacNair." The hard note—the note of uncompromising antagonism—had gone from her voice, and the man looked at her in surprise. It was the first time she had addressed him without prefixing the name Brute and emphasizing the prefix. He stood, regarding her calmly, waiting for her to proceed. Somehow, Chloe found that it had become very difficult for her to speak; to say the things to this man that she had intended to say. "I cannot understand you—your viewpoint."

"Why should you try? I ask no one to understand me. I care not what people think."

"About the Indians, I mean—"

"The Indians? What do you know of my viewpoint in regard to the Indians?" The man's face had hardened at her mention of the Indians.

"I know this!" exclaimed the girl. "That you are trading them whiskey! With my own eyes I saw Mr. Lapierre smash your kegs—the kegs that were cunningly disguised as bales of freight and marked with your name, and I saw the whiskey spilled out upon the ground."

She paused, expecting a denial, but MacNair remained silent and again she saw the peculiar twinkle in his eye as he waited for her to proceed. "And I—you, yourself told me that you would kill some of Mr. Lapierre's Indians! Do you call that justice—to kill men because they happen to be in the employ of a rival trader—one who has as much right to trade in the Northland as you have?"

Again she paused, but the man ignored her question.

"Go on," he said shortly.

"And you told me your Indians had to work so hard they had no time for book-learning, and that the souls of the Indians were black as—as hell."

"And I told you, also, that I have never owned any whiskey. Why do you believe me in some things and not in others? It would seem more consistent, Miss Chloe Elliston, for you either to believe or to disbelieve me."

"But, I *saw* the whiskey. And as for what you, yourself, told me—a man will scarcely make himself out worse than he is."

"At least, I can scarcely make myself out worse than you believe me to be." The twinkle was gone from MacNair's eyes now, and he spoke more gruffly. "Of what use is all this talk? You are firmly convinced of my character. Your opinion of me concerns me not at all. Even if I were to attempt to make my position clear to you, you would not believe anything I should tell you."

"What defence can there be to conduct such as yours?"

"Defence! Do you imagine I would stoop to defend my conduct to *you*—to one who is, either wittingly or unwittingly, hand in glove with Pierre Lapierre?"

The unconcealed scorn of the man's words stung Chloe to the quick.

"Pierre Lapierre is a man!" she cried with flashing eyes. "He is neither afraid nor ashamed to declare his principles. He is the friend of the Indians—and God knows they need a friend—living as they do by sufferance of such men as you, and the men of the Hudson Bay Company!"

"You believe that, I think," MacNair said quietly. "I wonder if you are really such a fool, or do you know Lapierre for what he is?"

"Yes!" exclaimed the girl, her face flushed. "I *do* know him for what he is! He is a *man*! He knows the North. I am learning the North, and together we will drive you and your kind out of the North."

"You cannot do that," he said. "Lapierre, I will crush as I would crush a snake. I bear you no ill will. As you say, you will learn the North—for you will remain in the North. I told you once that you would soon tire of your experiment, but I was wrong. Your eyes are the eyes of a fighting man."

"Thank you, Mr.—MacNair—"

"Why not Brute MacNair?"

Chloe shook her head. "No," she said. "Not that—not after—I think I shall call you Bob MacNair."

The man looked perplexed. "Women are not like men," he said, simply. "I do not understand you at times. Tell me—why did you come into the North?"

"I thought I had made that plain. I came to bring education to the Indians. To do what I can to lighten their burden and to make it possible for them to compete with the white man on the white man's terms when this country shall bow before the inevitable advance of civilization; when it has ceased to be the land beyond the outposts."

"We are working together then," answered, MacNair. "When you have learned the North we shall be—friends."

"Never! I—"

"Because you will have learned," he continued, ignoring her protest, "that education is the last thing the Indians need. If you can make better trappers and hunters of them; teach them to work in mines, timber, on the rivers, you will come nearer to solving their problem than by giving them all the education in the world. No, Miss Chloe Elliston, they can't play the white man's game—with the white man's chips."

"But they can! In the States we—"

"Why didn't you stay in the States?"

"Because the government looks after the education of the Indians—provides schools and universities, and—"

"And what do they turn out?"

"They turn out lawyers and doctors and engineers and ministers of the gospel, and educated men in all walks of life. We have Indians in Congress!"

"How many? And how many are lawyers and doctors and engineers and ministers of the gospel? And how many can truthfully be said to be 'educated men in all walks of life'? A mere handful! Where one succeeds, a hundred fail! And the others return to their reservation, dissolute, dissatisfied, to live on the bounty of your government; you, yourself, will admit that when an Indian does rise into a profession for which his education has fitted him, he is an object of wonder—a man to be written about in your newspapers and talked about in your homes. And then your sentimentalists—your fools—hold him up as a type! Not your educated Indians are reaping the benefit of your government's belated attention, but those who are following the calling for which nature has fitted them—stock-raising and small farming on their allotted reservations. The educated ones know that the government will feed and clothe them—why should they exert themselves?

"Here in the North, because the Indians have been dealt with sanely, and not herded onto restricted reservations, and subjected to the experiments of departmental fools well-intentioned—and otherwise—they are infinitely better off. They are free to roam the woods, to hunt and to trap and to fish, and they are contented. They remain at the posts only long enough to do their trading, and return again to the wilds. For the most part they are truthful and sober and honest. They can obtain sufficient clothing and enough to eat. The lakes and the rivers teem with fish, and the woods and the barrens abound with game,

"Contrast these with the Indians who have come more intimately into contact with the whites. You can see them hanging about the depots and the grogeries and rum shops of the railway towns, degenerate, diseased, reduced to beggary and petty thievery. And you do not have to go to the railway towns to see the effect of your civilization upon them. Follow the great trade rivers! From source to mouth, their banks are lined with the Indians who have come into contact with your civilization!

"Go to any mission centre! Do you find that the Indian has taken kindly to the doctrines it teaches? Do you find them happy, God-fearing Indians who embraced Christianity and are living in accord with its precepts? You do not! Except in a very few isolated cases, like your lawyers and doctors of the states, you will find at the very gates of the missions, be their denomination what they may, debauchery and rascality in its most vicious forms. Read your answer there in the vice-marked, ragged, emaciated hangers-on of the missions.

"I do not say that this harm is wrought wilfully—on the contrary, I know it is not. They are noble and well-meaning men and women who carry the gospel into the North.

Many of them I know and respect and admire—Father Desplaines, Father Crossett, the good Father O'Reiley, and Duncan Fitzgilbert, of my mother's faith. These men are good men; noble men, and the true friends of the Indians; in health and in sickness, in plague, famine, and adversity these men shoulder the red man's burden, feed, clothe, and doctor him, and nurse him back to health—or bury him. With these I have no quarrel, nor with the religion they teach—in its theory. It is not bad. It is good. These men are my friends. They visit me, and are welcome whenever they come.

"Each of these has begged me to allow him to establish a mission among my Indians. And my answer is always the same—'*No!*' And I point to the mission centres already established. It is then they tell me that the deplorable condition exists, not because of the mission, but *despite* it." He paused with a gesture of impatience. "*Because*! *Despite*! A quibble of words! If the *fact* remains, what difference does it make whether it is *because* or *despite*? It must be a great comfort to the unfortunate one who is degraded, diseased, damned, to know that his degradation, disease, and damnation, were wrought not *because*, but *despite*. I think God laughs—even as he pities. But, in spite of all they can do, the *fact* remains. I do not ask you to believe me. Go and see it with your own eyes, and then if you *dare*, come back and establish another plague spot in God's own wilderness. The Indian rapidly acquires all the white man's vices—and but few of his virtues.

"Stop and think what it means to experiment with the future of a people. To overthrow their traditions: to confute their beliefs and superstitions, and to subvert their gods! And what do you offer them in return? Other traditions; other beliefs; another God—and education! Do you dare to assume the responsibility? Do you dare to implant in the minds of these people an education—a culture—that will render them for ever dissatisfied with their lot, and send many of them to the land of the white man to engage in a feeble and hopeless struggle after that which is, for them, unattainable?"

"But it is *not* unattainable! They—"

"I know your sophisms; your fabrication of theory!" MacNair interrupted her almost fiercely. "The *facts*! I have seen the rum-sodden wrecks, the debauched and soul-warped men and women who hang about your frontier towns, diseased in body and mind, and whose greatest misfortune is that they live. These, Miss Chloe Elliston, are the real monuments to your education. Do you dare to drive one hundred to certain degradation that is worse than fiery hell, that you may point with pride to one who shall attain to the white man's standard of success?"

"That is not the truth! I do not believe it! I *will* not believe it!"

The steel-grey eyes of the man bored deep into the shining eyes of brown. "I know that you do not believe it. But you are wrong when you say that you *will* not believe it. You are honest and unafraid, and, therefore, you will learn, and now, one thing further.

"We will say that you succeed in keeping your school, or post, or mission, from this condition of debauchery—which you will not. What then? Suppose you educate your Indians? There are no employers in the North. None who buy education. The men who pay out money in the waste places pay it for bone and brawn, not for brains; they have brains—or something that answers the purpose—therefore, your educated Indian must do one of two things—he must go where he can use his education or he must remain where he is. In either event he will be the loser. If he seeks the land of the white man, he must compete with the white man on the white man's terms. He cannot do it. If he stays here in the North he must continue to hunt, or trap, or work on the river, or in the mines, or the timber, and he is ever afterward dissatisfied with his lot. More, he has wasted the time he spent in filling his brain with useless knowledge."

MacNair spoke rapidly and earnestly, and Chloe realized that he spoke from his heart and also that he spoke from a certain knowledge of his subject. She was at a loss for a reply. She could not dispute him, for he had told her not to believe him; to go see for herself. She did not believe MacNair, but in spite of herself she was impressed.

"The missionaries *are* doing good! Their reports show—"

"Their reports show! Of course their reports show! Why shouldn't they? Where do their reports go? To the people who pay them their salaries! Do not understand me to say that in all cases these reports are falsely made. They are not—that is, they are literally true. A mission reports so many converts to Christianity during a certain period of time. Well and good; the converts are there—they can produce them. The Indians are not fools. If the white men want them to profess Christianity, why they will profess Christianity—or Hinduism or Mohammedanism. They will worship any god the white man suggests—for a fancy waistcoat or a piece of salt pork. The white man gives many gifts of clothing, and sometimes of food—to his converts. Therefore, he shall not want for converts—while the clothing holds out!"

"And *your* Indians? Have they not suffered from their contact with you?"

"No. They have not suffered. I know them, their needs and requirements, and their virtues and failings. And they know me."

"Where is your fort?"

"Some distance above here on the shore of this lake."

"Will you take me there? Show me these Indians, that I may see for myself that you have spoken the truth?"

"No. I told you you were to have nothing to do with my Indians. I also warned my Indians against you—and your partner Lapierre. I cannot warn them against you and then take you among them."

"Very well. I shall go myself, then. I came up here to see your fort and the condition of your Indians. You knew I would come."

"No. I did not know that. I had not seen the fighting spirit in your eyes then. Now I know that you will come—but not while I am here. And when you do come you will be taken back to your own school. You will not be harmed, for you are honest in your purpose. But you will, nevertheless, be prevented from coming into contact with my Indians. I will have none of Lapierre's spies hanging about, to the injury of my people."

"Lapierre's spies! Do you think I am a spy? Lapierre's?"

"Not consciously, perhaps—but a spy, nevertheless. Lapierre may even now be lurking near for the furtherance of some evil design."

Chloe suddenly realized that MacNair's boring, steel-grey eyes were fixed upon her with a new intentness—as if to probe into the very thoughts of her brain.

"Mr. Lapierre is far to the Southward," she said—and then, upon the edge of the tiny clearing, a twig snapped. The man whirled, his rifle jerked into position, there was a loud report, and Bob MacNair sank slowly down upon the grass mound that was his mother's grave.

CHAPTER XI

BACK ON THE YELLOW KNIFE

The whole affair had been so sudden that Chloe scarcely realized what had happened before a man stepped quickly into the clearing, at the same time slipping a revolver into its holster. The girl gazed at him in amazement. It was Pierre Lapierre. He stepped forward, hat in hand. Chloe glanced swiftly from the dark, handsome features to the face of the man on the ground. The grey eyes opened for a second, and then closed; but in that brief, fleeting glance the girl read distrust, contempt, and silent reproach. The man's lips moved, but no sound came—and with a laboured, fluttering sigh, he sank into unconsciousness.

"Once more, it seems, my dear Miss Elliston, I have arrived just in time."

A sudden repulsion for this cruel, suave killer of men flashed into the girl's brain. "Get some water," she cried, and dropping to her knees began to unbutton MacNair's flannel shirt.

"But—" objected Lapierre.

"Will you get some water? This is no time to argue! You can explain later!" Lapierre turned and without a word, walked to the lake and, taking a pail from the canoe, filled it with water. When he returned, Chloe was tearing white bandages from a garment essentially feminine, while Big Lena endeavoured to stanch the flow of blood from a small wound high on the man's left breast, and another, more ragged wound where the bullet had torn through the thick muscles of his back.

The two women worked swiftly and capably, while Lapierre waited, frowning.

"Better hurry, Miss Elliston," he said, when the last of the bandages was in place. "This is no place for us to be found if some of MacNair's Indians happen along. Your canoe is ready. Mine is farther down the lake."

"But, this man—surely—"

"Leave him there. You have done all you can do for him. His Indians will find him."

"What!" cried Chloe. "Leave a wounded man to die in the bush!"

Lapierre stepped closer. "What would you do ?" he asked. "Surely you cannot remain here. His Indians would kill you as they would kill a *carcajo*." The man's face softened. "It is the way of the North," he said sadly. "I would gladly have spared him—even though he is my enemy. But when he whirled with his rifle upon my heart, his finger upon the trigger, and murder in his eye, I had no alternative. It was his life or mine. I am glad I did not kill him." The words and the tone reassured Chloe, and when she answered, it was to speak calmly.

"We will take him with us," she said. "The Indians could not care for him properly even if they found him. At home I have everything necessary for the handling of just such cases."

"But, my dear Miss Elliston—think of the portages and the added burden. His Indians—"

The girl interrupted him—"I am not asking you to help. I have a canoe here. If you are afraid of MacNair's Indians you need not remain."

The note of scorn in the girl's voice was not lost upon Lapierre. He flushed and answered with the quiet dignity that well became him: "I came here, Miss Elliston, with only three canoemen. I returned unexpectedly to your school, and when I learned that you had gone to Snare Lake, I followed—to save you, if possible, from the hand of the Brute."

Chloe interrupted him. "You came here for that?"

The man bowed low. "Knowing what you do of Brute MacNair, and of his hatred of me, you surely do not believe I came here for business—or pleasure." He drew closer, his black eyes glowing with suppressed passion. "There is one thing a man values more than life—the life and the safety of the woman he loves!"

Chloe's eyes dropped. "Forgive me!" she faltered. "I—I did not know—I—Oh! don't you see? It was all so sudden. I have had no time to think! I know you are not afraid. But, we can't leave him here—like this."

"As you please," answered Lapierre, gently.

"It is not the way of the North; but—"

"It is the way of humanity."

"It is *your* way—and, therefore, it is my way, also. But, let us not waste time!" He spoke sharply to Chloe's canoemen, who sprang to the unconscious form, and raising it from the ground, carried it to the water's edge and deposited it in the canoe.

"Make all possible speed," he said, as Chloe preceded Big Lena into the canoe; "I shall follow to cover your retreat."

The girl was about to protest, but at that moment the canoe shot swiftly out into the lake, and Lapierre disappeared into the bush.

There was small need for the quarter-breed's parting injunction. The four Indian canoemen evidently keenly alive to the desirability of placing distance between themselves and MacNair's retainers, bent to their paddles with a unanimity of purpose that fairly lifted the big canoe through the water and sent the white foam curling from its bow in tiny ripples of protest.

Hour after hour, as the craft drove southward, Chloe sat with the wounded man's head supported in her lap and pondered deeply the things he had told her. Now and again she gazed into the bearded face, calm, masklike in its repose of unconsciousness, as if to penetrate behind the mask and read the real nature of him. She realized with a feeling almost of fear, that here was no weakling—no plastic irresolute—whose will could be dominated by the will of a stronger; but a man, virile, indomitable; a man of iron will who, though he scorned to stoop to defend his position, was unashamed to vindicate it. A man whose words carried conviction, and whose eyes compelled attention, even respect, though the uncouth boorishness of him repelled.

Yet she knew that somewhere deep behind that rough exterior lay a finer sensitiveness, a gentleness of feeling, and a sympathy that had impelled him to a deed of unconscious chivalry of which no man need be ashamed. And in her heart Chloe knew that had she not witnessed with her own eyes the destruction of his whiskey, she would have been convinced of his sincerity, if not of his postulates. "He is bad, but not *all* bad," she murmured to herself. "A man who will fight hard, but fairly. At all events, my journey to Snare Lake has not been entirely in vain. He knows, now, that I have come into the North to stay; that I am not afraid of him, and will fight him. He knows that I am honest—"

Suddenly the very last words she had spoken to him flashed into her mind—"Mr. Lapierre is far to the Southward"—and then Chloe closed her eyes as if to shut out that look of mingled contempt and reproach with which the wounded man had sunk into unconsciousness. "He thinks I lied to him—that the whole thing was planned," she muttered, and was conscious of a swift anger against Lapierre. Her eyes swept backward to the brown spot in the distance which was Lapierre's canoe.

"He came up here because he thought I was in danger," she mused. "And MacNair would have killed him. Oh, it is terrible," she moaned. "This wild, hard wilderness, where human life is cheap; where men hate, and kill, and maim, and break all the laws of God and man; it is all *wrong*! Brutal, and savage, and wrong!"

The shadows lengthened, the canoe slipped into the river that leads to Reindeer Lake, and still the tireless canoemen bent unceasingly to their paddles. Reindeer Lake was crossed by moonlight, and a late camp was made a mile to the westward of the portage. The camp was fireless, and the men talked in whispers. Later Lapierre joined them, and at the first grey hint of dawn the outfit was again astir. By noon the five-mile portage had been negotiated, and the canoes headed down Carp Lake, which is the northmost reach of the Yellow Knife.

The following two days showed no diminution in the efforts of the canoemen. The wounded man's condition remained unchanged. Lapierre's canoe followed at a distance of a mile or two, and a hundred times a day Chloe found herself listening with strained expectancy for the sound of the shots that would proclaim that MacNair's Indians had overtaken them. But no shots were fired, and it was with a feeling of intense relief that the girl welcomed the sight of her own buildings as they loomed in the clearing on the evening of the third day.

That night Lapierre visited Chloe in the cottage, where he found her seated beside MacNair's bed, putting the finishing touches to a swathing of fresh bandages.

"How is he doing?" he asked, with a nod toward the injured man.

"There is no change," answered the girl, as she indicated a chair close beside a table, upon which were a tin basin, various bottles, and porcelain cups containing medicine, and a small pile of antiseptic tablets. For just an instant the man's glance rested upon the tablets, and then swiftly swept the room. It was untenanted except for the girl and the unconscious man on the bed.

"LeFroy, it seems, has improved his time," ventured Lapierre as he accepted the proffered chair and drew from his pocket a thick packet of papers. "His complete list of supplies," he smiled. "With these in your storehouse you may well expect to seriously menace the trade of both MacNair and the Hudson Bay Company's post at Fort Rae."

Chloe glanced at the list indifferently. "It seems, Mr.

Lapierre, that your mind is always upon trade—when it is not upon the killing of men."

The quarter-breed was quick to note the disapproval of her tone, and hastened to reply. "Surely, Miss Elliston, you cannot believe that I regard the killing of men as a pleasure; it is a matter of deep regret to me that twice during the short period of our acquaintance I have been called upon to shoot a fellow man."

"Only twice! How about the shot in the night—in the camp of the Indians, before you left for the Southward?" The sarcasm of the last four words was not lost upon the man. "Who fired that shot? And what was the thing that was lifted from your canoe and dropped into the river?"

Lapierre's eyes searched hers. Did she know the truth? The chance was against it.

"A most deplorable affair—a fight between Indians. One was killed and we buried him in the river. I had hoped to keep this from your ears. Such incidents are all too common in the Northland—"

"And the murderer—"

"Has escaped. But to return to the others. Both shots, as you well know, were fired on the instant, and in neither case did I draw first."

Chloe, who had been regarding him intently, was forced to admit the justice of his words. She noted the serious sadness of the handsome features, the deep regret in his voice, and suddenly realized that in both instances Lapierre's shots had been fired primarily in defence of her.

A sudden sense of shame—of helplessness—came over her.

Could it be that she did not fit the North? Surely, Lapierre was entitled to her gratitude, rather than her condemnation. Judged by his own standard, he had done well. With a shudder she wondered if she would ever reach the point where she could calmly regard the killing of men as a mere incident in the day's work? She thought not. And yet—what had men told her of Tiger Elliston? Without exception, almost, the deeds they recounted had been deeds of violence and bloodshed. When she replied, her voice had lost its note of disapproval.

"Forgive me," she said softly, "it has all been so different—so strange and new, and big. I have been unable to grasp it. All my life I have been taught to hold human life sacred. It is not you who are to blame! Nor, is it the others. It is the kill or be killed creed—the savage wolf creed—of the North."

The girl spoke rapidly, with her eyes upon the face of MacNair. So absorbed was she that she did not see the slim fingers of Lapierre steal softly across the table-top and extract two tablets from the little pile—failed also to see the swift motion with which those fingers dropped the tablets into a porcelain cup, across the rim of which rested a silver spoon.

The man arose at the conclusion of her words, and crossing to her side rested a slim hand upon the back of her chair. "No. Miss Elliston," he said gently, "I am not to blame nor, in a measure, are the others. It is, as you say, the North—the crushing, terrible, alluring North—in whose primitive creed a good man does not mean a moral one, but one who accomplishes his purpose, even though that purpose be bad. End, and not means, is the ethics of the lean, lone land, where human life sinks into insignificance, beneath the immutable law of savage might."

His eyes burned as he gazed down into the upturned face of the girl. His hands stole lightly from the chair back and rested upon her shoulder. For one long, intense moment, their eyes held, and then, with a movement as swift and lithe as the spring of a panther, the man was upon his knees beside her chair, his arms were about her, and with no thought of resistance, Chloe felt herself drawn close against his breast, felt the wild beating of his heart, and then—his lips were upon hers, and she felt herself struggling feebly against the embrace of the sinewy arms.

Only for a moment did Lapierre hold her. With a movement as sudden and impulsive as the movement that embraced her, the arms were withdrawn, and the man leaped swiftly to his feet. Too dazed to speak, Chloe sat motionless, her brain in a chaotic whirl of emotion, while in her breast outraged dignity and hot, fierce anger strove for the mastery over a thrill, so strange to her, so new, so intense that it stirred her to the innermost depths of her being.

Swiftly, unconsciously, her glance rested for a moment upon the lean, bearded face of MacNair; and beside her chair, Lapierre noted the glance, and the thin lips twisted into a smile—a cynical, sardonic smile, that faded on the instant, as his eyes flashed toward the doorway. For there, silent and grim as he had seen her once before, stood Big Lena, whose china-blue eyes were fixed upon him, in that same disconcerting, fishlike stare.

The hot blood mounted to his cheeks and suddenly receded, so that his face showed pallid and pasty in the gloom of the darkened room. He drew his hand uncertainly across his brow and found it damp with a cold, moist sweat. Was it fancy, or did the china-blue, fishlike eyes rest for just an instant upon the porcelain cup on the table? With an effort the man composed himself, and stooping, whispered a few hurried words into the ears of the girl who sat with her face buried in her hands.

"Forgive me, Miss Elliston; for the moment I forgot that I had no right. I love you! Love you more than life itself! More than my own life—or the lives of others. It was but the impulse of an unguarded moment that caused me to forget that I had not the right—forget that I am a gentleman. We love as we kill in the North. And now, good-by, I am going Southward. I will return, if it is within the power of man to return, before the ice skims the lakes and the rivers."

He paused, but the girl remained as though she had not heard him. He leaned closer, his lips almost upon her ear. "Please, Miss Elliston, can you not forgive me—wish me one last bon voyage?"

Slowly, as one in a dream, Chloe offered him her hand. "Good-by!" she said simply, in a dull, toneless voice. The man seized the hand, pressed it lightly, and turning abruptly, crossed to the table. As he drew his Stetson toward him, its brim came into violent contact with the porcelain medicine cup. The cup crashed to the floor, its contents splashing widely over the whip-sawed boards.

With a hurried word of apology he passed out of the door—passed close beside the form of Big Lena onto whose cold, fishlike eyes the black eyes stared insolently, even as the thin lips twisted into a smile—cynical, sardonic, mocking.

CHAPTER XII

A FIGHT IN THE NIGHT

The days immediately following Lapierre's departure were busy days for Chloe Elliston. The word had passed along the lakes and the rivers, and stolid, sullen-faced Indians stole in from the scrub to gaze apathetically at the buildings on the banks of the Yellow Knife. Chloe with pain-staking repetition, through LeFroy as interpreter, explained to each the object of her school; with the result that a goodly number remained and lost no time in installing themselves in the commodious barracks.

On the evening of the second day the girl tiptoed into the sick-room and, bending over MacNair, was startled to encounter the steady gaze of the steel-grey eyes. "I thought you never would come to," she smiled. "You see, I don't know much about surgery, and I was afraid perhaps—"

"Perhaps Lapierre had done his work well?"

Chloe started at the weak, almost gentle tones of the gruff voice she had learned to associate with this man of the North. She flushed as she met the steady, disconcerting stare of the grey eyes. "He shot on the spur of the moment. He thought you were going to shoot him."

"And he shot from—far to the Southward?"

"Oh! You do not think—you do not believe that I deliberately *lied* to you! That I *knew* Lapierre was on Snare Lake!" The words fell from her lips with an intense eagerness that carried the ring of sincerity. The hard look faded from the man's eyes, and the bearded lips suggested just the shadow of a smile.

"No," he answered weakly; "I do not think that. But tell me, how long have I been this way? And what has happened? For I remember nothing—after the world turned black. I am surprised that Lapierre missed me. He has the reputation for killing—at his own range."

"But he didn't miss you!" cried the girl in surprise. "It was his bullet that—that made the world turn black."

"Aye; but it was a miss, just the same, and a miss, I am thinking, that will cost him dear. He should have killed me."

"Please do not talk," said the girl in sudden alarm, and taking the medicine from the table, held the spoon to the man's lips. He swallowed its contents, and was about to speak when Chloe interrupted him. "Please do not talk," she begged, "and I'll tell you what happened. There is not much to tell: after we bound up your wounds we brought you here, where I could give you proper care. It took three days to do this, and two days have passed since we arrived."

"I knew I was in your—"

Chloe flushed deeply. "Yes, in my room," she hastened to interrupt him; "but you must not talk. It was the only place I knew where you could be quiet and—and safe."

"But, Lapierre—why did he allow it?"

Chloe flushed. "Allow it! I do not take orders from Mr. Lapierre, nor from you, nor from anybody else. This is my school; this cottage is mine; I'll do as I please with it, and I'll bring who I please into it without asking permission from any one."

While she was speaking, the man's glance strayed from her flashing eyes to the face of a tarnished, smoke-blackened portrait that showed indistinct in the dull lamplight of the little room. Chloe's glance followed MacNair's, and as the little clock ticked sharply, both stared in silence into the lean, lined features of Tiger Elliston.

"Your eyes," murmured the man—"sometimes they are like that." Suddenly his voice strengthened. He continued to gaze at the face in the dull gold frame. With an effort he withdrew an arm from beneath the cover and pointed with a finger that trembled weakly. "I should like to have known him," he said. "By God, yon is the face of a *man*!"

"My grandfather," muttered the girl.

"You'll love the North—when you know it," said MacNair. "Tell me, did Lapierre advise you to bring me here?"

"No," answered Chloe, "he did not. He—he said to leave you; that your Indians would care for you."

"And my Indians—did they not follow you?" Chloe shook her head. Once more MacNair bent a searching glance upon the girl's face. "Where is Lapierre?" he asked.

"He is gone," Chloe answered. "Two days ago he left for the—" She hesitated as there flashed through her brain the moment on Snare Lake when, once before, she had answered MacNair's question in almost the same words. "*He said* he was going to the southward," she corrected.

MacNair smiled. "I think, this time, he has gone. But why he left without killing me I cannot understand. Lapierre has made a mistake."

"You do him an injustice! Mr. Lapierre does not want to kill you. He is sorry he was forced to shoot; but, as he said, it was your life or his. And now please do be quiet, or I must leave you to yourself."

MacNair closed his eyes, and, seating herself by the table, Chloe stared silently into the face of the portrait until the man's deep, regular breathing told her that he slept.

Slowly the moments passed, and the girl's gaze roved from the face of the portrait along the walls of the little room. Suddenly her eyes dilated in horror; for there, tight pressed against an upper pane of the window, whose lower sash was daintily curtained with chintz, appeared a dark, scowling face—the face of an Indian, which she instantly recognized as one of the two who had accompanied MacNair upon his first visit to her clearing.

Even as she looked the face vanished, leaving the girl staring wide-eyed at the black square of the window. Curbing her impulse to awake MacNair, she stole softly from the room and, unlocking the outer door, sped swiftly through the darkness toward the little square of light that glowed from the window of the store.

The distance was not great from the door of the cottage to the soft square of radiance that showed distinctly in the darkness. But even as Chloe ran, the light was suddenly extinguished, and the outlines of the big storehouse loomed vague and huge and indistinct against the black background of the encircling scrub. The girl stopped abruptly and stared uncertainly into the darkness. Her heart beat wildly. A strange sense of terror came over her as she stood alone, surrounded by the blackness of the clearing. Why had LeFroy extinguished his light? And why was the night so still?

She strained to catch the familiar sounds of the wilderness—the little night sounds to which she had grown accustomed: the bellowing of frogs in the sedges, the chirp of tree-toads, and the harsh squawk of startled night-fowls. Even the air seemed unnaturally still, and the ceaseless drone of the mosquitoes served but to intensify the unnatural silence. The mosquitoes broke the spell of the nameless terror, and she slapped viciously at her face and neck.

"I'm a fool," she muttered; "a perfect fool! LeFroy puts out his light every night and—and what if there are no sounds? I'm just listening for something to be afraid of."

She glanced backward toward her own cottage where the light still glowed from the window. It was reassuring, that little square of yellow lamp-light that shone softly from the window of her room. She was not afraid now. She would return to the cottage and lock the door. She shuddered at the thought. Before her rose the vision of that dark, shadowy face, tight-pressed against the glass. Instinctively she knew that Indian was not alone. There were others, and—once more her eyes swept the blackness.

Suddenly the question flashed through her brain: Why should these Indians seek to avenge MacNair—the man who held the power of life and death over them—who had practically forced them into servitude? Then, swift as the question, flashed the answer: It was not to avenge MacNair they came, but, knowing he was helpless, to strike the blow that would free themselves from the yoke. Had Lapierre known this? Had he left, knowing that the man's own Indians would finish the work his bullet had only half completed? No! Lapierre would not have done that. Did he not say: "I am glad I did not kill him"? He was thinking only of my safety.

"We'll be safe enough till morning," she muttered. "Surely I have read somewhere that Indians never attack in the night. Tomorrow we must hide MacNair where they cannot find him. They will murder him, now that he is wounded. How they must hate him! Must hate the man who has oppressed and debauched and cheated them!"

The girl had nearly reached the door of the cottage when once more she halted, rooted in her tracks. Out of the unnatural silence of the night, close upon the edge of the clearing, boomed the cry of the great horned owl. It was a sound she had often heard here in the northern night—this hooting of an owl; but, somehow, this sound was different. Once more her heart thumped wildly against her ribs. Her fists clenched, and she peered tensely toward the wall of the scrub timber that showed silent and black and impenetrable in the little light of the stars. Again the portentous silence and then—was it fancy, or were there shapes, stealthy, elusive, shadowy, moving along the wall of the intense blackness?

A light suddenly flashed from the window of the storehouse. It disappeared. The great door banged sharply, and out of the blackness sounded a rush of moccasined feet, padding the earth as they ran.

From the edge of the timber—from the direction of the shadowy shapes—came a long, thin spurt of flame, and the silence was broken by the roar of a smooth-bore rifle. The next instant the roar was increased tenfold, and from the loopholes high on the walls of the storehouse flashed other thin red spurts of flame.

Terror-stricken, Chloe dashed for the cottage. Along the entire length of the timber-line, spikes of flame belched forth, and the crash and roar of rifles drowned the rush of the moccasin feet. A form dashed past her in the darkness, and then another, forcing Chloe from the path. The terrified girl realized that these forms were speeding straight for the door of the cottage. Her first thought was for MacNair. He would be murdered as he slept.

She redoubled her efforts, feeling blindly in the darkness for the path that led toward the square of light. In her ears sounded the sharp jangle of smashing glass. Her foot caught in a vine, and she crashed heavily forward almost at the door. All about her guns roared; from the edge of the scrub, from the river-bank, and from the corners of the long log dormitories. Bullets whined above her like angry mosquitoes, and thudded dully against the logs of the cottage.

Again sounded the sharp jangle of glass. She struggled to her knees, and was hurled backward as the huge form of an Indian tripped over her and sprawled, cursing, at her side. The door of the cottage burst suddenly open, and in the long quadrangle of light the forms of the two Indians who had passed her stood out distinctly. The girl gave a quick, short sob of relief. They were LeFroy's Indians! At the sound the man on the ground thrust his face close to hers and with a quick grunt of surprise scrambled to his feet. Chloe felt her arm seized, and realized that she was being dragged toward the door of the cottage through which the other two Indians had disappeared. She was jerked roughly across the threshold, and lay huddled up on the floor. The Indian released his hold on her arm and, stepping across her body, reached for the door.

Outside, the roar of the guns was incessant. Suddenly, close at hand, Chloe heard a quick, wicked spat, and the Indian reeled from the doorway, whirled as on a pivot, and crashed, face downward, across the table. There was a loud rattle of porcelain dishes, a rifle rang sharply upon the floor boards, and Chloe gazed in horrid fascination as the limp form of the Indian slipped slowly from the table. Its momentum increased, and the back of the man's head struck the floor with a sickening thump. The face turned toward her—a face wet and dripping with the rich red blood that oozed thickly from the irregular hole in the forehead where the soft, round ball from a smooth bore had torn into the brain. The wide eyes stared stonily into her own. The jaws sagged open, and the nearly severed tongue protruded from between the fang-like yellow teeth.

Someone blew out the lamp. The door slammed shut. Chloe felt strong hands beneath her shoulders; the voice of Big Lena sounded in her ears, and she was being guided through the pitch blackness to the door of her own room. The lamp by the bedside had also been extinguished, and the girl glanced toward the window, which showed in the feeble starlight a pattern of jagged panes. One of the Indians who had preceded her into the cottage thrust the barrel of a rifle through the aperture and fired rapidly at the flashes of flame in the clearing.

In the other room someone was shrieking, and Chloe recognized the voice of Harriet Penny. Big Lena left her side, and a moment later the shrieking ceased, or, rather, quieted to a series of terrified, choking grunts and muffled cries, as though something soft and thick had been forcibly applied as a gag. Chloe groped her way blindly toward the bed, where she had left the wounded man. Her feet stumbled awkwardly through the confusion of debris that was the wreck of the over-turned medicine table.

"Are you hurt?" she gasped as she sank trembling upon the

edge of the bed. Close beside her sounded the sharp snap of metal as the Indian jammed fresh cartridges into his magazine.

"No!" said a voice in her ear. "I'm not hurt. Are you?" Chloe shook her head, forgetting that in the intense blackness she had returned no answer. There was a movement upon the bed; a huge hand closed roughly about her arm. The Indian was firing again.

"Tell me, are you hurt?" rasped a voice in her ear. And her arm was shaken almost fiercely.

"No!" she managed to gasp, struggling to free herself. "But oh, it's all too, too horrible, too awful! There is a dead man in the other room. He is one of LeFroy's Indians. One of *my* Indians, and they shot him!"

"I'm damned glad of it!" growled MacNair thickly, and Chloe leaped from the bed. The coarse brutality of the man was inconceivable. In her mingled emotion of rage and loathing, she hated this man with a fierce, savage hatred that could kill. She knew now why men called him Brute MacNair. The name fitted! These Indians had rushed from the security of the fortlike storehouse upon the first intimation of danger to protect the defenseless quartet in the cottage—the three women and the wounded, helpless man. In the very doorway of the cottage one had been killed—killed facing the enemy—the savage blood-thirsty horde who, having learned of the plight of their oppressor, had taken the warpath to venge their wrongs. Surely MacNair must know that this man had died as much in the defense of him as of the women. And yet, when he learned of the death of this man, he had said: "I am damned glad of it!"

How long Chloe stood there speechless, trembling, with her heart fairly bursting with rage, she did not know. Time ceased to be. Suddenly she realized that the room was no longer in intense darkness. Objects appeared dim and indistinct: the bed with the wounded man, the contents of the table strewn in confusion upon the floor, and the Indian shooting from the window. Then the flare of flames met her eyes. The walls of the storehouse stood out distinctly from its black background of timber. Savage forms appeared in the clearing, gliding stealthily from stump to stump.

The light grew brighter. She could hear now, mingled with the sharp crack of the rifles, the dull roar of flames. The dormitories were burning! This added to her consuming rage. Her eyes seemed fairly to glow as she fixed them upon the pale face of MacNair, who had struggled to a sitting posture. She took a step toward the bed. A dull red spot showed on either cheek. A bullet ripped through the window and splintered the dull gold frame of Tiger Elliston's portrait, but the girl had lost all sense of fear. She shook her clenched fist in the bearded face of the man, and her voice quavered high and thin.

"You—you—*damn you*!" she cried. "I wish I'd left you back there to the mercy of your savages! You're a brute—a fiend! It would serve you right if I should give you up to them! He—the man who was killed—was trying to save you from the righteous wrath of those you have ground down and oppressed!"

MacNair ignored her words, and as his eyes met hers squarely, they betrayed not the slightest emotion. The pallid features showed tense and drawn in the growing firelight. His gaze projected past her to the lean face of Tiger Elliston.

"You are a fighter at heart," he said slowly addressing the girl. "You are his flesh and blood and he was a fighter. He won to victory over the bodies of his enemies. In his eyes I can see it."

"He was no coward!" flashed the girl. "He never won to victory over the bodies of his friends!" With an effort the man reached for his clothing, which hung from a peg near the head of the bed.

"Where are you going?" cried the girl sharply.

"I am going," MacNair answered gravely, looking straight into her eyes, "to take my Indians back to Snare Lake."

"They will kill you!" she cried impulsively.

"They will not!" MacNair smiled; "but if they do, you will be glad. Did you not say—"

The girl faced swiftly away, and at the same moment the Indian at the window staggered backward, dropping his rifle and cursing horribly in the only English he knew, as he clutched frantically at his shoulder. Chloe turned. MacNair was lacing his boots. He raised himself weakly to his feet, swaying uncertainly, with his hand pressed against his chest, and laughed harshly into the pain-twisted features of the Indian.

"When the last of yon dogs gets his bullet, I can leave this place in safety."

"What do you mean?" cried the girl, her eyes blazing.

"I mean," rasped the man, "that you are a fool! You have listened to Lapierre and you have easily become his dupe. There is no Indian in his employ who would not kill me. They have had their orders. Have you stopped to reflect that the brave Lapierre did not himself remain to stem this attack? To protect me from my Indians?"

The sneer in MacNair's voice was not lost upon the girl,

who drew herself up haughtily.

"Mr. Lapierre," she answered, "could hardly be charged with anticipating this attack, nor could he be blamed for not altering his plans to fight *your* battles."

MacNair laughed. "The idea of Lapierre fighting *my* battles is, indeed, unique. And you may be sure that Lapierre will not fight his own battles—as long as he can find others to fight them for him. Miss Elliston, this attack *was* anticipated. Lapierre knew to a certainty that when my Indians read the signs, and learned what had happened there on the shore of Snare Lake, their vengeance would not be delayed." He looked straight into the eyes of the girl. "Did you arm your Indians?"

"I did not!" answered Chloe. "I brought no guns."

"Then where did your Indians get their rifles?"

"Well, really, Mr. MacNair, I cannot tell you. Possibly at the same place your Indians got theirs. The Indians, who have come to me here are hunters and trappers. Is it so extraordinary that men who are hunters should own guns?"

"Your ignorance would be amusing, if it were not tragic!" retorted MacNair. And picking up the gun which the wounded Indian had dropped, held it before the eyes of the girl. "The hunters of the North, Miss Elliston, do not equip themselves with Mausers."

"With Mausers!" cried the girl. "You mean—"

"I mean just this," broke in MacNair, "that your Indians were armed to kill men, not animals. With, or without, your knowledge or sanction, your Indians have been supplied with the best rifles obtainable. Your school is Lapierre's fort!" Thrusting the rifle into the hands of the girl, he brushed past her and with difficulty made his way through the intervening room to the outer door, which he threw open.

Chloe followed. Outside the firing continued with undiminished intensity, but the girl was conscious of no sense of fear. Her eyes swept the room, flooded now by the glare of the flaring flames. Beside the stove stood Big Lena, an ax gripped tightly in her strong hands. The remaining Indian lay upon the floor, firing slowly through a loophole punched in the chinking. At the doorway MacNair turned, and in the strong light Chloe noticed that his face was haggard and drawn with pain.

"I thank you." he said, touching his bandaged chest, "for your nursing. It has probably saved my life."

"Come back! They will kill you!" MacNair ignored her warning. "You have one redeeming feature," cried the girl. "At least, you are as brutal toward yourself as toward others."

MacNair laughed harshly. "I thank you," he said and staggered out into the fire-lit clearing. Dully, Chloe noticed that the Indian who had been firing from the floor slipped stealthily through the doorway and, dropping to his knee, raised his rifle. The next instant the girl's eyes widened in horror. The gun was pointed squarely at MacNair's back. She tried to cry out, but no sound came. It seemed minutes that the Indian sighted as he knelt there in the clearing. And then—he pulled the trigger. There was a sharp, metallic click, followed by a muttered imprecation. The man jerked down the rifle and reaching into his pocket, produced long yellow cartridges, which he jammed into the magazine.

The horror of it! The diabolical deliberation of the man

spurred the girl to a fury she had never known. In that moment her one thought was to kill—to kill with her hands—to rend—to tear—and to maim! For the first time she realized that the thing in her hand was a gun.

Again the Indian was raising his rifle. The girl twisted and jerked at the bolt of her own gun. It was locked. The next instant, with a loud, animal-like cry, she leaped for the doorway, trampling, as she passed, with a wild, fierce joy upon the upturned staring face of the dead Indian.

Out in the clearing the flames roared and crackled. Rifles spat. And before her the Indian was again lining his sights. Grasping the heavy rifle by the barrel, Chloe whirled it high above her and brought it down with a crash upon the head of the kneeling savage. The man crumpled as dead men crumple—in an ugly, twisted heap. Fierce, swift exultation shot through the girl's brain as she stood beside the formless thing on the ground. She looked up—squarely into the eyes of MacNair, who had turned at the sound of her outcry.

"I said you would fight!" called the man. "I have seen it in your eyes. They are the eyes of the man on the wall."

Then, abruptly, he turned and disappeared in the direction of the river.

CHAPTER XIII

LAPIERRE RETURNS FROM THE SOUTH

When Pierre Lapierre left Chloe Elliston's school after the completion of the buildings, he proceeded at once to his own rendezvous on Lac du Mort.

This shrewdly chosen stronghold was situated on a high, jutting point that rose abruptly from the waters of the inland lake, which surrounded it upon three sides. The land side was protected by an enormous black spruce swamp. This headland terminated in a small, rock-rimmed plateau, perhaps three acres in extent, and was so situated as to be practically impregnable against the attack of an ordinary force; the rim-rocks forming a natural barricade which reduced the necessity for artificial fortification to a minimum. Across the neck of the tiny peninsula, Lapierre had thrown a strong stockade of logs, and from the lake access was had only by means of a narrow, one-man trail that slanted and twisted among the rocks of the precipitous cliff side.

The plateau itself was sparsely covered with a growth of stunted spruce and banskian, which served as a screen both for the stockade and the long, low, fort-like building of logs, which was Lapierre's main cache for the storing of fur, goods of barter, and contraband whiskey. The fort was provisioned to withstand a siege, and it was there that the crafty quarter-breed had succeeded in storing two hundred Mauser rifles and many cases of ammunition. Among Lapierre's followers it was known as the "Bastile du Mort." A safe haven of refuge for the hard-pressed, and, in event of necessity, the one place in all the North where they might hope indefinitely to defy their enemies.

The secret of this fort had been well guarded, and outside of Lapierre's organized band, but one man knew its location—and few even guessed its existence. There were vague rumours about the Hudson Bay posts, and in the barracks of the Mounted, that Lapierre maintained such a fort, but its location was accredited to one of the numerous islands of the extreme western arm of Great Slave Lake.

Bob MacNair knew of the fort, and the rifles, and the whiskey. He knew, also, that Lapierre did not know that he knew, and therein, at the proper time, would lie his advantage. The Hudson Bay Company had no vital interest in verifying the rumour, nor had the men of the Mounted, for as yet Lapierre had succeeded in avoiding suspicion except in the minds of a very few. And these few, realizing that if Lapierre was an outlaw, he was by far the shrewdest and most dangerous outlaw with whom they had ever been called upon to deal, were very careful to keep their suspicions to themselves, until such time as they could catch him with the goods—after that would come the business of tracking him to his lair. And they knew to a certainty that the men would not be wanting who could do this—no matter how shrewdly that lair was concealed.

Upon arriving at Lac du Mort, Lapierre ordered the canoe-men to load the fur, proceed at once to the mouth of Slave River, transfer it to the scows, and immediately start upon the track-line journey to Athabasca Landing. His own canoe he loaded with rifles and ammunition, and returned to the

Yellow Knife. It was then he learned that Chloe had gone to Snare Lake, and while he little relished an incursion into MacNair's domain, he secreted the rifles in the store-house and set out forthwith to overtake her. Despite the fact that he knew the girl to be strongly prejudiced against MacNair, Lapierre had no wish for her to see his colony in its normal condition of peace and prosperity. And so, pushing his canoemen to the limit of their endurance, he overtook her as she talked with MacNair by the side of his mother's grave.

Creeping noiselessly through the scrub to the very edge of the tiny clearing, Lapierre satisfied himself that MacNair was unattended by his Indians. The man's back was turned toward him, and the quarter-breed noticed that, as he talked, he leaned upon his rifle. It was a chance in a thousand. Never before had he caught MacNair unprepared—and the man's blood would be upon his own head. Drawing the revolver from its holster, he timed his movements to the fraction of a second; and deliberately snapped a twig, MacNair whirled like a flash, and Lapierre fired. His bullet went an inch too high, and when Chloe insisted upon carrying the wounded man to the school, Lapierre could but feebly protest.

The journey down the Yellow Knife was a nightmare for the quarter-breed, who momentarily expected an attack from MacNair's Indians. Upon their safe arrival, however, his black eyes glittered wickedly—at last MacNair was *his*. Fate had played directly into his hands. He knew the attack was inevitable, and during the excitement—well, LeFroy could be trusted to attend to MacNair. With the rifles in the storehouse, MacNair's Indians would be beaten back, and in the event of an investigation by the Mounted, the responsibility would be laid at MacNair's door. But of that MacNair would never know, for MacNair would have passed beyond.

Knowing that the vengeance of MacNair's Indians would not be long delayed, Lapierre determined to be well away from the Yellow Knife when the attack came. However, he had no wish to leave without first assuring himself that the shooting of MacNair stood justified in the eyes of the girl, and to that end he had called upon her in her cottage.

Then it was that chance seemed to offer a safe and certain means of putting MacNair away, and he dropped the poisonous antiseptic tablets into the medicine, only to have his plan frustrated by the unexpected presence of Big Lena. He was not sure that the woman had seen his action. But he took no chances, and with an apparent awkward movement of his hat, destroyed the evidence, sought out LeFroy, who had already been warned of the impending attack, and ordered him to place three or four of his most dependable Indians in the cottage, with instructions not only to protect Chloe, but to kill MacNair.

Then he hastened southward to overtake his scowmen, who were toiling at the track-lines somewhere among the turbulent rapids of the Slave. And indeed there was need of haste. The summer was well advanced. Six hundred miles of track-line and portage lay between Great Slave Lake and Athabasca Landing. And if he was to return with the many scow-loads of supplies for Chloe Elliston's store before the water-way became ice-locked, he had not a day nor an hour to lose.

At Point Brule he overtook the fur-laden scows, and at Smith Landing an Indian runner reported the result of the fight, and the escape of MacNair. Lapierre smothered his rage, and with twenty men at the track-line of each scow, bored his way southward.

A month later the gaunt, hard-bitten outfit tied up at the Landing. Lapierre disposed of his fur, purchased the supplies, and within a week the outfit was again upon the river.

At the mouth of La Biche a half-dozen burlapped pieces were removed from a *cache* in a thicket of balsam and added to the outfit. And at Fort Chippewayan the scows with their contents were examined by two officers of the Mounted, and allowed to proceed on their way.

On the Yellow Knife, Chloe Elliston anxiously awaited Lapierre's return. Under LeFroy's supervision the dormitories had been rebuilt, and a few sorry-looking, one-room cabins erected, in which families of Indians had taken up their abode.

Through the long days of the late summer and early fall, Indians had passed and repassed upon the river, and always, in answer to the girl's questioning, they spoke of the brutality of MacNair. Of how men were made to work from daylight to dark in his mines. And of the fact that no matter how hard they worked, they were always in his debt. They told how he plied them with whiskey, and the hunger and misery of the women and children. All this the girl learned through her interpreter, LeFroy; and not a few of these Indians remained to take up their abode in dormitories or cabins, until the little settlement boasted some thirty or forty colonists.

It was hard, discouraging work, this striving to implant the rudiments of education in the minds of the sullen, apathetic savages, whose chief ambition was to gorge themselves into stupidity with food from the storehouse. With the adults the case seemed hopeless. And, indeed, the girl attempted little beyond instruction in the simplest principles of personal and domestic cleanliness and order. Even this met with no response, until she established a daily inspection, and it became known that the filthy should also go hungry.

With the children, Chloe made some slight headway, but only at the expense of unceasing, monotonous repetition, and even she was forced to admit that the results were far from encouraging. The little savages had no slightest conception of any pride or interest in their daily tasks, but followed unvaryingly the line of least resistance as delineated by a simple system of rewards and punishments.

The men had shown no aptitude for work of any kind, and now when the ice skimmed thinly the edges of the lake and rivers, they collected their traps and disappeared into the timber, cheerfully leaving the women and children to be fed and cared for at the school. As the days shortened and the nights grew longer, the girl realized, with bitterness in her heart, that almost the only thing she had accomplished along educational lines was the imperfect smattering of the Indian tongue that she herself had acquired.

But her chiefest anxiety was a more material one, and Lapierre's appearance with the supplies became a matter of the gravest importance, for upon their departure the trappers had drawn heavily upon the slender remaining stores, with a result that the little colony on the Yellow Knife was already reduced to half rations, and was entirely dependent upon the scows for the winter's supply of provisions.

Not since the night of the battle had Chloe heard directly from MacNair. He had not visited the school, nor had he expressed a word of regret or apology for the outrage. He ignored her existence completely, and the girl guessed that many of the Indians who refused her invitation to camp in the clearing, as they passed and repassed upon the river, did so in obedience to MacNair's command.

In spite of her abhorrence for the man, she resented his total disregard of her existence. Indeed, she would have welcomed a visit from him, if for no other reason than because he was a white man. She spent many hours in framing bitter denunciations to be used in event of his appearance. But he did not appear, and resentment added to the anger in her heart, until in her mind he became the embodiment of all that was despicable, and brutish, and evil.

More than once she was upon the point of attempting another visit to Snare Lake, and in all probability would have done so had not Big Lena flatly refused to accompany her under any circumstances whatever. And this attitude the huge Swedish woman stubbornly maintained, preserving a haughty indifference alike to Chloe's taunts of cowardice, promise of reward, and threats of dismissal. Whereupon Chloe broached the subject to Harriet Penny, and that valiant soul promptly flew into hysteria, so that for three days Chloe did double duty in the school. After that she nursed her wrath in silence and brooded upon the wrongs of MacNair's Indians.

This continued brooding was not without its effect upon the girl, and slowly but surely destroyed her sense of proportion. No longer was the education and civilization of the Indians the uppermost thought in her mind. With Lapierre, she came to regard the crushing of MacNair's power as the most important and altogether desirable undertaking that could possibly be consummated.

While in this frame of mind, just at sunset of a keen October day, the cry of "*la brigade! la brigade!*" reached her ears as she sat alone in her room in the cottage, and rushing to the river bank she joined the Indians who swarmed to the water's edge to welcome the huge freight canoe that had rounded the point below the clearing. Chloe clapped her hands in sheer joy and relief, for there, proud and erect, in the bow of the canoe stood Lapierre, and behind him from bank to bank the Yellow Knife fairly swarmed with other full-freighted canoes. The supplies had arrived!

Even as the bow of his canoe scraped the bank, Lapierre was at her side. Chloe felt her hand pressed between his—felt the grip of his strong fingers, and flushed deeply as she realized that not alone because of the supplies was she glad that he had come. And then, his voice was in her ears, and she was listening as he told her how good it was to stand once more at her side, and look into the face whose image had spurred him to almost super-human effort, throughout the days and the nights of the long river trail.

Lightly she answered him, and Lapierre's heart bounded at the warmth of her welcome. He turned with a word to his canoemen, and Chloe noted with admiration, how one and all they sprang to do his bidding. She marvelled at his authority. Why did these men leap to obey his slightest command, when LeFroy, to obtain even the half-hearted obedience she required of her Indians, was forced to brow-beat and bully them? Her heart warmed to the man as she thought of the slovenly progress of her school. Here was one who could help her. One who could point with the finger of a master of men to the weak spots in her system.

Suddenly her brow clouded. For, as she looked upon Lapierre, the words of MacNair flashed through her mind, as he stood weak from his wounds, in the dimness of her fire-lit room. Her eyes hardened, and unconsciously her chin thrust outward, as she realized that before she could ask this man's aid, there were things he must explain.

Darkness settled, and at a word from Lapierre, fires flared out on the beach and in the clearing, and by their light the long line of canoemen conveyed the pieces upon their heads into the wide door of the storehouse. It was a weird, fantastic scene. The long line of pack-laden men, toiling up the bank between the rows of flaring fires, to disappear in the storehouse; and the long line returning empty-handed to toil again, to the storehouse. After a time Lapierre called LeFroy to his side and uttered a few terse commands. The man nodded, and took Lapierre's place at the head of the steep slope to the river. The quarter-breed turned to the girl.

"Come," he said, smiling, "LeFroy can handle them now. May we not go to your cottage? I would hear of your progress—the progress of your school. And also," he bowed, "is it not possible that the great, what do you call her, Lena, has prepared supper? I've eaten nothing since morning."

"Forgive me!" cried the girl. "I had completely forgotten supper. But, the men? Have they not eaten since morning?"

Lapierre smiled. "They will eat," he answered, "when their work is done."

Supper over, the two seated themselves upon the little veranda. Along the beach the fires still flared, and still the men, like a huge, slow-moving endless chain, carried the supplies to the store-house. Lapierre waved his hand toward the scene.

"You see now," he smiled, "why I built the storehouse so large?"

Chloe nodded, and regarded him intently. "Yes, I see that," she answered gravely, "but there are things I do not see. Of course you have heard of the attack by MacNair's Indians?"

Lapierre assented. "At Smith Landing I heard it," he answered, and waited for her to proceed.

"Had you expected this attack?"

Lapierre glanced at her in well-feigned surprise.

"Had I expected it, Miss Elliston, do you think I would have gone to the Southward? Would I have left you to the mercy of those brutes? When I thought you were in danger on Snare Lake, did I—"

The girl interrupted him with a gesture. "No! No! I do not think you anticipated the attack, but—"

Lapierre finished her sentence. "But, MacNair told you I did, and that I had timed accurately my trip to the Southward? What else did he tell you?"

"He told me," answered Chloe, "that had you not anticipated the attack you would not have armed my Indians with Mausers. He said that my Indians were armed to kill men, not animals." She paused and looked directly into his eyes. "Mr. Lapierre, where did those rifles come from?"

Lapierre answered without a moment's hesitation. "From my—*cache* to the westward." He leaned closer. "I told you once before," he said, "that I could place a hundred guns in the hands of your Indians, and you forbade me. While I could remain in the North, I bowed to your wishes. I know the North and its people, and I knew you would be safer with the rifles than without them. In event of an emergency, the fact that your Indians were armed with guns that would shoot farther, and harder, and faster, than the guns of your enemies, would offset, in a great measure, their advantage in numbers. It seems that my judgment was vindicated. I disobeyed you flatly. But, surely, you will not blame me! Oh! If you knew—"

Chloe interrupted him.

"Don't!" she cried sharply. "Please—not that! I—I think I

understand. But there are still things I do not understand. Why did one of my own Indians attempt to murder MacNair? And how did MacNair know that he would attempt to murder him? He said you had ordered it so. And the man was one of your Indians—one of those you left with LeFroy."

Lapierre nodded. "Do you not see, Miss Elliston, that MacNair is trying by every means in his power to discredit me in your eyes? Apatawa, the Indian you—" Chloe shuddered as he paused, and he hastened on—"The Indian who attempted to shoot MacNair, was originally one of MacNair's own Indians—one of the few who dared to desert him. And, for the wrongs he had suffered, he had sworn to kill MacNair."

"But, knowing that, why did LeFroy send him to the cottage?"

"That," answered Lapierre gravely, "is something I do not know. I must first question LeFroy, and if I find that he thus treacherously endangered the life of a wounded man, even though that man was MacNair, who is his enemy, and likewise my enemy, I will teach him a lesson he will not soon forget."

Chloe heaved a sigh of relief. "I am glad," she breathed softly, "that you feel that way."

"Could you doubt it?" asked the man.

Chloe hesitated. "Yes," she answered, "I *did* doubt it. How could I help but doubt, when he warned me what would happen, and it all came about as he said? I—I could not help but believe him. And now, one thing more. Can you tell me why MacNair's Indians are willing to fight to the death to save him from harm? If the things you tell me are true, and I know that they are true, because during the summer I have questioned many of MacNair's Indians, and they all tell the same story; why do they fight for him?"

Lapierre considered. "That is one of those things," he answered, "that men cannot explain. It is because of his hold upon them. Great generals have had it—this power to sway men—to command them to certain death, even though those men cursed the very ground their commanders stood upon. MacNair is a powerful personality. In all the North there is not his equal. I cannot explain it. It is a psychological problem none can explain. For, although his Indians hate him, they make no attempt to free themselves from his yoke, and they will fight to the death in defense of him."

"It is hard to believe," answered Chloe, "hard to understand. And yet, I think I do understand. He said of my grandfather, as he looked into the eyes of his portrait on the wall: 'He was a fighter. He won to victory over the bodies of his enemies.' That is MacNair's idea of greatness."

Lapierre nodded, and when he looked into the face of the girl he noted that her eyes flashed with purpose.

"Tell me," she continued almost sharply, "you are not afraid of MacNair?"

For just an instant Lapierre hesitated. "No!" he answered. "I am not afraid."

Chloe leaned toward him eagerly and placed a hand upon his arm, while her eyes seemed to search his very thoughts. "Then you will go with me to Snare Lake—to carry our war into the heart of the enemy's country?"

"To Snare Lake!" gasped the man.

"Yes, to Snare Lake. I shall never rest now until MacNair's power over these poor savages is broken forever. Until they are free from the yoke of oppression."

"But it would be suicide!" objected Lapierre. "No possible good can come of it! To kill a lion, one does not thrust his head into the lion's mouth in an effort to choke him to death. There are other ways."

Chloe laughed. "He will not harm us," she answered. "I am not going to kill him as one would kill a lion. There has been blood enough spilled already. As you say, there are other ways. We are going to Snare Lake for the purpose of procuring evidence that will convict this man in the courts."

"The courts!" cried Lapierre. "Where are the courts north of sixty?"

"North of sixty, or south of sixty, what matters it? There are courts, and there are prisons awaiting such as he. Will you go with me, or must I go alone?"

Lapierre glanced toward the flaring fires, where the endless line of canoemen still toiled from the river to the storehouse. Slowly he arose from his chair and extended his hand.

"I will go with you," he answered simply, "and now I will say good night."

CHAPTER XIV

THE WHISKEY RUNNERS

When Lapierre left Chloe Elliston's cottage after promising to accompany her to Snare Lake, he immediately sought out LeFroy, who was superintending the distribution of the last of the supplies in the storehouse.

The two proceeded to LeFroy's room, and at the end of an hour sought the camp of the canoemen. Ten minutes later, two lean-bodied scouts took the trail for the Northward, with orders to report immediately the whereabouts of MacNair. If luck favoured him, Lapierre knew that MacNair accompanied by the pick of his hunters, would be far from Snare Lake, upon his semi annual pilgrimage to intercept the fall migration of the caribou herd, along the northernmost reaches of the barren grounds.

If MacNair had not yet started upon the fall hunt, the journey to Snare Lake must be delayed. For the crafty Lapierre had no intention whatever of risking a meeting with MacNair in the heart of his own domain. Neither had he any intention of journeying to Snare Lake for the purpose of securing evidence against MacNair to be used in a court of law. His plans for crushing MacNair's power included no aid from constituted authority.

He noted with keen satisfaction that the girl's hatred for MacNair had been greatly intensified, not so much by the attack upon her school, as by the stories she heard from the lips of Indians who passed back and forth upon the river. The posting of those Indians had been a happy bit of forethought on the part of Lapierre; and their stories had lost nothing in LeFroy's interpretation.

Lapierre contrived to make the succeeding days busy ones. By arrangement with Chloe, a system of credits had been established, and from daylight to dark he was busy about the storehouse, paying off and outfitting his canoemen, who were to fare North upon the trap-lines until the breaking up of the ice in the spring would call them once more to the lakes and the rivers, to move Lapierre's freight, handle his furs, and deliver his contraband whiskey.

Each evening Lapierre repaired to the cottage, and LeFroy at his post in the storehouse nodded sagely to himself as the notes of the girl's rich contralto floated loud and clear above the twang of the accompanying guitar.

Always the quarter-breed spoke eagerly to Chloe of the proposed trip to Snare Lake, and bitterly he regretted the enforced delay incident to outfitting the trappers. And always, with the skill and finesse of the born intriguer, by a smile, a suggestion, or an adroitly worded question, he managed to foster and to intensify her hatred for Brute MacNair.

On the sixth day after their departure, the scouts returned from the Northward and reported that MacNair had travelled for many days across the barrens, in search of the caribou herds. Followed, then, another conference with LeFroy. The remaining canoemen were outfitted with surprising celerity. And at midnight a big freight canoe, loaded to the gunwale with an assortment of cheap knives and hatchets, bolts of gay-coloured cloth, and cheaper whiskey broke through the ever thickening skim of shore ice, and headed Northward under the personal direction of that master of all whiskey runners, Louis LeFroy.

The next day Lapierre, with a great show of eagerness, informed Chloe that he was ready to undertake the journey to Snare Lake. Enthusiastically the girl set about her preparation, and the following morning, accompanied by Big Lena and Lapierre, took her place in a canoe manned by four lean-shouldered paddlers.

Just below "the narrows," on the northeastern shore of Snare Lake, and almost upon the site of Old Fort Enterprise, erected and occupied by Lieutenant, later Sir John Franklin during the second winter of his first Arctic expedition, Bob MacNair had built his fort. The fort itself differed in no important particular from many of the log trading forts of the Hudson Bay Company. Grouped about the long, low building, within the enclosure of the log stockade, were the cabins of Indians who had forsaken the vicissitudes of the lean, barren grounds and attached themselves permanently to MacNair's colony.

Under his tutelage, they learned to convert the work of their hands into something more nearly approaching the comforts of existence than anything they had ever known. Where, as trappers of fur, they had succeeded, by dint of untold hardship and privation and suffering, in obtaining the barest necessities of life from the great fur company, they now found themselves housed in warm, comfortable cabins, eating good food, and clothing their bodies, and the bodies of their wives and children, in thick, warm clothing that defied the rigours of the Arctic winters.

While to the credit of each man, upon MacNair's books, stood an amount in tokens of "made beaver," which to any trapper in all the Northland would have spelled wealth beyond wildest dreams. And so they came to respect this stern, rugged man who dealt with them fairly—to love him, and also to fear him. And upon Snare Lake his word became the law, from which there was no appeal. Tender as a woman in sickness, counting no cost or hardship too dear in the rendering of assistance to the needy, he was at the same time hard and unbending toward wilful offenders, and a very real terror to the enemies of his people.

He had killed men for selling whiskey to his Indians. And those of his own people who drank the whiskey, he had flogged with dog-whips—floggings that had been administered in no half-hearted or uncertain manner, and that had ceased only upon the tiring of his arm. And many there were among his Indians who could testify that the arm was slow to tire.

To this little colony, upon the fourth day after his departure from Chloe Elliston's school on the Yellow Knife, came LeFroy with his freighted canoe. And because it was not his first trip among them, all knew his mission.

It so happened that at the time MacNair left for the barren grounds, Sotenah, the leader of the young men, the orator who had lauded MacNair to the skies and counselled a summary wiping out of Chloe Elliston's school, chanced to be laid up with an injury to his foot. And, as he could not accompany the hunters, MacNair placed him in charge of the fort during his absence. Upon his back Sotenah carried scars of many floggings. And the memory of these remained with him long after the deadly effects of the cheap whiskey that begot them had passed away. And now, as he stood upon the shore of the lake surrounded by the old men, and the boys who were not yet permitted to take the caribou trail, his face was sullen and black as he greeted LeFroy. For the feel of the bite of the gut-lash was strong upon him.

"*B'jo! B'jo! Nitchi!*" greeted LeFroy, smiling into the scowling face.

"*B'jo!*" grunted the younger man with evident lack of enthusiasm.

"*Kah* MacNair?"

The Indian returned a noncommittal shrug.

LeFroy repeated his question, at the same time taking from his pocket a cheap clasp-knife which he extended toward the Indian. The other regarded the knife in silence; then, reaching out his hand, took it from LeFroy and examined it gravely.

"How much?" he asked. LeFroy laughed.

"You ke'p," he said, and stepping to the canoe, threw back the blanket, exposing to the covetous eyes of the assembled Indians the huge pile of similar knives, and the hatchets, and the bolts of gay-coloured goods.

A few moments of adroit questioning sufficed to acquaint LeFroy with MacNair's prices for similar goods; and the barter began.

Where MacNair and the Hudson Bay Company charged ten "skins," or "made beaver," for an article, LeFroy charged five, or four, or even three, until the crowding Indians became half-crazed with the excitement of barter. And while this excitement was at its height, with scarcely half of his goods disposed of, LeFroy suddenly declared he would sell no more, and stepping into the canoe pushed out from the bank.

He turned a deaf ear to the frantic clamourings of those who had been unable to secure the wonderful bargains, and ordering his canoemen to paddle down the lake some two or three hundred yards, deliberately prepared to camp. Hardly had his canoe touched the shore before he was again surrounded by the clamouring mob. Whereupon he faced them and, striking an attitude, harangued them in their own tongue.

He had come, he said, hoping to find MacNair and to plead with him to deal fairly with his people. It is true that MacNair pays more for the labour of their hands than the company does for their furs, and in doing so he has proved himself a friend of the Indians. But he can well afford to pay more. Is not the *pil chickimin*—the gold—worth more even than the finest of skins?

He reached beneath the blankets and, drawing forth one of the cheap knives, held it aloft. For years, he told them, the great fur company has been robbing the Indians. Has been charging them two, three, four, and even ten times the real value of the goods they offer in barter. But the Indians have not known this. Even he, LeFroy, did not know it until the *kloshe kloochman*—the good white woman—came into the North and built a school at the mouth of the Yellow Knife. She is the real friend of the Indians. For she brought goods, even more goods than are found in the largest of the Hudson Bay posts, and she sells them at prices unheard of—at their real value in the land of the white man.

"See now!" he cried, holding the knife aloft, "in the store of MacNair, for this knife you will pay eight skins. Who will buy it for two?"

A dozen Indians crowded forward, and the knife passed into the hands of an old squaw. Other knives and hatchets changed hands, and yards of bolt goods were sold at prices that caused the black eyes of the purchasers to glitter with greed.

"Why do you stay here?" cried LeFroy suddenly. "Oh! my people, why do you remain to toil all your lives in the mines—to be robbed of the work of your hands? Come to the Yellow Knife and join those who are already enjoying the fruits of their labours! Where all have plenty, and none are asked to toil and dig in the dirt of the mines. Where all that is required is to sit in the school and learn from books, and become wise in the ways of the white man."

The half-breed paused, swaying his body to and fro as he gazed intently into the eyes of the greed-crazed horde. Suddenly his voice arose almost to a shriek. "You are free men—dwellers in a free land! Who is MacNair, that he should hold you in servitude? Why should you toil to enrich him? Why should you bow down beneath his tyranny? Who is *he* to make laws that you shall obey?" He shifted his gaze to the upturned face of Sotenah. "Who is he to say: 'You shall drink no firewater'? And who is he to flog you when you break that law? I tell you in the great storehouse on the Yellow Knife is firewater for all! The white man's drink! The drink that makes men strong—and happy—and wise as gods!"

He called loudly. Two of his canoemen rolled a cask to his feet, and, upending it, broached in the head. Seizing a tin cup, LeFroy plunged it into the cask and drank with a great smacking of lips. Then, refilling the cup, he passed it to Sotenah.

"See!" he cried, "it is a present from the *kloshe kloochman* to the people of MacNair! The people who are down-trodden and oppressed!" Under the spell of the man's words, all fear of the wrath of MacNair vanished, and Sotenah greedily seized the cup and drank, while about him crowded the others rendering the night hideous with their frenzied cries of exultation.

The cask was quickly emptied, and another broached. Old men, women, and children, all drank—and fighting, and leaping, and dancing, and yelling, returned to drink again. For, never within the memory of the oldest, had any Indian drunk the white man's whiskey for which he had not paid.

Darkness fell. Fires were lighted upon the beach, and the wild orgy continued. Other casks were opened, and the drink-crazed Indians yelled and fought and sang in a perfect frenzy of delirium. Fire-brands were hurled high into the air, to fall whirling among the cabins. And it was these whirling brands that riveted the attention of the occupants of the big canoe that approached swiftly along the shore from the direction of the Yellow Knife. LeFroy had timed his work well. In the bow, Lapierre, with a grim smile upon his thin lips, watched the arcs of the whirling brands, while from their position amidship, Chloe and Big Lena stared fascinated upon the scene.

"What are they doing?" cried the girl in amazement. Lapierre turned and smiled into her eyes.

"We have come," he answered, "at a most opportune time. You are about to see MacNair's Indians at their worst. For they seem to be even more drunk than usual. It is MacNair's way—to make them drunk while he looks on and laughs."

"Do you mean," cried the girl in horror, "that they are drunk?"

Lapierre smiled. "Very drunk," he answered dryly. "It is the only way MacNair can hold them—by allowing them free license at frequent intervals. For well the Indians know that nowhere else in all the North would this thing be permitted. Therefore, they remain with MacNair."

The canoe had drawn close now, and the figures of the Indians were plainly discernible. Many were lying sprawled upon the ground, while others leaped and danced in the red flare of the flames. At frequent intervals, above the sound of the frenzied shouts and weird chants, arose the sharp rattle of shots, as the Indians fired recklessly into the air.

At a signal from Lapierre the canoemen ceased paddling. Chloe's eyes flashed an inquiry, and Lapierre shook his head.

"We can venture no closer," he explained. "At such times their deviltry knows no bounds. They would make short shrift of anyone who would venture among them this night."

Chloe nodded. "I have no wish to go farther!" she cried. "I have seen enough, and more than enough! When this night's work shall become known in Ottawa, its echo shall ring from Labrador to the Yukon until throughout all Canada the name of MacNair shall be hated and despised!"

At the words, Lapierre glanced into her flushed face, and, removing his hat, bowed reverently. "God grant that your prophecy may be fulfilled. And I speak, not because of any hatred for MacNair, but from a heart overflowing with love and compassion for my people. For their welfare, it is my earnest prayer that this man's just punishment shall not long be delayed."

While he was yet speaking, from the midst of the turmoil red flames shot high into the air. The yelling increased tenfold, and the frenzied horde surged toward the walls of the stockade. The cabins of the Indians were burning! Wider and higher flared the fire, and louder and fiercer swelled the sounds of yelling and the firing of rifles. The walls of the stockade ignited. The fire was eating its way toward the long, log storehouse. Instantly through the girl's mind flashed the memory of that other night when the sky glowed red, and the crash of rifles mingled with the hoarse roar of flames. She gazed in fascination as the fire licked and curled above the roof of the storehouse. Upon the shore, even the canoes were burning.

Suddenly a wild shriek was borne to her ears. The firing of guns ceased abruptly, and around the corner of the burning storehouse dashed a figure of terror, hatless and coatless, with long hair streaming wildly in the firelight. Tall, broad, and gaunt it appeared in the light of the flaring flames, and instantly Chloe recognized the form of Bob MacNair. Lapierre also recognized it, and gasped audibly. For at that moment he knew MacNair should have been far across the barrens on the trail of the caribou herd.

"Look! Look!" cried the girl. "What is he doing?" And watched in horror as the big man charged among the Indians, smashing, driving and kicking his way through the howling, rum-crazed horde. At every lashing blow of his fist, every kick of his high-laced boot, men went down. Others reeled drunkenly from his path screaming aloud in their fright; while across the open space in the foreground four or five men could be seen dashing frantically for the protection of the timber. MacNair ripped the gun from the hand of a reeling Indian and, throwing it to his shoulder, fired. Of those who ran, one dropped, rose to his knees, and sank backward. MacNair fired again, and another crashed forward, and rolled over and over upon the ground.

Lapierre watched with breathless interest while the others gained the shelter of the timber. He wondered whether one of the two men who fell was LeFroy.

"Oh!" cried Chloe in horror. "He's killing them!"

Lapierre made a swift sign to his paddlers, and the canoe shot behind a low sand-point where, in response to a tense command, the canoemen turned its bow southward; and, for the second time, Chloe Elliston found herself being driven by willing hands southward upon Snare Lake.

"He pounded—and kicked—and beat them!" sobbed the girl hysterically. "And two of them he killed!"

Lapierre nodded. "Yes," he answered sadly, "and he will kill more of them. It seems that this time they got beyond even his control. For the destruction of his buildings and his goods, he will take his toll in lives and in the sufferings of his Indians."

While the canoe shot southward through the darkness, Chloe sat huddled upon her blankets. And as she watched the dull-red glow fade from the sky above MacNair's burning fort, her heart cried out for vengeance against this brute of the North.

One hour, two hours, the canoe plowed the black waters of the lake, and then, because men must rest, Lapierre reluctantly gave the order to camp, and the tired canoemen turned the bow shoreward.

Hardly had they taken a dozen strokes when the canoe ground sharply against the thin, shore ice. There was the sound of ripping bark, where the knifelike edge of the ice tore through the side of the frail craft. Water gushed in, and Lapierre, stifling a curse that rose to his lips, seized a paddle, and leaning over the bow began to chop frantically at the ice. Two of the canoemen with their paddles held her head on, while the other two, with the help of Chloe and Big Lena endeavoured to stay the inrush of water with blankets and fragments of clothing.

Progress was slow. The ice thickened as they neared the shore, and Lapierre's paddle-blade, battered upon its point and edges to a soft, fibrous pulp, thudded softly upon the ice without breaking it. He threw the paddle overboard and seized another. A few more yards were won, but the shore loomed black and forbidding, and many yards away. Despite the utmost efforts of the women and the two canoemen, the water gained rapidly. Lapierre redoubled his exertion, chopping and stabbing at the ever thickening shore-ice. And then suddenly his paddle crashed through, and with a short cry of relief he rose to his feet, and leaped into the black water, where he sank only to his middle. The canoemen followed. And the canoe, relieved of the bulk of its burden, floated more easily.

Slowly they pushed shoreward through the shallow water, the men breaking the ice before them. And a few minutes later, wet and chilled to the bone, they stepped onto the gravel.

Within the shelter of a small thicket a fire was built, and while the men returned to examine the damaged canoe, the two women wrung out their dripping garments and, returning them wet, huddled close to the tiny blaze. The men returned to the fire, where a meal was prepared and eaten in silence. As he ate, Chloe noticed that Lapierre seemed ill at ease.

"Did you repair the canoe?" she asked. The man shook his head.

"No. It is damaged beyond any thought of repair. We removed the food and such of its contents as are necessary, and, loading it with rocks, sank it in the lake."

"Sank it in the lake!" cried the girl in amazement.

"Yes," answered Lapierre. "For even if it were not damaged, it would be of no further use to us. Tonight the lake will freeze."

"What are we going to do?" cried the girl.

"There is only one thing to do," answered Lapierre quickly. "Walk to the school. It is not such a long trail—a hundred miles or so. And you can take it easy. You have plenty of provisions."

"I!" cried the girl. "And what will you do?"

"It is necessary," answered the man, "that I should make a forced march."

"You are going to leave me?"

Lapierre smiled at the evident note of alarm in her voice. "I am going to take two of the canoemen and return in all haste to your school. Do you realize that MacNair, now that he has lost his winter provisions, will stop at nothing to obtain more?"

"He would not dare!" cried the girl, her eyes flashing.

Lapierre laughed. "You do not know MacNair. You, personally, he would not venture to molest. He will doubtless try to buy supplies from you or from the Hudson Bay Company. But, in the meantime, while he is upon this errand, his Indians, with no one to hold them in check, and knowing that the supplies are in your storehouse, will swoop down upon it, and your own Indians, without a leader, will fall an easy prey to the hungry horde."

"But surely," cried the girl, "LeFroy is capable—"

"Possibly, if he were at the school," interrupted Lapierre. "But unfortunately the day before we ourselves departed, I sent LeFroy upon an important mission to the eastward. I think you will agree with me upon the importance of the mission when I tell you that, as I swung out of the mouth of Slave River at the head of the canoe brigade, I saw a fast canoe slipping stealthily along the shore to the eastward. In that canoe, with the aid of my binoculars, I made out two men whom I have long suspected of being engaged in the nefarious and hellish business of peddling whiskey among the Indians. I knew it was useless to try to overtake them with my heavily loaded canoe, and so upon my arrival at the school, as soon as we had concluded the outfitting of the trappers, I dispatched LeFroy to hunt these men down, to destroy any liquor found in their possession, and to deal with them as he saw fit."

He paused and gazed steadily into the girl's face. "This may seem to you a lawless and high-handed proceeding, Miss Elliston," he went on; "but you have just witnessed one exhibition of the tragedy that whiskey can work among my people. In my opinion, the end justifies the means."

The girl regarded him with shining eyes. "Indeed it does!" she cried. "Oh, there is nothing—no punishment—too severe for such brutes, such devils, as these! I—I hope LeFroy will catch them. I hope—almost—he will kill them."

Lapierre nodded. "Yes, Miss Elliston," he answered gravely, "one could sometimes almost wish so, but I have forbidden it. The taking of a human life is a serious matter; and in the North the exigencies of the moment all too frequently make this imperative. As a last resort only should we kill."

"You are right," echoed the girl. "Only after the scene we have just witnessed, it seemed that I myself could kill deliberately, and be glad I killed. Truly the North breeds savagery. For I, too, have killed on the spur of the moment!" The words fell rapidly from her lips, and she cried out as in physical pain. "And to think that I killed in defence of *him*! Oh, if I had let the Indian shoot that night, all this"—she waved her hand to the northward—"would never have happened."

"Very true, Miss Elliston," answered Lapierre softly. "But do not blame yourself. Under the circumstances, you could not have done otherwise."

As he talked, two of the canoemen made up light packs from the outfit of the wrecked canoe. Seeing that they had concluded, Lapierre arose, and taking Chloe's hand in both of his, looked straight into her eyes.

"Good-by," he said simply. "These Indians will conduct you in safety to your school." And, without waiting for a reply, turned and followed the two canoemen into the brush.

Chloe sat for a long time staring into the flames of the tiny fire before creeping between her damp blankets. Despite the utter body-weariness of her long canoe-trip, the girl slept but fitfully in her cold bed.

In the early grey of the morning she started up nervously. Surely a sound had awakened her. She heard it distinctly now, the sound of approaching footsteps. She strained to locate the sound, and instantly realized it was not the tread of moccasined feet. She threw off the frost-stiffened blankets and leaped to her feet, shivering in the keen air of the biting dawn.

The sounds of the footsteps grew louder, plainer, as though someone had turned suddenly from the shore and approached the thicket with long, heavy strides. With muscles tense and heart bounding wildly the girl waited. Then, scarce ten feet from her side, the thick scrub parted with a vicious swish, and a man, hatless, glaring, and white-faced, stood before her. The man was MacNair.

CHAPTER XV

"ARREST THAT MAN!"

Seconds passed—tense, portentous seconds—as the two stood facing each other over the dead ashes of the little fire. Seconds in which the white drawn features of the man engraved themselves indelibly upon Chloe Elliston's brain. She noted the knotted muscles of the clenched hands and the glare of the sunken eyes. Noted, also, the cringing fear-stricken forms of the two Indians, who had awakened and lay cowering upon their blankets. And Big Lena, whose pale-blue, fishlike eyes stared first at one and then the other from out a face absolutely devoid of expression.

Suddenly a fierce, consuming anger welled into the girl's heart, and words fell from her lips in a veritable hiss of scorn: "Have you come to kill me, too?"

"By God, it would be a good thing for the North if I should kill you!"

"A good thing for MacNair, you mean!" taunted the girl. "Yes, I think it would. Well, there is nothing to hinder you. Of course, you would have to kill these, also." She indicated Big Lena and the Indians. "But what are mere lives to you?"

"They are nothing to me when the fate of my people is at

stake! And at this very moment their fate—their whole future—the future of their children and their children's children—is at stake, as it has never been at stake before. Many times in my life have I faced crises: but never such a crisis as this. And always I have won, regardless of cost—but the cost only *I* have ever known."

His eyes glared, and he seemed a madman in his berserk rage. He drove a huge fist into his upturned palm and fairly shouted his words: "I am MacNair! And if there is a God in heaven, I will win! From this moment, it is my life or Lapierre's! Since last night's outrage there can be no truce—no quibbling—no parleying—no half-way measures! My friends are my friends, and his friends are my enemies! The war is on—and it will be a fight to the finish. A fight that may well disrupt the North!" He shook his clenched fist before the face of the girl. "I have taken the man-trail! I am MacNair! And at the end of that trail will lie a dead man—myself or Pierre Lapierre!"

"And at the beginning of the trail lie *two* dead men," sneered Chloe. "Those who started for the timber—"

"And, by God, if necessary, the trail will be *paved with dead men*! For Lapierre, the day of reckoning is at hand."

Chloe took a step forward, and with blazing eyes stood trembling with anger before the man. "And how about *your own* day of reckoning? You have told me that I am a fool; but it is you who are the fool! You killer of helpless men! You debaucher of women and children! You trader in souls! As you say, the day of reckoning is at hand—not for Lapierre, but for *you*! Until this day you have not taken me seriously. I *have* been a fool—a blind, trusting fool. You have succeeded, in spite of what I have heard—in spite of my better judgment—in spite even of what I have seen, in making me believe that, possibly you had been misunderstood; had been painted blacker than you really are. At times I almost *believed* in you; but I have since learned enough from the mouths of your own Indians to convince me of my folly. And after what I saw last night—" She paused in very horror of the thought, and MacNair glared into her outraged eyes.

"You saw that? You stood by and witnessed the ruination of my Indians? Deliberately watched them changed from sober, industrious, simple-hearted children of the wild into a howling, drink-crazed horde of beasts that thirsted for blood—tore at each other's throats—and, in the frenzy of their madness, burned their own homes, and their winter's supplies and provisions? You stood by and saw them glutted with the whiskey from your storehouse—by your own paid creatures—"

"Whiskey from my storehouse!" The girl's voice rose to a scream, and MacNair interrupted her savagely:

"Aye, whiskey from your storehouse! Brought in by Lapierre, and by Lapierre cunningly and freely given out to my Indians."

"You are crazy! You are mad! You do not know what you are saying? But if you *do* know, you are the most consummate liar on the face of the earth! Of all things absurd! Is it possible that you hope by any such preposterous and flimsy fabrication to escape the punishment which will surely and swiftly be meted out to you? Will, you tell that to the Mounted? And will you tell it to the judge and the jury? What will they say when I have told my story, and have had it corroborated by your own Indians—those Indians who have fled to my school to seek a haven of refuge from your tyranny? I have my manifest. My goods were inspected and passed by the Mounted—"

"Inspected and passed! And why? Because they were *your* goods, and the men of the Mounted have yet to suspect you. The inspection was perfunctorily made. And as for the manifest—I did not say it was your whiskey. I said, 'whiskey from your storehouse.' It was Lapierre's whiskey. And he succeeded in running it in by the boldest, and at the same time the cleverest and safest method—disguised as your freight. Tell me this: Did you check your pieces upon their arrival at your storehouse?"

"No; Lapierre did that, or LeFroy."

"And Lapierre, having first ascertained that I was far on the caribou trail, succeeded in slipping the whiskey to my Indians, but he—"

"Mr. Lapierre was with me! Accuse him and you accuse me, also. He brought me here because I wished to see for myself the condition of your Indians—the condition of which I had so often heard."

"Was LeFroy, also, with you?"

"LeFroy was away upon a mission, and that mission was to capture two others of your ilk—two whiskey-runners!"

MacNair laughed harshly. "Good LeFroy!" he exclaimed in derision. "Great God, you are a fool! You yourself saw LeFroy and his satellites rushing wildly for the shelter of the timber, when I unexpectedly appeared among them." The light of exultation leaped into his eyes. "I killed two of them, but LeFroy escaped. Lapierre timed his work well. And had it not been that one of my Indians, who was a spy in Lapierre's camp, learned of his plan and followed me across the barrens, Lapierre would have had ample time, after the destruction of my fort, to have scattered my Indians to the four winds. When I learned of his plot, I forced the trail as I never had forced a trail, in the hope of arriving in time to prevent the catastrophe. I reached the fort too late to save my Indians from your human wolf-pack, their homes from the flames, and my buildings and my property from destruction. But, thank God, it is not too late to wreck my vengeance upon the enemies of my people! For the trail is hot, and I will follow it, if need be, to the end of the earth."

"Your love for your Indians is, indeed, touching. I witnessed a demonstration of that love last night, when you battered and kicked and hurled them about in their drunken and helpless condition. But, tell me, what will become of them while you are following your trail of blood—the trail you so fondly imagine will terminate in the death of Lapierre, but which will, as surely and inevitably as justice itself, lead you to a prison cell, if not the gallows?"

MacNair regarded the girl almost fiercely. "I must leave my Indians," he answered, "for the present, to their own devices. For the simple reason that I cannot be in two places at the same time."

"But their supplies were burned! They will starve!" cried the girl. "It would seem that one who really loved his Indians would have his first thought for their welfare. But no; you prefer to take the trail and kill men; men who may at some future time tell their story upon the witness-stand; a story that will not sound pretty in the telling, and that will mark the crash of your reign of tyranny. 'Safety first' is your slogan, and your Indians may starve while you murder men." The girl paused and suddenly became conscious that MacNair was regarding her with a strange look in his eyes. And at his next words she could scarcely believe her ears.

"Will you care for my Indians?"

The question staggered her. "What!" she managed to gasp.

"Just what I said," answered MacNair gruffly. "Will you care for my Indians until such time as I shall return to them—until I have ridded the North of Lapierre?"

"Do you mean," cried the astonished girl, "will I care for your Indians—the same Indians who attacked my school—who only last night fought like fiends among themselves, and burned their own homes?"

"Just that!" answered MacNair. "The Indian who warned me of Lapierre's plot told me, also, of the arrival of your supplies—sufficient, he said, to feed the whole North. You will not lose by it. Name your own price, and I shall pay whatever you ask."

"Price!" flashed the girl. "Do you think I would take your gold—the gold that has been wrung from the hearts' blood of your Indians?"

"On your own terms, then," answered MacNair. "Will you take them? Surely this arrangement should be to your liking. Did you not tell me yourself, upon the occasion of our first meeting, that you intended to use every means in your power to induce my Indians to attend your school? That you would teach them that they are free? That they owe allegiance and servitude to no man? That you would educate and show them they were being robbed and cheated and forced into serfdom? That you intended to appeal to their better natures, to their manhood and womanhood? I think those were your words. Did you not say that? And did you mean it? Or was it the idle boast of an angry woman?"

Chloe interrupted him. "Yes, I said that, and I meant it! And I mean it now!"

"You have your chance," growled MacNair, "I impose no restrictions. I shall command them to obey you; even to attend your school, if you wish! You will hardly have time to do them much harm. As I told you, the North is not ready for your education. But I know that you are honest. You are a fool, and the time is not far distant when you yourself will realize this; when you will learn that you have become the unwitting dupe of one of the shrewdest and most diabolical scoundrels that ever drew breath. Again I tell you that some day you and I shall be friends! At this moment you hate me. But I know it is through ignorance you hate. I have small patience with your ignorance; but, also, at this moment you are the only person in all the North with whom I would trust my Indians. Lapierre, from now on, will be past charming them. I shall see to it that he is kept so busy in the matter of saving his own hide that he will have scant time for deviltry."

Still Chloe appeared to hesitate. And through MacNair's mind flashed the memory of the rapier-blade eyes that stared from out the dull gold frame of the portrait that hung upon the wall of the little cottage—eyes that were the eyes of the girl before him.

"Well," he asked with evident impatience, "are you *afraid* of these Indians?"

The flashing eyes of the girl told him that the shot had struck home. "No!" she cried. "I am not afraid! Send your Indians to me, if you will; and when you send them, bid good-by to them forever."

MacNair nodded. "I will send them," he answered, and, turning abruptly upon his heel, disappeared into the scrub.

The journey down the Yellow Knife consumed six days, and it was a journey fraught with many hardships for Chloe

Elliston, unaccustomed as she was to trail travel. The little-used trail, following closely the bank of the stream, climbed low, rock-ribbed ridges, traversed black spruce swamps, and threaded endlessly in and out of the scrub timber. Nevertheless, the girl held doggedly to the slow pace set by the canoemen.

When at last, foot-sore and weary, with nerves a-jangle, and with every muscle in her body protesting with its own devilishly ingenious ache against the overstrain of the long, rough miles and the chill misery of damp blankets, she arrived at the school, Lapierre was nowhere to be found. For the wily quarter-breed, knowing that MacNair would instantly suspect the source of the whiskey, had, upon his arrival, removed the remaining casks from the storehouse, and conveyed them with all haste to his stronghold on Lac du Mort.

Upon her table in the cottage, Chloe found a brief note to the effect that Lapierre had been, forced to hasten to the eastward to aid LeFroy in dealing with the whiskey-runners. The girl had scant time to think of Lapierre, however, for upon the morning after her arrival, MacNair appeared, accompanied by a hundred or more dejected and woe-begone Indians. Despite the fact that Chloe had known them only as fierce roisterers she was forced to admit that they looked harmless and peaceful enough, under the chastening effect of a week of starvation.

MacNair wasted no time, but striding up to the girl, who stood upon the veranda of her cottage, plunged unceremoniously into the business at hand.

"Do not misunderstand me," he began gruffly. "I did not bring my Indians here to receive the benefits of your education, nor as a sop to your anger, nor for any other reason than to procure for them food and shelter until such time as I myself can provide for them. If they were trappers this would be unnecessary. But they have long since abandoned the trap-lines, and in the whole village there could not be found enough traps to supply one tenth of their number with the actual necessities of life. I have sent runners to the young men upon the barren grounds, with orders to continue the caribou kill and bring the meat to you here. I have given my Indians their instructions. They will cause you no trouble, and will be subject absolutely to your commands. And now, I must be on my way. I must pick up the trail of Lapierre. And when I return, I shall confront you with evidence that will prove to you beyond a doubt that the words I have spoken are true!"

"And I will confront you," retorted the girl, "with evidence that will place you behind prison bars for the rest of your life!" Again Chloe saw in the grey eyes the twinkle that held more than the suspicion of a smile.

"I think I would make but a poor prisoner," the man answered. "But if I am to be a prisoner I warn you that I will run the prison. I am MacNair!" Something in the man's look—he was gazing straight into her eyes with a peculiar intense gaze—caused the girl to start, while a sudden indescribable feeling of fear, of helplessness before this man, flashed over her. The feeling passed in an instant and she sneered boldly into MacNair's face.

"My, how you hate yourself!" she cried. "And how long is it, Mr. Brute MacNair—" was it fancy, or did the man wince at the emphasis of the name? She repeated, with added emphasis, "Mr. Brute MacNair, since you have deemed it worth your while to furnish me with evidence? You told me once, I believe, that you cared nothing for my opinion. Is it possible that you hope at this late day to flatter me with my own importance?"

MacNair, in no wise perturbed, regarded her gravely. "No," he answered "It is not that, it is—" He paused as if at a loss for words. "I do not know why," he continued, "unless, perhaps, it is because—because you have no fear of me. That you do not fear to take your life into your hands in defence of what you think is right. It may be that I have learned a certain respect for you. Certainly I do not pity you. At times you have made me very angry with your foolish blundering, until I remember it is honest blundering, and that some day you will know the North, and will know that north of sixty, men are not measured by your little rule of thumb. Always I have gone my way, caring no more for the approval of others than I have for their hatred or scoffing. I know the North! Why should I care for the opinion of others? If they do not know, so much the worse for them. The reputation of being a fool injures no one. Had I not been thought a fool by the men of the Hudson Bay Company they would not have sold me the barren grounds whose sands are loaded with gold."

"And yet you said *I* was a fool," interrupted Chloe. "According to your theory, that fact should redound to my credit."

MacNair answered without a smile. "I did not say that *being* a fool injured no one. You *are* a fool. Of your reputation I know nothing, nor care." He turned abruptly on his heel and walked to the storehouse, leaving the girl, speechless with anger, standing upon the veranda of the cottage, as she watched his swinging shoulders disappear from sight around the corner of the log building.

With flushed face, Chloe turned toward the river, and instantly her attention centred upon the figure of a man, who swung out of the timber and approached across the clearing in long, easy strides. She regarded the man closely. Certainly he was no one she had ever seen before. He was very near now, and at the distance of a few feet, paused and bowed, as he swept the Stetson from his head. The girl's heart gave a wild bound of joy. The man wore the uniform of the Mounted!

"Miss Elliston?" he asked.

"Yes," answered Chloe, as her glance noted the clear-cut, almost boyish lines of the weather-bronzed face.

"I am Corporal Ripley, ma'am, at your service. I happened on a Fort Rae Injun—a Dog Rib, a few days since, and he told me some kind of a yarn about a band of Yellow Knives that had attacked your post some time during the summer. I couldn't get much out of him because he could speak only a few words of English, and I can't speak any Dog Rib. Besides, you can't go much on what an Indian tells you. When you come to sift down their dope, it generally turns out to be nine parts lies and the other part divided between truth, superstition, and guess-work. Constable Darling, at Fort Resolution, said he'd received no complaint, so I didn't hurry through."

With a swift glance toward the storehouse, into which MacNair had disappeared, Chloe motioned the man into the cottage. "The—the attack was nothing," she hastened to assure him. "But there is something—a complaint that I wish to make against a man who is, and has been for years, doing all in his power to debauch and brutalize the Indians of the North." The girl paced nervously up and down as she spoke, and she noted that the youthful officer leaned forward expectantly, his wide boyish eyes narrowed to slits.

"Yes," he urged eagerly, "who is this man? And have you got the evidence to back your charge? For I take it from your words you intend to make a charge."

"Yes," answered Chloe. "I do intend to make a charge, and I have my evidence. The man is MacNair. Brute MacNair he is called—"

"What! MacNair of Snare Lake—Bob MacNair of the barren grounds?"

"Yes, Bob MacNair of the barren grounds." A moment of silence followed her words. A silence during which the officer's face assumed a troubled expression.

"You are sure there is no mistake?" he asked at length.

"There is no mistake!" flashed the girl. "With my own eyes I have seen enough to convict a dozen men!"

Even as she spoke, a form passed the window, and a heavy tread sounded on the veranda. Stepping quickly to the door, Chloe flung it open, and pointing toward MacNair, who stood, rifle in hand, cried; "Officer, arrest that man!"

Corporal Ripley, who had risen to his feet, stood gazing from one to the other; while MacNair, speechless, stared straight into the eyes of the girl.

CHAPTER XVI

MACNAIR GOES TO JAIL

The silence in the little room became almost painful. MacNair uttered no word as his glance strayed from the flushed, excited face of the girl to the figure of Corporal Ripley, who stood hat in hand, gazing from one to the other with eyes plainly troubled by doubt and perplexity.

"Well, why don't you do something?" cried the girl, at length. "It seems to me if I were a man I could think of something to do besides stand and gape!"

Corporal Ripley cleared his throat. "Do I understand," he began stiffly, "that you intend to prefer certain charges against MacNair—that you demand his arrest?"

"I should *think* you would understand it!" retorted the girl. "I have told you three or four times."

The officer flushed slightly and shifted the hat from his right to his left hand.

"Just step inside, MacNair," he said, and then to the girl: "I'll listen to you now, if you please. You must make specific charges, you know—not just hearsay. Arresting a man in this country is a serious matter, Miss Elliston. We are seven hundred miles from a jail, and the law expects us to use discretion in making an arrest. It don't do us any good at headquarters to bring in a man unless we can back up our charge with strong evidence, because the item of transportation of witnesses and prisoner may easily run up into big money. On the other hand it's just as bad if we fail or delay in bringing a guilty man to book. What we want is specific evidence. I don't tell you this to discourage any just complaint, but only to show you that we've got to have direct and specific evidence. Now, Miss Elliston, I'll hear what you've got to say."

Chloe sank into a chair and motioned the others to be seated. "We may as well sit down while we talk. I will try to tell you only the facts as I myself have seen them—only such as I could swear to on a witness stand." The officer bowed, and Chloe plunged directly into the subject.

"In the first place," she began, "when I brought my outfit in I noticed in the scows, certain pieces with the name of MacNair painted on the burlap. The rest of the outfit, I think, consisted wholly of my own freight. I wondered at the time who MacNair was, but didn't make any inquiries until I happened to mention the matter to Mr. Lapierre. That was on Slave River. Mr. Lapierre seemed very much surprised that any of MacNair's goods should be in his scows. He examined the pieces and then with an ax smashed them in. They contained whiskey."

"And he destroyed it? Can you swear it was whiskey?" asked the officer.

"Certainly, I can swear it was whiskey! I saw it and *smelled* it."

"Can you explain why Lapierre did not know of these pieces, until you called his attention to them?"

Chloe hesitated a moment and tapped nervously on the table with her fingers. "Yes," she answered, "I can. Mr. Lapierre took charge of the outfit only that morning."

"Who was the boss scowman? Who took the scows down the Athabasca?"

"A man named Vermilion. He was a half-breed, I think. Anyway, he was a horrible creature."

"Where is Vermilion now?"

Again Chloe hesitated. "He is dead," she answered. "Mr. Lapierre shot him. He shot him in self-defence, after Vermilion had shot another man."

The officer nodded, and Chloe called upon Big Lena to corroborate the statement that Lapierre had destroyed certain whiskey upon the bank of Slave Lake. "Is that all?" asked the officer.

"No, indeed!" answered Chloe. "That isn't all! Only last week, I went to visit MacNair's fort on Snare Lake in company with Mr. Lapierre and Lena, and four canoemen. We got there shortly after dark. Fires had been built on the beach—many of them almost against the walls of the stockade. As we drew near, we heard loud yells and howlings that sounded like the cries of animals, rather than of human beings. We approached very close to the shore where the figures of the Indians were distinctly visible by the light of the leaping names. It was then we realized that a wild orgy of indescribable debauchery was in progress. The Indians were raving drunk. Some lay upon the ground in a stupor—others danced and howled and threw fire-brands about in reckless abandon.

"We dared not land, but held the canoe off shore and

watched the horrible scene. We had not long to wait before the inevitable happened. The whirling fire-brands falling among the cabins and against the walls of the stockade started a conflagration, which soon spread to the storehouse. And then MacNair appeared on the scene, rushing madly among the Indians, striking, kicking, and hurling them about. A few sought to save themselves by escaping to the timber. And, jerking a rifle from the hand of an Indian, MacNair fired twice at the fleeing men. Two of them fell and the others escaped into the timber."

"You did not see any whiskey in the possession of these Indians?" asked Corporal Ripley. "You merely surmised they were drunk by their actions?"

Chloe nodded. "Yes," she admitted, "but certainly there can be no doubt that they were drunk. Men who are not drunk do not—"

MacNair interrupted her. "They were drunk," he said quietly, "very drunk."

"You admit that?" asked the officer in surprise. "I must warn you, MacNair, that anything you say may be used against you." MacNair nodded.

"And, as to the killing of the men," continued Chloe, "I charge MacNair with their murder."

"Murder is a very serious charge, Miss Elliston. Let's go over the facts again. You say you were in a canoe near the shore—you saw a man you say was MacNair grab a rifle from an Indian and kill two men. Stop and think, now—it was night and you saw all this by firelight—are you sure the man who fired the shots was MacNair?"

"Absolutely!" cried the girl, with a trace of irritation.

"It was I who shot," interrupted MacNair.

The officer regarded him curiously and again addressed the girl. "Once more, Miss Elliston, do you know that the men you saw fall are dead? Mere shooting won't sustain a charge of murder."

Chloe hesitated. "No," she admitted reluctantly. "I did not examine their dead bodies, if that is what you mean. But MacNair afterward told me that he killed them, and I can swear to having seen them fall."

"The men are dead," said MacNair.

The officer stared in astonishment. Chloe also was puzzled by the frank admission of the man, and she gazed into his face as though striving to pierce its mask and discover an ulterior motive. MacNair returned her gaze unflinchingly and again the girl felt an indescribable sense of smallness—of helplessness before this man of the North, whose very presence breathed strength and indomitable man-power.

"Was it possible," she wondered, "that he would dare to flaunt this strength in the very face of the law?" She turned to Corporal Ripley, who was making notes with a pencil in a little note-book. "Well," she asked, "is my evidence *specific* enough to warrant this man's arrest?"

The officer nodded slowly. "Yes," he answered gravely. "The evidence warrants an arrest. Very probably several arrests."

"You mean," asked the girl, "that you think he may have—an accomplice?"

"No, Miss Elliston, I don't mean that. In spite of your evidence and his own words, I don't think MacNair is guilty. There is something queer here. I guess there is no doubt that whiskey has been run into the territory, and that it has been supplied to the Indians. You charge MacNair with these crimes, and I've got to arrest him."

Chloe was about to retort, when the officer interrupted her with a gesture.

"Just a moment, please," he said quietly; "I'm not sure I can make myself plain to you, but you see in the North we know something of MacNair's work. Of what he has done in spite of the odds. We know the North needs men like MacNair. You claim to be a friend of the Indians. Do you realize that up on Snare Lake, right now, are a bunch of Indians who depend on MacNair for their existence? MacNair's absence will cause suffering among them and even death. If his storehouse has been burned, what are they going to eat? On your statements I've got to enter charges against MacNair. First and foremost the charge of murder. He will also be charged with importing liquor, having liquor in prohibited territory, smuggling whiskey, and supplying liquor to the Indians.

"Now, Miss Elliston, for the good of those Indians on Snare Lake I want you to withdraw the charge of murder. The other offences are bailable ones, and in my judgment he should be allowed to return to his Indians. Then, when his trial comes up at the spring assizes, the charge of murder can be placed against him. I'll bet a year's pay, MacNair isn't to blame. In the meantime we will get busy and comb the barrens for the real criminals. I've got a hunch. And you can take my word that justice shall be done, no matter where the blow falls."

Suddenly, through Chloe's mind flashed the memory of what Lapierre had told her of the Mounted. She arose to her feet and, drawing herself up haughtily, glared into the face of the officer. When she spoke, her voice rang hard with scorn.

"It is very evident that you don't want to arrest MacNair. I have heard that he is a law unto himself—that he would defy arrest—that he has the Mounted subsidized. I did not believe it at the time. I regarded it merely as the exaggerated statement of a man who justly hates him. But it seems this man was right. You need not trouble yourself about MacNair's Indians. I will stand sponsor for their welfare. They are my Indians now. I warn you that the day of MacNair is past. I refuse to withdraw a single word of my charges against him, and you will either arrest him, or I shall go straight to Ottawa. And I shall never rest until I have blazoned before the world the whole truth about your rotten system! What will Canada say, when she learns that the Mounted—the men who have been held up before all the world as models of bravery, efficiency, and honour—are as crooked and grafting as—as the police of New York?"

Corporal Ripley's face showed red through the tan, and he started to his feet with an exclamation of anger. "Hold on, Corporal." The voice of MacNair was the quiet voice with which one sooths a petulant child. He remained seated and pushed the Stetson toward the back of his head. "She really believes it. Don't hold it against her. It is not her fault. When the smoke has cleared away and she gets her bearings, we're all going to like her. In fact, I'm thinking that the time is coming when the only one who will hate her will be herself. I like her now; though she is not what you'd call my friend. I mean—not yet."

Corporal Ripley gazed in astonishment at MacNair and then very frigidly he turned to Chloe. "Then the charge of murder stands?"

"Yes, it does," answered the girl. "If he were allowed to go free now there would be three murders instead of two by the time of the spring assizes or whatever you call them, for he is even now upon the trail of a man he has threatened to kill. I can give you his exact words. He said: 'I have taken the man-trail . . . and at the end of that trail will lie a dead man—myself or Pierre Lapierre!'"

"Lapierre!" exclaimed the officer. "What has he got to do with it?" He turned to MacNair as if expecting an answer. But MacNair remained silent. "Why don't you charge Lapierre with the crimes you told me he was guilty of?" taunted the girl. Again she saw that baffling twinkle in the grey eyes of the man. Then the eyes hardened.

"The last thing I desire is the arrest of Lapierre," he answered. "Lapierre must answer to me." The words, pronounced slowly and distinctly, rasped hard. In spite of herself, Chloe shuddered.

Corporal Ripley shifted uneasily. "We'd better be going, MacNair," he said. "There's something queer about this whole business—something I don't quite understand. It's up to me to take you up the river; but, believe me, I'm coming back! I'll get at the bottom of this thing if it takes me five years. Are you ready?"

MacNair nodded.

"I can let you have some Indians," suggested the girl.

"What for?"

"Why, for a guard, of course; to help you with your prisoner."

Ripley drew himself up and answered abruptly: "The Mounted is quite capable of managing its own affairs, Miss Elliston. I don't need your Indians, thank you."

Chloe glanced wrathfully into the boyish face of the officer. "Suit yourself," she answered sweetly. "But if I were you, I'd want a whole regiment of Indians. Because if MacNair wants to, he'll eat you up."

"He won't want to," snapped Ripley. "I don't taste good."

As they passed out of the door, MacNair turned. "Good-by, Miss Elliston," he said gravely. "Beware of Pierre Lapierre." Chloe made no reply and as MacNair turned to go, he chanced to glance into the wide, expressionless face of Big Lena, who had stood throughout the interview leaning heavily against the jamb of the kitchen door. Something inscrutable in the stare of the fishlike, china-blue eyes clung in his memory, and try as he would in the days that followed, MacNair could not fathom the meaning of that stare, if indeed it had any meaning. MacNair did not know why, but in some inexplainable manner the memory of that look eased many a weary mile.

CHAPTER XVII

A FRAME-UP

News, of a kind, travels on the wings of the wind across wastes of the farther land. Principalities may fall, nations crash, and kingdoms sink into oblivion, and the North will neither know nor care. For the North has its own problems—vital problems, human problems—and therefore big. Elemental, portentous problems, having to do with life and the eating of meat.

In the crash and shift of man-made governments; in the redistribution of man-constituted authority, and man-gathered surplus of increment, the North has no part. On the cold side of sixty there is no surplus, and men think in terms of meat, and their possessions are meat-getting possessions. Guns, nets, and traps, even of the best, insure but a bare existence. And in the lean years, which are the seventh years—the years of the rabbit plague—starvation stalks in the teepees, and gaunt, sunken-eyed forms, dry-lipped, and with the skin drawn tightly over protruding ribs, stiffen between shoddy blankets. For even the philosophers of the land of God and the H.B.C. must eat to live—if not this week, at least once next week.

The H.B.C., taking wise cognizance of the seventh year, extends it credit—"debt" it is called in the outlands—but it puts no more wool in its blankets, and for lack of food the body-fires burn low. But the cold remains inexorable. And with the thermometer at seventy degrees below zero, even in the years of plenty, when the philosophers eat almost daily, there is little of comfort. With the thermometer at seventy in the lean years, the suffering is diminished by the passing of many philosophers.

The arrest of Bob MacNair was a matter of sovereign import to the dwellers of the frozen places, and word of it swept like wildfire through the land of the lakes and rivers. Yet in all the North those upon whom it made the least impression were those most vitally concerned—MacNair's own Indians. So quietly had the incident passed that not one of them realized its importance.

With them MacNair was *God*. He was the *law*. He had taught them to work, so that even in the lean years they and their wives and their babies ate twice each day. He had said that they should continue to eat twice each day, and therefore his departure was a matter of no moment. They knew only that he had gone southward with the man of the soldier-police. This was doubtless as he had commanded. They could conceive of MacNair only as commanding. Therefore the soldier-policeman had obeyed and accompanied him to the southward.

With no such complacency, however, was the arrest of MacNair regarded by the henchmen of Lapierre. To them MacNair was not God, nor was he the law. For these men knew well the long arm of the Mounted and what lay at the end of the trail. Lean forms sped through the woods, and the word passed from lip to lip in far places. It was whispered upon the Slave, the Mackenzie, and the Athabasca, and it was told in the provinces before MacNair and Ripley reached Fort Chippewayan. Along the river, men talked excitedly, and impatiently awaited word from Lapierre, while their eyes snapped with greed and their thoughts flew to the gold in the sands of the barren grounds.

In the Bastile du Mort, a hundred miles to the eastward, Lapierre heard the news from the lips of a breathless runner, but a scant ten hours after Corporal Ripley and MacNair stepped from the door of the cottage. And within the hour the quarter-breed was upon the trail, travelling light, in company with LeFroy, who, fearing swift vengeance, had also sought safety in the stronghold of the outlaws.

Chloe Elliston stood in the doorway and watched the broad form of Bob MacNair swing across the clearing in company with Corporal Ripley. As the men disappeared in the timber, a fierce joy of victory surged through her veins. She had bared the mailed fist! Had wrested a people from the hand of their oppressor! The Snare Lake Indians were henceforth to be *her* Indians! She had ridded the North of MacNair! Every fibre of her sang with the exultation of it as she turned into the room and encountered the fishlike stare of Big Lena.

The woman leaned, ponderous and silent, against the jamb of the door giving into the kitchen. Her huge arms were folded tightly across her breast, and, for some inexplicable reason, Chloe found the stare disconcerting. The enthusiasm of her victory damped perceptibly. For if the fish-eyed stare held nothing of reproach, it certainly held nothing of approbation. Almost the girl read a condescending pity in the stare of the china-blue eyes. The thought stung, and she faced the other wrathfully.

"Well, for Heaven's sake say something! Don't stand there and stare like a—a billikin! Can't you talk?"

"Yah, Ay tank Ay kin; but Ay von't—not yat."

"What do you mean?" cried the exasperated girl, as she flung herself into a chair. But without deigning to answer, Big Lena turned heavily into the kitchen, and closed the door with a bang that impoverished invective—for volumes may be spoken—in the banging of a door. The moment was inauspicious for the entrance of Harriet Penny. At best, Chloe merely endured the little spinster, with her whining, hysterical outbursts, and abject, unreasoning fear of God, man, the devil, and everything else. "Oh, my dear, I am so glad!" piped the little woman, rushing to the girl's side: "we need never fear him again, need we?"

"Nobody ever did fear him but you," retorted Chloe.

"But, Mr. Lapierre said—"

The girl arose with a gesture of impatience, and Miss Penny returned to MacNair. "He is so big, and coarse, and horrible! I am sure even his looks are enough to frighten a person to death."

Chloe sniffed. "I think he is handsome, and he is big and strong. I like big people."

"But, my dear!" cried the horrified Miss Penny. "He—he kills Indians!"

"So do I!" snapped the girl, and stamped angrily into her own room, where she threw herself upon the bed and gave way to bitter reflections. She hated everyone. She hated MacNair, and Big Lena, and Harriet Penny, and the officer of the Mounted. She hated Lapierre and the Indians, too. And then, realizing the folly of her blind hatred, she hated herself for hating. With an effort she regained her poise.

"MacNair is out of the way; and that's the main thing," she murmured. She remembered his last words: "Beware of

Pierre Lapierre," and her eyes sought the man's hastily scribbled note that lay upon the table where he had left it. She reread the note, and crumpling it in her hand threw it to the floor. "He always manages to be some place else when anything happens!" she exclaimed. "Oh, why couldn't it have been the other way around? Why couldn't MacNair have been the one to have the interest of the Indians at heart? And why couldn't Lapierre have been the one to browbeat and bully them?"

She paced angrily up and down the room, and kicked viciously at the little ball of paper that was Lapierre's note. "He couldn't browbeat anything!" she exclaimed. "He's—he's—sometimes, I think, he's almost *sneaking*, with his bland, courtly manners, and his suave tongue. Oh, how I could hate that man! And how I—" she stopped suddenly, and with clenched fists fixed her gaze upon the portrait of Tiger Elliston, and as she looked the thin features that returned her stare seemed to resolve into the rugged outlines of the face of Bob MacNair.

"He's big and strong, and he's not afraid," she murmured, and started nervously at the knock with which Big Lena announced supper.

When Chloe appeared at the table five minutes later she was quite her usual self. She even laughed at Harriet Penny's horrified narrative of the fact that she had discovered several Indians in the act of affixing runners to the collapsible bathtubs in anticipation of the coming snow.

Chloe spent an almost sleepless night, and it was with a feeling of distinct relief that she arose to find Lapierre upon the veranda. She noted a certain intense eagerness in the quarter-breed's voice as he greeted her.

"Ah, Miss Elliston!" he cried, seizing both her hands. "It

seems that during my brief absence you have accomplished wonders! May I ask how you managed to bring about the downfall of the brute of the North, and at the same time win his Indians to your school?"

Under the enthusiasm of his words the girl's heart once more quickened with the sense of victory. She withdrew her hands from his clasp and gave a brief account of all that had happened since their parting on Snare Lake.

"Wonderful," breathed Lapierre at the conclusion of the recital. "And you are sure he was duly charged with the murder of the two Indians?"

Chloe nodded. "Yes, indeed I am sure!" she exclaimed. "The officer, Corporal Ripley, tried to get me to put off this charge until his other trial came up at the spring assizes. He said MacNair could give bail and secure his liberty on the liquor charges, and thus return to the North—and to his Indians."

Lapierre nodded eagerly. "Ah, did I not tell you, Miss Elliston, that the men of the Mounted are with him heart and soul? He owns them! You have done well not to withdraw the charge of murder."

"I offered to furnish him with an escort of Indians, but he refused them. I don't see how in the world he can expect to take MacNair to jail. He's a mere boy."

Lapierre laughed. "He'll take him to jail all right, you may rest assured as to that. He will not dare to allow him to escape, nor will MacNair try to escape. We have nothing to fear now until the trial. It is extremely doubtful if we can make the murder charge stick, but it will serve to hold him during the winter, and I have no doubt when his case comes up in the spring we will be able to produce evidence that will insure conviction on the whiskey charges, which will mean at least a year or two in jail and the exaction of a heavy fine.

"In the meantime you will have succeeded in educating the Indians to a realization of the fact that they owe allegiance to no man. MacNair's power is broken. He will be discredited by the authorities, and hated by his own Indians—a veritable pariah of the wilderness. And now, Miss Elliston, I must hasten at once to the rivers. My interests there have long been neglected. I shall return as soon as possible, but my absence will necessarily be prolonged, for beside my own trading affairs and the getting out of the timber for new scows, I hope to procure such additional evidence as will insure the conviction of MacNair. LeFroy will remain with you here."

"Did you catch the whiskey runners?" Chloe asked.

Lapierre shook his head. "No," he answered, "they succeeded in eluding us among the islands at the eastern end of the lake. We were about to push our search to a conclusion when news reached us of MacNair's arrest, and we returned with all speed to the Yellow Knife."

Somehow, the man's words sounded unconvincing—the glib reply was too ready—too like the studied answer to an anticipated question. She regarded him searchingly, but the simple directness of his gaze caused her own eyes to falter, and she turned into the house with a deep breath that was very like a sigh.

The sense of elation and self-confidence inspired by Lapierre's first words ebbed as it had ebbed before the unspoken rebuke of Big Lena, leaving her strangely depressed. With the joy of accomplishment dead within her, she drove herself to her work without enthusiasm. In all the world, nothing seemed worth while. She was unsure—unsure of Lapierre; unsure of herself; unsure of Big Lena—and, worst of all, unbelievable and preposterous as it seemed in the light of what she had witnessed with her own eyes, unsure of MacNair—of his villainy!

Before noon the first snow of the season started in a fall of light, feathery flakes, which gradually resolved themselves into fine, hard particles that were hurled and buffeted about by the blasts of a fitful wind.

For three days the blizzard raged—days in which Lapierre contrived to spend much time in Chloe's company, and during which the girl set about deliberately to study the quarter-breed, in the hope of placing definitely the defect in his make-up, the tangible reason for the growing sense of distrust with which she was coming to regard him. But, try as she would, she could find no cause, no justification, for the uncomfortable and indefinable *something* that was gradually developing into an actual doubt of his sincerity. She knew that the man had himself well in hand, for never by word or look did he express any open avowal of love, although a dozen times a day he managed subtly to show that his love had in no wise abated.

On the morning of the fourth day, with forest and lake and river buried beneath three feet of snow, Lapierre took the trail for the southward. Before leaving, he sought out LeFroy in the storehouse.

"We have things our own way, but we must lie low for a while, at least. MacNair is not licked yet—by a damn' sight! He knows we furnished the booze to his Indians, and he will yell his head off to the Mounted, and we will have them dropping in on us all the winter. In the meantime leave the liquor where it is. Don't bring a gallon of it into this clearing. It will keep, and we can't take chances with the

Mounted. There will be enough in it for us, with what we can knock down here, and what the boys can take out of MacNair's diggings. They know the gold is there; most of them were in on the stampede when MacNair drove them back a few years ago. And when they find out that MacNair is in jail, there will be another stampede. And we will clean up big all around."

LeFroy, a man of few words, nodded sombrely, and Lapierre, who was impatient to be off to the rivers, failed to note that the nod was far more sombre than usual—failed, also, to note the pair of china-blue, fishlike eyes that stared impassively at him from behind the goods piled high upon the huge counter.

Once upon the trail, Lapierre lost no time. As passed the word upon the Mackenzie, where the men who had heard of the arrest of MacNair waited in a frenzy of impatience for the signal that would send them flying over the snow to Snare Lake. Day and night the man travelled; from the Mackenzie southward the length of Slave and up the Athabasca. And in his wake men, whose eyes fairly bulged with the greed of gold, jammed their outfits into packs and headed into the North.

At Athabasca Landing he sent a crew into the timber, and hastened on to Edmonton where he purchased a railway ticket for a point that had nothing whatever to do with his destination. That same night he boarded an east-bound train, and in an early hour of the morning, when the engine paused for water beside a tank that was the most conspicuous building of a little flat town in the heart of a peaceful farming community, he stepped unnoticed from the day coach and proceeded at once to the low, wooden hotel, where he was cautiously admitted through a rear door by the landlord himself, who was, incidentally, Lapierre's shrewdest and most effective whiskey runner.

It was this Tostoff: Russian by birth, and crook by nature, whose business it was to disguise the contraband whiskey into innocent-looking freight pieces. And, it was Tostoff who selected the men and stood responsible for the contraband's safe conduct over the first stage of its journey to the North.

Tostoff objected strenuously to the running of a consignment in winter, but Lapierre persisted, covering the ground step by step while the other listened with a scowl.

"It's this way, Tostoff: For years MacNair has been our chief stumbling-block. God knows we have trouble enough running the stuff past the Dominion police and the Mounted. But the danger from the authorities is small in comparison with the danger from MacNair." Tostoff growled an assent. "And now," continued Lapierre, "for the first time we have him where we want him."

The Russian looked sceptical. "We got MacNair where we want him if he's dead," he grunted. "Who killed him?"

Lapierre made a gesture of impatience. "He is not dead. He's locked up in the Fort Saskatchewan jail."

For the first time Tostoff showed real interest. "What's against him?" he asked eagerly.

"Murder, for one thing," answered Lapierre. "That will hold him without bail until the spring assizes. He will probably get out of that, though. But they are holding him also on four or five liquor charges."

"Liquor charges!" cried Tostoff, with an angry snort. "O-ho! so that's his game? That's why he's been bucking us—because he's got a line of his own!"

Lapierre laughed. "Not so fast, Tostoff, not so fast. It is a frame-up. That is, the charges are not, but the evidence is. I attended to that myself. I think we have enough on him to keep him out of the cold for a couple of winters to come. But you can't tell. And while we have him we will put the screws to him for all there is in it. It is the chance of a lifetime. What we want now is evidence—and more evidence.

"Here is the scheme: You fix up a consignment, five or ten gallons, the usual way, and instead of shooting it in by the Athabasca, cut into the old trail on the Beaver and take it across the Methye portage to a *cache* on the Clearwater. Brown's old cabin will about fill the bill. We ought to be able to *cache* the stuff by Christmas.

"In the meantime, I will slip up the river and tip it off to the Mounted at Fort McMurray that I got it straight from down below that MacNair is going to run in a batch over the Methye trail, and that it is to be *cached* on the bank of the Clearwater on New Year's Day. That will give your packers a week to make their getaway. And on New Year's Day the Mounted will find the stuff in the *cache*. There will be nobody to arrest, but they will have the evidence that will clinch the case against MacNair. And with MacNair behind the bars we will have things our own way north of sixty."

Tostoff shook his head dubiously.

"Bad business, Lapierre," he warned. "Winter trailing is bad business. The snow tells tales. We haven't been caught yet. Why? Not because we've been lucky, but because we've been careful. Water leaves no trail. We've always run our stuff in in the summer. You say you've got the goods on MacNair. I say, let well enough alone. The Mounted ain't fools—they can read the sign in the snow."

Lapierre arose with a curse. "You white-livered clod!" he cried. "Who is running this scheme? You or I? Who delivers the whiskey to the Indians? And who pays you your money? I do the thinking for this outfit. I didn't come down here to *ask* you to run this consignment. I came here to *tell* you to do it. This thing of playing safe is all right. I never told you to run a batch in the winter before, but this time you have got to take the chance."

Lapierre leaned closer and fixed the heavy-faced Russian with his gleaming black eyes. He spoke slowly so that the words fell distinctly from his lips. "You *cache* that liquor on the Clearwater on Christmas Day. If you fail—well, you will join the others that have been dismissed from my service—see?"

Tostoff's only reply was a ponderous but expressive shrug, and without a word Lapierre turned and stepped out into the night.

CHAPTER XVIII

WHAT HAPPENED AT BROWN'S

It was the middle of December. Storm after storm had left the North cold and silent beneath its white covering of snow. A dog-team swung across the surface of the ice-locked Athabasca, and took the steep slope at Fort McMurray on a long slant.

Leaving the dogs in care of the musher, Pierre Lapierre loosened the thongs of his rackets, and, pushing open the door, stamped noisily into the detachment quarters of the Mounted and advanced to the stove where two men were mending dog-harness. The men looked up.

"Speaking of the devil," grinned Constable Craig, with a glance toward Corporal Ripley, who greeted the newcomer with a curt nod. "Well, Lapierre, where'd you come from?"

Lapierre jerked his thumb toward the southward. "Up river," he answered. "Getting out timber for my scows." Removing his cap and mittens, the quarter-breed loosened his heavy moose-hide *parka*, beat the clinging snow from the coarse hair, and drew a chair to the stove.

"Come through from the Landing on the river?" asked Ripley, as he filled a short black pipe with the tobacco he shaved from a plug. "How's the trail?"

"Good and hard, except for the slush at the Boiler and another stretch just below the Cascade." Lapierre rolled a cigarette. "Hear you caught MacNair with the goods at last," he ventured.

Ripley nodded.

"Looks like it," he admitted. "But what do you mean, 'at last'?"

The quarter-breed laughed lightly and blew a cloud of cigarette-smoke ceilingward. "I mean he has had things pretty much his own way the last six or eight years."

"Meanin' he's been runnin' whiskey all that time?" asked Craig.

Lapierre nodded. "He has run booze enough into the North to float a canoe from here to Port Chippewayan."

It was Ripley's turn to laugh. "If you are so all-fired wise, why haven't you made a complaint?" he asked. "Seems like I never heard you and MacNair were such good friends,"

Lapierre shrugged. "I know a whole lot of men who have got their full growth because they minded their own business," he answered. "I am not in the Mounted. That's what you are paid for."

Ripley flushed. "We'll earn our pay on this job all right. We've got the goods on him this time. And, by the way, Lapierre, if you've got anything in the way of evidence, we'll be wanting it at the trial. Better show up in May, and save somebody goin' after you. If you run onto any Indians that know anything, bring them along."

"I will be there," smiled the other. "And since we are on the subject, I can put you wise to a little deal that will net you some first-hand evidence." The officers looked interested, and Lapierre continued: "You know where Brown's old cabin is, just this side of the Methye portage?" Ripley nodded. "Well, if you should happen to be at Brown's on New Year's Day, just pull up the puncheons under the bunk and see what you find."

"What will we find?" asked Craig.

Lapierre shrugged. "If I were you fellows I wouldn't overlook any bets," he answered meaningly.

"Why New Year's Day any more than Christmas, or any other day?"

"Because," answered Lapierre, "on Christmas Day, or any other day before New Year's Day, you won't find a damned thing but an empty hole—that is why. Well, I must be going." He fastened the throat of his *parka* and drew on his cap and mittens. "So long! See you in the spring. Shouldn't wonder if I will run onto some Indians, this winter, who will tell what they know, now that MacNair is out of the way. I know plenty of them that can talk, if they will."

"So long!" answered Ripley as Lapierre left the room. "Much obliged for the tip. Hope your hunch is good."

"Play it and see," smiled Lapierre, and banged the door behind him.

Moving slowly northward upon a course that paralleled but studiously avoided the old Methye trail, two men and a dog-team plodded heavily through the snow at the close of a shortening day. Ostensibly, these men were trappers; and, save for a single freight piece bound securely upon the sled, their outfit varied in no particular from the outfits of others who each winter fare into the North to engage in the taking of fur. A close observer might have noted that the eyes of these men were hard, and the frequent glances they cast over the back-trail were tense with concern.

The larger and stronger of the two, one Xavier, a sullen riverman of evil countenance, paused at the top of a ridge and pointed across a snow-swept beaver meadow. "T'night we camp on dees side. T'mor' we cross to de mout' of de leetle creek, and two pipe beyon' we com' on de cabin of Baptiste Chambre."

The smaller man frowned. He, too, was a riverman, tough and wiry and small. A man whose pinched, wizened body was a fitting cloister for the warped soul that flashed malignantly from the beady, snakelike eyes.

"*Non, non*!" he cried, and the venomous glance of the beady eyes was not unmingled with fear. "We ke'p straight on pas' de beeg swamp. Me—I'm no lak' dees wintaire trail." He pointed meaningly toward the marks of the sled in the snow.

The other laughed derisively. "*Sacre*! you leetle man, you Du Mont, you 'fraid!"

The other shrugged. "I'm 'fraid, *Oui*, I'm lak' I ke'p out de jail. Tostoff, she say, you com' on de cabin of Brown de Chrees'mas Day. *Bien*! Tostoff, she sma't mans. Lapierre, too. Tostoff, she 'fraid for de wintaire trail, but she 'fraid for Lapierre mor'."

Xavier interrupted him. "*Tra la*, Chrees'mas Day! Ain't we got de easy trail? Two days befor' Chrees'mas we com' on de cabin of Brown. Baptiste Chambre, she got de beeg jug rum. We mak' de grand dronk—one day—one night. Den we hit de trail an com' on de Clearwater Chrees'mas Day sam' lak' now. Tostoff, de Russ, she nevair know, Lapierre, she nevair know. *Voila*!"

Still the other objected. "Mebe so com' de storm. What den? We was'e de time wit' Baptiste Chambre. We no mak' de Clearwater de Chrees'mas Day—eh?"

Xavier growled. "De Chrees'mas Day, damn! We no mak' de Chrees'mas Day, we mak' som' odder day. Lapierre's damn' Injuns com' for de wheeskey on Chrees'mas Day, she haf to wait. Me—I'm goin' to Baptiste Chambre. I'm goin' for mak' de beeg dronk. If de snow com' and de dog can't pull, I'm tak' dees leetle piece on ma back to the Clearwater."

He reached down contemptuously and swung the piece containing ten gallons of whiskey to his shoulder with one hand, then lowered it again to the sled.

"You know w'at I'm hear on de revair?" he asked, stepping closer to Du Mont's side and lowering his voice. "I'm hearin' MacNair ees een de jail. I'm hearin' Lapierre she pass de word to hit for Snare Lake, for deeg de gol'."

"Did Lapierre tell you to deeg de gol', or me? *Non*. He say, you go to Tostoff." The snakelike eyes of the smaller man glittered at the mention of gold. He clutched at the other's arm and cried out sharply:

"MacNair arres'! *Sacre*! Com', we tak' de wheeskey to de Clearwater an' go on to Snare Lake."

This time it was Xavier's eyes that flashed a hint of fear. "*Non*!" he answered quickly. "Lapierre, she—"

The other silenced him, speaking rapidly. "Lapierre, she

t'ink she mak' us w'at you call, de double cross!" Xavier noted that the malignant eyes flashed dangerously—"Lapierre, she sma't but me—I'm sma't too. Dere's plent' men 'long de revair lak' to see de las' of Pierre Lapierre. And plent' Injun in de Nort' dey lak' dat too. But dey 'fraid to keel him. We do de work—Lapierre she tak' de money. *Sacre*! Me—I'm 'fraid, too." He paused and shrugged significantly. "But som' day I'm git de chance an' den leetle Du Mont she dismees Lapierre from de serveece. Den me—I'm de bos'. *Bien*!"

The other glanced at him in admiration.

"Me, I'm goin' 'long to Snare Lake," he said, "but firs' we stop on Baptiste Chambre an' mak' de beeg dronk, eh!" The smaller man nodded, and the two sought their blankets and were soon sleeping silently beside the blazing fire.

A week later the two rivermen paused at the edge of a thicket that commanded the approach to Brown's abandoned cabin on the Clearwater. The threatened storm had broken while they were still at Baptiste Chambre's cabin, and the two days' debauch had lengthened into five.

Chambre's jug had been emptied and several times refilled from the contents of Tostoff's concealed cask, which had been skilfully tapped and as skilfully replenished as to weight by the addition of snow water.

The effect of their protracted orgy was plainly visible in the bloodshot eyes and heavy movements of both men. And it was more from force of long habit than from any sense of alertness or premonition of danger that they crouched in the thicket and watched the smoke curl from the little iron stovepipe that protruded above the roof of the cabin.

"Dem Injun she wait," growled Xavier. "Com' on, me—I'm

lak' for ketch som' sleep." The two swung boldly into the open and, pausing only long enough to remove their rackets, pushed open the door of the cabin.

An instant later Du Mont, who was in the lead, leaped swiftly backward and, crashing into the heavier and clumsier Xavier bowled him over into the snow, where both wallowed helplessly, held down by Xavier's heavy pack.

It was but the work of a moment for the wiry Du Mont to free himself, and when he leaped to his feet, cursing like a fiend, it was to look squarely into the muzzle of Corporal Ripley's service revolver, while Constable Craig loosened the pack straps and allowed Xavier to arise.

"Caught with the goods, eh?" grinned Ripley, when the two prisoners were seated side by side upon the pole bunk.

The sullen-faced Xavier glowered in surly silence, but the malignant, beady eyes of Du Mont regarded the officer keenly. "You patrol de Clearwater now, eh?"

Ripley laughed. "When there's anything doin' we do."

"How you fin' dat out? Dem Injun she squeal? I'm lak' to know 'bout dat."

"Well, it wasn't exactly an Indian this time," answered Ripley; "that is, it wasn't a regular Indian. Pierre Lapierre put us on to this little deal."

"*Pierre*—LAPIERRE!"

The little wizened man fairly shrieked the name and, leaping to his feet, bounded about the room like an animated rubber ball, while from his lips poured a steady stream of vile epithets, mingled with every curse and gem of profanity known to two languages.

"That's goin' some," enthused Constable Craig, when the other finally paused for breath. "An' come to think about it, I believe you're right. I like to hear a man speak his mind, an' from your remarks it seems like you're oncommon peeved with this here little deal. It ain't nothin' to get so worked up over. You'll serve your time an' in a couple of years or so they'll turn you loose again."

At the mention of the prison term the burly Xavier moved uneasily upon the bunk. He seemed about to speak, but was forestalled by the quicker witted Du Mont.

"Two years, eh!" asked the outraged Metis, addressing Ripley. "Mebe so you mak' w'at you call de deal. Mebe so I'm tell you who's de boss. Mebe so I'm name de man dat run de wheeskey into de Nort'. De man dat plans de cattle raids on de bordair. De man dat keels mor' Injun dan mos' men keels deer, eh! Wat den? Mebe so den you turn us loose, eh?"

Ripley laughed. "You think I'm goin' to pay you to tell me the name of the man we've already got locked up?"

"You got MacNair lock up," Du Mont leered knowingly. "*Bien*! You t'ink MacNair run de wheeskey. But MacNair, she ain't run no wheeskey. You mak' de deal wit' me. Ba Gos'! I'm not jus' tell you de name, I'm tell you so you fin' w'at you call de proof! I no fin' de proof—you no turn me loose. *Voila*!"

Corporal Ripley was a keen judge of men, and he knew that the vindictive and outraged Metis was in just the right mood to tell all he knew. Also Ripley believed that the man knew much. Therefore, he made the deal. And it is a tribute to the Mounted that the crafty and suspicious Metis accepted, without question, the word of the corporal when he promised to do all in his power to secure their liberty in return for the evidence that would convict "the man higher up."

Corporal Ripley was a man of quick decision; with him to decide was to act. Within an hour from the time Du Mont concluded his story the two officers with their prisoners were headed for Fort Saskatchewan. Both Du Mont and Xavier realized that their only hope for clemency lay in their ability to aid the authorities in building up a clear case against Lapierre, and during the ten days of snow-trail that ended at Athabasca Landing each tried to outdo the other in explaining what he knew of the workings of Lapierre's intricate system.

At the Landing, Ripley reported to the superintendent commanding N Division, who immediately sent for the prisoners and submitted them to a cross-examination that lasted far into the night, and the following morning the corporal escorted them to Fort Saskatchewan, where they were to remain in jail to await the verification of their story.

Division commanders are a law unto themselves, and much to his surprise, two days later, Bob MacNair was released upon his own recognizance. Whereupon, without a moment's delay, he bought the best dog-team obtainable and headed into the North accompanied by Corporal Ripley, who was armed with a warrant for the arrest of Pierre Lapierre.

CHAPTER XIX

THE LOUCHOUX GIRL

Winter laid a heavy hand upon the country of the Great Slave. Blizzard after howling blizzard came out of the North until the buildings of Chloe Elliston's school lay drifted to the eaves in the centre of the snow-swept clearing.

With the drifting snows and the bitter, intense cold that isolated the little colony from the great world to the southward, came a sense of peace and quietude that contrasted sharply with the turbulent, surcharged atmosphere with which the girl had been surrounded from the moment she had unwittingly become a factor in the machinations of the warring masters of wolf-land.

With MacNair safely behind the bars of a jail far to the southward, and Lapierre somewhere upon the distant rivers, the Indians for the first time relaxed from the strain of tense expectancy. Of her own original Indians, those who had remained at the school by command of the crafty Lapierre, there remained only LeFroy and a few of the older men who were unfit to go on the trap-lines, together with the women and children.

MacNair's Indians, who had long since laid down their traps to pick up the white man's tools, stayed at the school.

And much to the girl's surprise, under the direction of the refractory Sotenah, and Old Elk, and Wee Johnnie Tamarack, not only performed with a will the necessary work of the camp—the chopping and storing of firewood, the shovelling of paths through the huge drifts, and the drawing of water from the river—but took upon themselves numerous other labours of their own initiative.

An ice-house was built and filled upon the bank of the river. Trees were felled, and the logs ranked upon miniature rollways, where all through the short days the Indians busied themselves in the rude whip-sawing of lumber.

Their women and children daily attended the school and worked faithfully under the untiring tutelage of Chloe and Harriet Penny, who entered into the work with new enthusiasm engendered by the interest and the aptness of the Snare Lake Indians—absent qualities among the wives and children of Lapierre's trappers.

LeFroy was kept busy in the storehouse, and with the passing of the days Chloe noticed that he managed to spend more and more time in company with Big Lena. At first she gave the matter no thought. But when night after night she heard the voices of the two as they sat about the kitchen-stove long after she had retired, she began to consider the matter seriously.

At first she dismissed it with a laugh. Of all people in the world, she thought, these two, the heavy, unimaginative Swedish woman, and the leathern-skinned, taciturn wood-rover, would be the last to listen to the call of romance.

Chloe was really fond of the huge, silent woman who had followed her without question into the unknown wilderness of the Northland, even as she had accompanied her without protest through the maze of the far South Seas. With all her averseness to speech and her vacuous, fishy stare, the girl had long since learned that Big Lena was both loyal and efficient and shrewd. But, Big Lena as a wife! Chloe smiled broadly at the thought.

"Poor LeFroy," she pitied. "But it would be the best thing in the world for him. 'The perpetuity of the red race will be attained only through its amalgamation with the white,'" she quoted; the trite banality of one of the numerous theorists she had studied before starting into the North.

Of LeFroy she knew little. He seemed a half-breed of more than average intelligence, and as for the rest—she would leave that to Lena. On the whole, she rather approved of the arrangement, not alone upon the amalgamation theory, but because she entertained not the slightest doubt as to who would rule the prospective family. She could depend upon Big Lena's loyalty, and her marriage to one of their number would therefore become a very important factor in the attitude of the Indians towards the school.

Gradually, the women of the Slave Lake Indians taking the cue from their northern sisters, began to show an appreciation of the girl's efforts in their behalf. An appreciation that manifested itself in little tokens of friendship, exquisitely beaded moccasins, shyly presented, and a pair of quill-embroidered leggings laid upon her desk by a squaw who slipped hurriedly away. Thus the way was paved for a closer intimacy which quickly grew into an eager willingness among the Indians to help her in the mastering of their own language.

As this intimacy grew, the barrier which is the chief stumbling-block of missionaries and teachers who seek to carry enlightenment into the lean lone land, gradually dissolved. The women with whom Chloe came in contact ceased to be Indians *en masse*; they became *people*—

personalities—each with her own capability and propensity for the working of good or harm. With this realization vanished the last vestige of aloofness and reserve. And, thereafter, many of the women broke bread by invitation at Chloe's own table.

The one thing that remained incomprehensible to the girl was the idolatrous regard in which MacNair was held by his own Indians. To them he was a superman—the one great man among all white men. His word was accepted without question. Upon leaving for the southward MacNair had told the men to work, therefore they worked unceasingly. Also he had told the women and the children to obey without question the words of the white *kloochman*, and therefore they absorbed her teaching with painstaking care.

Time and again the girl tried to obtain the admission that MacNair was in the habit of supplying his Indians with whiskey, and always she received the same answer. "MacNair sells no whiskey. He hates whiskey. And many times has he killed men for selling whiskey to his people."

At first these replies exasperated the girl beyond measure. She set them down as stereotyped answers in which they had been carefully coached. But as time went on and the women, whose word she had come to hold in regard, remained unshaken in their statements, an uncomfortable doubt assailed her—a doubt that, despite herself, she fostered. A doubt that caused her to ponder long of nights as she lay in her little room listening to the droning voices of LeFroy and Big Lena as they talked by the stove in the kitchen.

Strange fancies and pictures the girl built up as she lay, half waking, half dreaming between her blankets. Pictures in which MacNair, misjudged, hated, fighting against fearful odds, came clean through the ruck and muck with which his enemies had endeavoured to smother him, and proved himself the man he might have been; fancies and pictures that dulled into a pain that was very like a heartache, as the vivid picture—the real picture—which she herself had seen with her own eyes that night on Snare Lake, arose always to her mind.

The tang of the northern air bit into the girl's blood. She spent much time in the open and became proficient and tireless in the use of snowshoes and skis. Daily her excursions into the surrounding timber grew longer, and she was never so happy as when swinging with strong, wide strides on her fat thong-strung rackets, or sliding with the speed of the wind down some steep slope of the river-bank, on her smoothly polished skis.

It was upon one of these solitary excursions, when her steps had carried her many miles along the winding course of a small tributary of the Yellow Knife, that the girl became so fascinated in her exploration she failed utterly to note the passage of time until a sharp bend of the little river brought her face to face with the low-hung winter sun, which was just on the point of disappearing behind the shrub pines of a long, low ridge.

With a start she brought up short and glanced fearfully about her. Darkness was very near, and she had travelled straight into the wilderness almost since early dawn. Without a moment's delay she turned and retraced her steps. But even as her hurrying feet carried her over the back-trail she realized that night would overtake her before she could hope to reach the larger river.

The thought of a night spent alone in the timber at first terrified her. She sought to increase her pace, but her muscles were tired, her footsteps dragged, and the rackets clung to her feet like inexorable weights which sought to drag her down, down into the soft whiteness of the snow.

Darkness gathered, and the back-trail dimmed. Twice she fell and regained her feet with an effort. Suddenly rounding a sharp bend, she crashed heavily among the dead branches of a fallen tree. When at length she regained her feet, the last vestige of daylight had vanished. Her own snowshoe tracks were indiscernible upon the white snow. She was off the trail!

Something warm and wet trickled along her cheek. She jerked off her mittens and with fingers tingling in the cold, keen air, picked bits of bark from the edges of the ragged wound where the end of a broken branch had snagged the soft flesh of her face. The wound stung, and she held a handful of snow against it until the pain dulled under the numbing chill.

Stories of the night-prowling wolf-pack, and the sinister, man-eating *loup cervier*, crowded her brain. She must build a fire. She felt through her pocket for the glass bottle of matches, only to find that her fingers were too numb to remove the cork. She replaced the vial and, drawing on her mittens, beat her hands together until the blood tingled to her finger-tips. How she wished now that she had heeded the advice of LeFroy, who had cautioned against venturing into the woods without a light camp ax slung to her belt.

Laboriously she set about gathering bark and light twigs which she piled in the shelter of a cut-bank, and when at last a feeble flame flickered weakly among the thin twigs she added larger branches which she broke and twisted from the limbs of the dead trees. Her camp-fire assumed a healthy proportion, and the flare of it upon the snow was encouraging.

At the end of an hour, Chloe removed her rackets and

dropped wearily onto the snow beside the fire-wood which she had piled conveniently close to the blaze. Never in her life had she been so utterly weary, but she realized that for her that night there could be no sleep. And no sooner had the realization forced itself upon her than she fell sound asleep with her head upon the pile of fire-wood.

She awoke with a start, sitting bolt upright, staring in bewilderment at her fire—and beyond the fire where, only a few feet distant, a hooded shape stood dimly outlined against the snow. Chloe's garments, dampened by the exertion of the earlier hours, had chilled her through while she slept, and as she stared wide-eyed at the apparition beyond the fire, the figure drew closer and the chill of the dampened garments seemed to clutch with icy fingers at her heart. She nerved herself for a supreme effort and arose stiffly to her knees, and then suddenly the figure resolved itself into the form of a girl—an Indian girl—but a girl as different from the Indians of her school as day is different from night.

As the girl advanced she smiled, and Chloe noted that her teeth were strong and even and white, and that dark eyes glowed softly from a face as light almost as her own.

"Do not 'fraid," said the girl in a low, rich voice. "I'm not hurt you. I'm see you fire, I'm com' 'cross to fin'. Den, ver' queek you com' 'wake, an' I'm see you de one I'm want."

"The one you want!" cried Chloe, edging closer to the fire. "What do you mean? Who are you? And why should you want me?"

"Me—I'm Mary. I'm com' ver' far. I'm com' from de people of my modder. De Louchoux on de lower Mackenzie. I'm com' to fin' de school. I'm hear about dat school."

"The lower Mackenzie!" cried Chloe in astonishment. "I should think you have come very far."

The girl nodded. "Ver' far," she repeated. "T'irty-two sleep I'm on de trail."

"Alone!"

"Alone," she assented. "I'm com' for learn de ways of de white women."

Chloe motioned the girl closer, and then, seized by a sudden chill, shivered violently. The girl noticed the paroxysm, and, dropping to her knees by Chloe's side, spoke hurriedly.

"You col'," she said. "You got no blanket. You los'."

Without waiting for a reply, she hurried to a light pack-sled which stood nearby upon the snow. A moment later she returned with a heavy pair of blankets which she spread at Chloe's side, and then, throwing more wood upon the fire, began rapidly to remove the girl's clothing. Within a very short space of time, Chloe found herself lying warm and comfortable between the blankets, while her damp garments were drying upon sticks thrust close to the blaze. She watched the Indian girl as she moved swiftly and capably about her task, and when the last garment was hung upon its stick she motioned the girl to her side.

"Why did you come so far to my school?" she asked. "Surely you have been to school. You speak English. You are not a full-blood Indian."

The girl's eyes sought the shadows beyond the firelight, and, as her lips framed a reply, Chloe marvelled at the weird beauty of her.

"I go to school on de Mission, two years at Fort MacPherson. I learn to spik de Englis'. My fadder, heem Englis', but I'm never see heem. Many years ago he com' in de beeg boat dat com' for ketch de whale an' got lock in de ice in de Bufort Sea. In de spring de boat go 'way, an' my fadder go 'long, too. He tell my modder he com' back nex' winter. Dat many years ago—nineteen years. Many boats com' every year, but my fadder no com' back. My modder she t'ink he com' back som' day, an' every fall my modder she tak' me 'way from Fort MacPherson and we go up on de coast an' build de *igloo*. An' every day she set an' watch while de ships com' in, but my fadder no com' back. My modder t'ink he sure com' back, he fin' her waitin' when he com'. She say, mebe so he ketch 'm many whale. Mebe so he get reech so we got plen' money to buy de grub."

The girl paused and her brows contracted thoughtfully. She threw a fresh stick upon the fire and shook her head slowly. "I don' know," she said softly, "mebe so he com' back—but heem been gone long tam'."

"Where is your mother now?" asked Chloe, when the girl had finished.

"She up on de coast in de little *igloo*. Many ships com' into Bufort Sea las' fall. She say, sure dis winter my fadder com' back. She got to wait for heem."

Chloe cleared her throat sharply. "And you?" she asked, "why did you come clear to the Yellow Knife? Why did you not go back to school at the Mission?"

A troubled expression crept into the eyes of the Louchoux girl, and she seemed at a loss to explain. "Eet ees," she answered at length, "dat my man, too, he not com' back lak' my fadder."

"Your man!" cried Chloe in astonishment. "Do you mean you are married? Why, you are nothing but a child!"

The girl regarded her gravely. "Yes," she answered, "I'm marry. Two years ago I git marry, up on de Anderson Reever. My man, heem free-trader, an' all summer we got plent' to eat. In de fall he tak' me back to de *igloo*. He say, he mus' got to go to de land of de white man to buy supplies. I lak' to go, too, to de land of de white man, but he say no, you Injun, you stay in de Nort', an' by-m-by I com' back again. Den he go up de reever, an' all winter I stay in de igloo wit' my modder an' look out over de ice-pack at de boats in de Bufort Sea. In de spreeng my man he don' com' back, my fadder he don' com' back neider. We not have got mooch grub to eat dat winter, and den we go to Fort MacPherson. I go back to de school, and I'm tell de pries' my man he no com' back. De pries' he ver' angry. He say, I'm not got marry, but de pries' he ees a man—he don' un'stan'.

"All summer I'm stay on de Mackenzie, an' I'm watch de canoes an' I'm wait for my man to com' back, but he don' com' back. An' in de fall my modder she go Nort' again to watch de ships in de Bufort Sea. She say, com' 'long, but I don' go, so she go 'lone and I'm stay on de Mackenzie. I'm stay 'til de reever freeze, an' no more canoe can com'. Den I'm wait for de snow. Mebe so my man com' wit' de dog-team. Den I'm hear 'bout de school de white woman build on de Yellow Knife. Always I'm hear 'bout de white women, but I'm never seen none—only de white men. My man, he mos' white.

"Den I'm say, mebe so my man lak' de white women more dan de Injun. He not com' back dis winter, an' I'm go on de school and learn de ways of de white women, an' in de spreeng when my man com' back he lak' me good, an' nex' winter mebe he tak' me 'long to de land of de white women.

But, eet's a long trail to de Yellow Knife, an' I'm got no money to buy de grub an' de outfit. I'm go once mor' to de pries' an' I'm tell heem 'bout dat school. An' I'm say, mebe so I'm learn de ways of de white women, my man tak' me 'long nex' tam'.

"De pries' he t'ink 'bout dat a long tam'. Den he go over to de Hudson Bay Pos' an' talk to McTavish, de factor, an' by-m-by he com' back and tak' me over to de pos' store an' give me de outfit so I'm com' to de school on de Yellow Knife. Plent' grub an' warm blankets dey give me. An' t'irty-two sleep I'm travel de snow-trail. Las' night I'm mak' my camp in de scrub cross de reever. I'm go 'sleep, an' by-m-by I'm wake up an' see you fire an' I'm com' 'long to fin' out who camp here."

As she listened, Chloe's hand stole from beneath the blankets and closed softly about the fingers of the Louchoux girl. "And so you have come to live with me?" she whispered softly.

The girl's face lighted up. "You let me com'?" she asked eagerly, "an' you teach me de ways of de white women, so I ain't jus' be Injun girl? So when my man com' back, he lak' me an' I got plent' to eat in de winter?"

"Yes, dear," answered Chloe, "you shall come to live with me always."

Followed then a long silence which was broken at last by the Indian girl.

"You don' say lak' de pries'," she asked, "you not marry, you bad?"

"No! No! No! You poor child!" cried Chloe, "of course you are not bad! You are going to live with me. You will learn many things."

"An' som' tam', we fin' my man?" she asked eagerly.

Chloe's voice sounded suddenly harsh. "Yes, indeed, we will find him!" she cried. "We will find him and bring him back—" she stopped suddenly. "We will speak of that later. And now that my clothes are dry you can help me put them on, and if you have any grub left in your pack let's eat. I'm starving."

While Chloe finished dressing, the Louchoux girl boiled a pot of tea and fried some bacon, and an hour later the two girls were fast asleep in each other's arms, beneath the warm folds of the big Hudson Bay blankets.

The following morning they had proceeded but a short distance upon the back-trail when they were met by a searching party from the school. The return was made without incident, and Chloe, who had taken a great fancy to the Louchoux girl, immediately established her as a member of her own household.

During the days which followed, the girl plunged with an intense eagerness into the task of learning the ways of the white women. Nothing was too trivial or unimportant to escape her attention. She learned to copy with almost pathetic exactness each of Chloe's little acts and mannerisms, even to the arranging of her hair. With the other two inmates of the cottage the girl became hardly less a favourite than with Chloe herself.

Her progress in learning to speak English, her skill with the needle and the rapidity with which she learned to make her own clothing delighted Harriet Penny. While Big Lena never tired of instructing her in the mysteries of the culinary department. In return the girl looked upon the three women with an adoration that bordered upon idolatry. She would sit by the hour listening to Chloe's accounts of the wondrous cities of the white men and of the doings of the white men's women.

Chloe never mentioned the girl's secret to either Harriet Penny or Big Lena, and carefully avoided any allusion to the subject to the girl herself. Nothing could be done, she reasoned, until the ice went out of the rivers, and in the meantime she would do all in her power to instil into the girl's mind an understanding of the white women's ethics, so that when the time came she would be able to choose intelligently for herself whether she would return to her free-trader lover or prosecute him for his treachery.

Chloe knew that the girl had done no wrong, and in her heart she hoped that she could be brought to a realization of the true character of the man and repudiate him. If not—if she really loved him, and was determined to remain his wife—Chloe made up her mind to insist upon a ceremony which should meet the sanction of Church and State.

Christmas and New Year's passed, and Lapierre did not return to the school. Chloe was not surprised at this, for he had told her that his absence would be prolonged; and in her heart of hearts she was really glad, for the veiled suspicion of the man's sincerity had grown into an actual distrust of him—a distrust that would have been increased a thousand-fold could she have known that the quarter-breed was even then upon Snare Lake at the head of a gang of outlaws who were thawing out MacNair's gravel and shovelling it into dumps for an early clean-up; instead of looking after his "neglected interests" upon the rivers.

But she did not know that, nor did she know of his midnight visit to Tostoff, nor of what happened at Brown's cabin, nor of the release of MacNair.

CHAPTER XX

ON THE TRAIL OF PIERRE LAPIERRE

Bob MacNair drove a terrific trail. He was known throughout the Northland as a hard man to follow at any time. His huge muscles were tireless at the paddle, and upon the rackets his long swinging stride ate up the miles of the snow-trails. And when Bob MacNair was an a hurry the man who undertook to keep up with him had his work cut out.

When he headed northward after his release from the Fort Saskatchewan Jail, MacNair was in very much of a hurry. From daylight until far into the dark he urged his malamutes to their utmost. And Corporal Ripley, who was by no means a *chechako*, found himself taxed to the limit of his endurance, although never by word or sign did he indicate that the pace was other than of his own choosing.

Fort McMurray, a ten- to fourteen-day trip under good conditions, was reached in seven days. Fort Chippewayan in three days more, and Fort Resolution a week later—seventeen days from Athabasca Landing to Fort Resolution—a record trip for a dog-train!

MacNair was known as a man of few words, but Ripley wondered at the ominous silence with which his every attempt at conversation was met. During the whole seventeen days of the snow-trail, MacNair scarcely addressed a word to him—seemed almost oblivious to his presence.

Upon the last day, with the log buildings of Fort Resolution in sight, MacNair suddenly halted the dogs and faced Corporal Ripley.

"Well, what's your program?" he asked shortly.

"My program," returned the other, "is to arrest Pierre Lapierre,"

"How are you going to do it?"

"I've got to locate him first, the details will work out later. I've been counting a lot on your help and judgment in the matter."

"Don't do it!" snapped MacNair.

The other gazed at him in astonishment.

"What do you mean?"

"I mean that I'm not going to help you arrest Lapierre. He's mine! I have sworn to get him, and, by God, I *will* get him! From now on we are working against each other."

Ripley flushed, and his eyes narrowed. "You mean," he exclaimed, "that you defy the Mounted! That you refuse to help when you're called on?"

MacNair laughed. "You might put it that way, I suppose, but it don't sound well. You know me, Ripley. You know when my word has passed—when I've once started a thing—I'll see it through to the limit. I've sworn to get

Lapierre. And I tell you, he's mine! Unless you get him first. You're a good man, Ripley, and you may do it—but if you do, when you get back with him, you'll know you've been somewhere."

The lines of Ripley's face softened; as a sporting proposition the situation appealed to him. He thrust out his hand. "It's a go, MacNair," he said, "and let the best man win!"

MacNair wrung the officer's hand in a mighty grip, and then just as he was on the point of starting his dogs, paused and gazed thoughtfully after the other who was making his way toward the little buildings of Fort Resolution.

"Oh, Ripley," he called. The officer turned and retraced his steps. "You've heard of Lapierre's fort to the eastward. Have you ever been there?"

Ripley shook his head. "No, but I've heard he has one somewhere around the east end of the lake."

MacNair laughed. "Yes, and if you hunted the east end of the lake for it you could hunt a year without finding it. If you really want to know where it is, come along, I'll show you. I happen to be going there."

"What's the idea?" asked the officer, regarding MacNair quizzically.

"The idea is just this. Lapierre's no fool. He's got as good a chance of getting me as I have of getting him. And if anything happens to me you fellows will lose a lot of valuable time before you can locate that fort. I don't know myself exactly why I'm taking you there, except that—well, if anything should happen to me, Lapierre would—you see, he might—that is—Damn it!" he broke out wrathfully. "Can't you see he'll have things his own way with *her*?"

Ripley grinned broadly. "Oh! So that's it, eh? Well, a fellow ought to look out for his friends. She seemed right anxious to have *you* put where nothing would hurt you."

"Shut up!" growled MacNair shortly. "And before we start there's one little condition you must agree to. If we find Lapierre at the fort, in return for my showing you the place, you've got to promise to make no attempt to arrest him without first returning to Fort Resolution. If I can't get him in the meantime I ought to lose."

"You're on," grinned Ripley, "I promise. But man, if he's there he won't be alone! What chance will you have single-handed against a whole gang of outlaws?"

MacNair smiled grimly. "That's my lookout. Remember, your word has passed, and when we locate Lapierre, you head back for Fort Resolution."

The other nodded regretfully, and when MacNair turned away from the fort and headed eastward along the south shore of the lake, the officer fell silently in behind the dogs.

They camped late in a thicket on the shore of South Bay, and at daylight headed straight across the vast snow-level, that stretched for sixty miles in an unbroken surface of white. That night they camped on the ice, and toward noon of the following day drew into the scrub timber directly north of the extremity of Peththenneh Island.

Long after dark they made a fireless camp directly opposite the stronghold of the outlaws on the shore of Lac du Mort. Circling the lake next morning, they reconnoitred the black spruce swamp, and working their way, inch by inch, passed cautiously between the dense evergreens in the direction of the high promontory upon which Lapierre had built his "Bastile du Mort."

Silence enveloped the swamp. An intense, all-pervading stillness, accentuated by the low-hung snow-weighted branches through which the men moved like dark phantoms in the grey half-light of the dawn. They moved not with the stealthy, gliding movement of the Indian, but with the slow caution of trained woodsmen, pausing every few moments to scrutinize their surroundings, and to strain their ears for a sound that would tell them that other lurking forms glided among the silent aisles and vistas of the snow-shrouded swamp. But no sounds came to them through the motionless air, and after an hour of stealthy advance, they drew into the shelter of a huge spruce and peered through the interstices of its snow-laden branches toward the log stockade that Lapierre had thrown across the neck of his lofty peninsula.

Silent and grey and deserted loomed the barrier so cunningly devised as to be almost indistinguishable at a distance of fifty yards. Snow lay upon its top, and vertical ridges of snow clung to the crevices of the upstanding palings.

A half-hour passed, while the two men remained motionless, and then, satisfied that the fort was unoccupied, they stepped cautiously from the shelter of their tree. The next instant, loud and clear, shattering the intense silence with one sharp explosion of sound, rang a shot. And Corporal Ripley, who was following close at the heels of MacNair, staggered, clawed wildly for the butt of his service revolver which protruded from its holster, and, with an imprecation on his lips that ended in an unintelligible snarl, crashed headlong into the snow.

MacNair whirled as if upon a pivot, and with hardly a glance at the prostrate form, dashed over the back-trail with the curious lumbering strides of the man who would hurry on rackets. He had jerked off his heavy mitten at the sound of the shot, and his bared hand clutched firmly the butt of a blue-black automatic. A spruce-branch, suddenly relieved of its snow, sprang upward with a swish, thirty yards away. MacNair fired three times in rapid succession.

There was no answering shot, and he leaped forward, charging directly toward the tree that concealed the hidden foe before the man could reload; for by the roar of its discharge, MacNair knew that the weapon was an old Hudson Bay muzzle-loading smoothbore—a primitive weapon of the old North, but in the hands of an Indian, a weapon of terrible execution at short range, where a roughly moulded bullet or a slug rudely hammered from the solder melted from old tin cans tears its way through the flesh, driven by three fingers of black powder.

Near the tree MacNair found the gun where its owner had hurled it into the snow—found also the tracks of a pair of snowshoes, which headed into the heart of the black spruce swamp. The tracks showed at a glance that the lurking assassin was an Indian, that he was travelling light, and that the chance of running him down was extremely remote. Whereupon MacNair returned his automatic to its holster and bethought himself of Ripley, who was lying back by the stockade with his face buried in the snow.

Swiftly he retraced his steps, and, kneeling beside the wounded man, raised him from the snow. Blood oozed from the corners of the officer's lips, and, mingling with the snow, formed a red slush which clung to the boyish cheek. With his knife MacNair cut through the clothing and disclosed an ugly hole below the right shoulder-blade. He bound up the wound, plugging the hole with suet chewed from a lump which he carried in his pocket. Leaving Ripley upon his face to prevent strangulation from the blood in his throat, he hastened to the camp on the shore of the lake, harnessed the dogs, and returned to the prostrate man; it was the work of a few moments to bind him securely upon the sled. Skilfully MacNair guided his dogs through the maze of the black spruce swamp, and, throwing caution to the winds, crossed the lake, struck into the timber, and headed straight for Chloe Elliston's school.

In the living-room of the little cottage on the Yellow Knife, Harriet Penny and Mary, the Louchoux girl, sat sewing, while Chloe Elliston, with chair pulled close to the table, read by the light of an oil-lamp from a year-old magazine. If the Louchoux girl failed to follow the intricacies of the plot, an observer would scarcely have known it. Nor would he have guessed that less than two short months before this girl had been a skin-clad native of the North who had mushed for thirty days unattended through the heart of the barren grounds. So marvellously had the girl improved and so desirously had she applied her needle, that save for the beaded moccasins upon her feet, her clothing differed in no essential detail from that of Chloe Elliston or of Harriet Penny.

Chloe paused in her reading, and the three occupants of the little room stared inquiringly into each other's faces as a rough-voiced "Whoa!" sounded from beyond the door. A moment of silence followed the command, and then came the sounds of a heavy footfall upon the veranda. The Louchoux girl sprang to the door, and as she wrenched it open the yellow lamplight threw into bold relief the huge figure of a man, who, bearing a blanket-wrapped form in his arms, staggered into the room, and, without a word deposited his burden upon the floor. The man looked up, and Chloe Elliston started back with an exclamation of angry amazement. The man was Bob MacNair! And Chloe noticed that the Louchoux girl, after one terrified glance into his face, fled incontinently to the kitchen.

"You! You!" cried Chloe, groping for words.

The man interrupted her gruffly. "This is no time to talk. Corporal Ripley has been shot. For three days I have burned up the snow getting him here. He's hard hit, but the bleeding has stopped, and a good bed and good nursing will pull him through."

As he snapped out the words, MacNair busied himself in removing the wounded man's blankets and outer garments. Chloe gave some hurried orders to Big Lena, and followed MacNair into her own room, where he laid the wounded man upon her bed—the same he, himself, had once occupied while recovering from the effect of Lapierre's bullet. Then he straightened and faced Chloe, who stood regarding him with flashing eyes.

"So you did get away from him after all?" she said, "and when he followed you, you shot him! Just a boy—and you shot him in the back!" The voice trembled with the scorn of her words. MacNair pushed roughly past her.

"Don't be a damn fool!" he growled, and called over his shoulder: "Better rest him up for three or four days, and send him down to Fort Resolution. He'll stand the trip all right by that time, and the doctor may want to poke around for that bullet." Suddenly he whirled and faced her. "Where is Lapierre?" The words were a snarl.

"So you want to kill him, too? Do you think I would tell you if I knew? You—you *murderer*! Oh, if I—" But the sentence was cut short by the loud banging of the door. MacNair had returned into the night.

An hour later, when she and Big Lena quitted the bedroom, Corporal Ripley was breathing easily. Her thoughts turned at once to the Louchoux girl. She recalled the look of terror that had crept into the girl's eyes as she gazed into the upturned face of MacNair. With the force of a blow a thought flashed through her brain, and she clutched at the edge of the table for support. What was it the girl had told her about the man who had deceived her into believing she was his wife? He was a free-trader! MacNair was a free-trader! Could it be—

"No, no!" she gasped—"and yet—"

With an effort she crossed to the door of the girl's room and, pushing it open, entered to find her cowering, wide-eyed between her blankets. The sight of the beautiful, terrorized face did not need the corroboration of the low, half-moaned words, "Oh, please, please, don't let him get me!" to tell Chloe that her worst fears were realized.

"Do not be afraid, my dear," she faltered. "He cannot harm you now," and hurriedly closing the door, staggered across the living-room, threw herself into a chair beside the table, and buried her face in her arms.

Harriet Penny opened her door and glanced timidly at the still figure of the girl, and, deciding it were the better part of prudence not to intrude, noiselessly closed her door. Hours later, Big Lena, entering from the kitchen, regarded her mistress with a long vacant-faced stare, and returned again to the kitchen. All through the night Chloe dozed fitfully beside the table, but for the most part she was widely—painfully—awake. Bitterly she reproached herself. Only she knew the pain the discovery of MacNair's treachery had caused her. And only she knew why the discovery had caused her pain.

Always she had believed she had hated this man. By all standards, she should hate him. This great, elemental brute of the North who had first attempted to ignore, and later to ridicule and to bully her. This man who ruled his Indians with a rod of iron, who allowed them full license in their debauchery, and then shot them down in cold blood, who shot a boy in the back while in the act of doing his duty, and who had called her a "damn fool" in her own house, and was even then off on the trail of another man he had sworn to kill on sight. By all the laws of justice, equity, and decency, she should hate this man! She was conscious of no other feeling toward him than a burning, unquenchable hate. And yet, deep down in her heart she knew—by the pain of her discovery of his treachery—she knew she loved him, and utterly she despised herself that this could be so.

Daylight softly dimmed the yellow lamplight of the room. The girl arose, and, after a hurried glance at the sleeping Ripley, bathed her eyes in cold water and passed into the kitchen, where Big Lena was busy in the preparation of breakfast.

"Send LeFroy to me at once!" she ordered, and five minutes later, when the man stood before her, she ordered him to summon all of MacNair's Indians.

The man shifted his weight uneasily from one foot to the other as he faced her upon the tiny veranda. "MacNair Injuns," he answered, "dem gon' las' night. Dem gon' 'long wit' MacNair. Heem gon' for hunt Pierre Lapierre!"

CHAPTER XXI

LAPIERRE PAYS A VISIT

Up on Snare Lake the men to whom Lapierre had passed the word had taken possession of MacNair's burned and abandoned fort, and there the leader had joined them after stopping at Fort McMurray to tip off to Ripley and Craig the bit of evidence that he hoped would clinch the case against MacNair. More men joined the Snare Lake stampede—flat-faced breeds from the lower Mackenzie, evil-visaged rivermen from the country of the Athabasca and the Slave, and the renegade white men who were Lapierre's underlings.

By dog-train and on foot they came, dragging their outfits behind them, and in the eyes of each was the gleam of the greed of gold. The few cabins which had escaped the conflagration had been pre-empted by the first-comers, while the later arrivals pitched their tents and shelter tarps close against the logs of the unburned portion of MacNair's stockade.

At the time of Lapierre's arrival the colony had assumed the aspect of a typical gold camp. The drifted snow had been removed from MacNair's diggings, and the night-fires that thawed out the gravel glared red and illuminated the clearing with a ruddy glow in which the dumps loomed black and ugly, like unclean wens upon the white surface of the trampled snow.

Lapierre, a master of organization, saw almost at the moment of his arrival that the gold-camp system of two-man partnerships could be vastly improved upon. Therefore, he formed the men into shifts: eight hours in the gravel and tending the fires, eight hours chopping cord-wood and digging in the ruins of MacNair's storehouse for the remains of unburned grub, and eight hours' rest. Always night and day, the seemingly tireless leader moved about the camp encouraging, cursing, bullying, urging; forcing the utmost atom of man-power into the channels of greatest efficiency. For well the quarter-breed knew that his tenure of the Snare Lake diggings was a tenure wholly by sufferance of circumstances—over which he, Lapierre, had no control.

With MacNair safely lodged in the Fort Saskatchewan jail, he felt safe from interference, at least until late in the spring. This would allow plenty of time for the melting snows to furnish the water necessary for the cleaning up of the dumps. After that the fate of his colony hung upon the decision of a judge somewhere down in the provinces. Thus Lapierre crowded his men to the utmost, and the increasing size of the black dump-heaps bespoke a record-breaking clean-up when the waters of the melting snow should be turned into sluices in the spring.

With his mind easy in his fancied security, and in order that every moment of time and every ounce of man-power should be devoted to the digging of gold, Lapierre had neglected to bring his rifles and ammunition from the Lac du Mort rendezvous and from the storehouse of Chloe Elliston's school. An omission for which he cursed himself roundly upon an evening, early in February when an Indian, gaunt and wide-eyed from the strain of a forced snow-trail, staggered from the black shadow of the bush into the glare of the blazing night-fires, and in a frenzied gibberish of jargon proclaimed that Bob MacNair had returned to the Northland. And not only that he had returned, but had visited Lac du Mort in company with a man of the Mounted.

At first Lapierre flatly refused to credit the Indian's yarn, but when upon pain of death the man refused to alter his statement, and added the information that he himself had fired at MacNair from the shelter of a snow-ridden spruce, and that just as he pulled the trigger the man of the soldier-police had intervened and stopped the speeding bullet, Lapierre knew that the Indian spoke the truth.

In the twinkling of an eye the quarter-breed realized the extreme danger of his position. His wrath knew no bounds. Up and down he raged in his fury, cursing like a madman, while all about him—blaming, reviling, advising—cursed the men of his ill-favoured crew. For not a man among them but knew that somewhere someone had blundered. And for some inexplicable reason their situation had suddenly shifted from comparative security to extreme hazard. They needed not to be told that with MacNair at large in the Northland their lives hung by a slender thread. For at that very moment Brute MacNair was, in all probability, upon the Yellow Knife leading his armed Indians toward Snare Lake.

In addition to this was the certain knowledge that the vengeance of the Mounted would fall in full measure upon the heads of all who were in any way associated with Pierre Lapierre. An officer had been shot, and the men of Lapierre were outlawed from Ungava to the Western sea. The intricate system had crumbled in the batting of an eye. Else why should a man of the Mounted have been found before the barricade of the Bastile du Mort in company with Brute MacNair?

The quick-witted Lapierre was the first to recover from the shock of the stunning blow. Leaping onto the charred logs of MacNair's storehouse, he called loudly to his men, who in a panic were wildly throwing their outfits onto sleds. Despite their mad haste they crowded close and listened to the words of the man upon whose judgment they had learned to rely, and from whose dreaded "dismissal from service" they had cowered in fear. They swarmed about Lapierre a hundred strong, and his voice rang harsh.

"You dogs! You *canaille*!" he cried, and they shrank from the baleful glare of his black eyes. "What would you do? Where would you go? Do you think that, single-handed, you can escape from MacNair's Indians, who will follow your trails like hounds and kill you as they would kill a snared rabbit? I tell you your trails will be short. A dead man will lie at the end of each. But even if you succeed in escaping the Indians, what, then, of the Mounted? One by one, upon the rivers and lakes of the Northland, upon wide snow-steeps of the barren grounds, even to the shores of the frozen sea, you will be hunted and gathered in. Or you will be shot like dogs, and your bones left to crunch in the jaws of the wolf-pack. We are outlaws, all! Not a man of us will dare show his face in any post or settlement or city in all Canada."

The men shrank before the words, for they knew them to be true. Again the leader was speaking, and hope gleamed in fear-strained eyes.

"We have yet one chance; I, Pierre Lapierre, have not played my last card. We will stand or fall together! In the Bastile du Mort are many rifles, and ammunition and provisions for half a year. Once behind the barricade, we shall be safe from any attack. We can defy MacNair's Indians and stand off the Mounted until such time as we are in a position to dictate our own terms. If we stand man to man together, we have everything to gain and nothing to lose. We are outlawed, every one. There is no turning back!"

Lapierre's bold assurance averted the threatened panic, and with a yell the men fell to work packing their outfits for the journey to Lac du Mort. The quarter-breed despatched scouts to the southward to ascertain the whereabouts of MacNair, and, if possible, to find out whether or not the officer of the Mounted had been killed by the shot of the Indian.

At early dawn the outfit crossed Snare Lake and headed for Lac du Mort by way of Grizzly Bear, Lake Mackay, and Du Rocher. Upon the evening of the fourth day, when they threaded the black-spruce swamp and pulled wearily into the fort on Lac du Mort, Lapierre found a scout awaiting him with the news that MacNair had headed northward with his Indians, and that LeFroy was soon to start for Fort Resolution with the wounded man of the Mounted. Whereupon he selected the fastest and freshest dog-team available and, accompanied by a half-dozen of his most trusted lieutenants, took the trail for Chloe Elliston's school on-the Yellow Knife, after issuing orders as to the conduct of defence in case of an attack by MacNair's Indians.

Affairs at the school were at a standstill. From a busy hive of activity, with the women and children showing marked improvement at their tasks, and the men happy in the felling of logs and the whip-sawing of lumber, the settlement had suddenly slumped into a disorganized hodge-podge of unrest and anxiety. MacNair's Indians had followed him into the North; their women and children brooded sullenly, and a feeling of unrest and expectancy pervaded the entire colony.

Among the inmates of the cottage the condition was even worse. With Harriet Penny hysterical and excited, Big Lena more glum and taciturn than usual, the Louchoux girl cowering in mortal dread of impending disaster, and Chloe herself disgusted, discouraged, nursing in her heart a consuming rage against Brute MacNair, the man who had wrought the harm, and who had been her evil genius since she had first set foot into the North.

Upon the afternoon of the day she despatched LeFroy to Fort Resolution with the wounded officer of the Mounted, Chloe stood at her little window gazing out over the wide sweep of the river and wondering how it all would end. Would MacNair find Lapierre, and would he kill him? Or would the Mounted heed the urgent appeal she despatched in care of LeFroy and arrive in time to recapture MacNair before he came upon his victim?

"If I only knew where to find him," she muttered, "I could warn him of his danger."

The next moment her eyes widened with amazement, and she pressed her face close against the glass; across the clearing from the direction of the river dashed a dog-team, with three men running before and three behind, while upon the sled, jaunty and smiling, and debonair as ever, sat Pierre Lapierre himself. With a flourish he swung the dogs up to the tiny veranda and stepped from the sled, and the next moment Chloe found herself standing in the little living-room with Lapierre bowing low over her hand. Harriet Penny was in the schoolhouse; the Louchoux girl was helping Big Lena in the kitchen, and for the first time in many moons Chloe Elliston felt glad that she was alone with Lapierre.

When at length she removed her hand from his grasp she stood for some moments regarding the clean-cut lines of his features, and then she smiled as she noted the trivial fact that he had removed his hat, and that he stood humbly before her with bared head. A great surge of feeling rushed over her as she realized how clean and good—how perfect this man seemed in comparison with the hulking brutality of MacNair. She motioned him to a seat beside the table, and drawing her chair close to his side, poured into his attentive and sympathetic ears all that she knew of MacNair's escape, of the shooting of Corporal Ripley, and his departure in the night with his Indians.

Lapierre listened, smiling inwardly at her version of the affair, and at the conclusion of her words leaned forward and took one of the slim brown hands in his. For a long, long time the girl listened in silence to the pleading of his lips; and the little room was filled with the passion of his low-voiced eloquence.

Neither was aware of the noiseless opening of a door, nor of the wide-eyed, girlish face that stared at them through the aperture, nor was either aware that the man's words were borne distinctly to the ears of the Louchoux girl. Nor could they note the change from an expression of startled surprise to slitlike, venomous points of fire that took place in the eyes of the listening girl—nor the clenching fists. Nor did they hear the soft, catlike tread with which the girl quit the door and crossed to the kitchen table. Nor could they see the cruel snarl of her lips as her fingers closed tightly about the haft of the huge butcher-knife, whose point was sharp and whose blade was keen. Nor did they hear the noiseless tread with which the girl again approached the door, swung wider now to admit the passage of her tense, lithe body. Nor did they see her crouch for a spring with the tight-clutched knife upraised and the gleaming slitlike eyes focused upon a point mid-way between Lapierre's shoulder-blades as his arm unconsciously came to rest upon the back of Chloe Elliston's chair.

For a long moment the girl poised, gloating—enjoying in its fulness the measure of her revenge. Before her, leaning in just the right attitude to receive upon his defenceless back the full force of the blow, sat the man who had deceived her. For not until she had listened to the low-voiced, impassioned words had she realized there had been any deception. With the realization came the hot, fierce flame of anger that seared her very soul. An anger engendered by her own wrong, and fanned to its fiercest by the knowledge that the man was at that moment seeking to deceive the white woman—the woman who had taught her much, and who with the keenest interest and gentleness had treated her as an equal.

She had come to love this white woman with the love that was greater than the love of life. And the words to which this woman was now listening were the same words, from the same lips, to which she herself had listened beside the cold waters of the far-off Mackenzie. Thus the Louchoux girl faced suddenly her first great problem. And to the half-savage mind of her the solution of the problem seemed very simple, very direct, and, had Big Lena not entered by way of the outer door at the precise moment that the girl crouched with uplifted knife, it would doubtless have been very effective.

But Big Lena did enter, and, with a swiftness of perception that belied the vacuous stare of the fishlike eyes, took in the situation at a glance; for LeFroy had already hinted to her of the relation which existed between his erstwhile superior and this girl from the land of the midnight sun. Whereupon Big Lena had kept her own counsel and had patiently bided her time, and now her time had come, and she was in no wise minded that the fulness of her vengeance should be marred by the untimely taking off of Lapierre. Swiftly she crossed the room, and as her strong fingers closed about the wrist of the Indian girl's upraised knife-arm, the other hand reached beyond and noiselessly closed the door between the two rooms.

The Louchoux girl whirled like a flash and sank her strong, white teeth deep in the rolled-sleeved forearm of the huge Swedish woman. But a thumb, inserted dextrously and with pressure in the little hollow behind the girl's ear, caused her jaws instantly to relax, and she stood trembling before the big woman, who regarded her with a tolerant grin, and the next moment laid a friendly hand upon her shoulder and, turning her gently about, guided her to a chair at the farther side of the room.

Followed then a quarter of an hour of earnest conversation, in which the older woman managed to convey, through the medium of her broken English, a realization that Lapierre's discomfiture could be encompassed much more effectively and in a thoroughly orthodox and less sanguinary manner.

The ethics of Big Lena's argument were undoubtedly beyond the Louchoux girl's comprehension; but because this woman had been good to her, and because she seemed greatly to desire this thing, the girl consented to abstain from violence, at least for the time being. A few minutes later, when Chloe Elliston opened the door and announced that Mr. Lapierre would join them at supper, she found the two women busily engaged in the final preparation of the meal.

Big Lena passed into the dining-room, which was also the living-room, and without deigning to notice Lapierre's presence, proceeded to lay the table for supper. Returning to the kitchen, she despatched the Indian girl to the storehouse upon an errand which would insure her absence until after Chloe and Lapierre and Harriet Penny had taken their places at the table.

Since her arrival at the school the Louchoux girl had been treated as "one of the family," and it was with a look of inquiry toward the girl's empty chair that Chloe seated herself with the others. Interpreting the look, Big Lena assured her that the girl would return in a few moments; and Chloe had just launched into an impassioned account of the virtues and the accomplishments of her ward, when the door opened and the girl herself entered the room and crossed swiftly to her accustomed place. As she stood with her hand on the back of her chair, Lapierre for the first time glanced into her face.

The quarter-breed was a man trained as few men are trained to meet emergencies, to face crises with an impassiveness of countenance that would shame the Sphinx. He had lost thousands across the green cloth of gambling-tables without batting an eye. He had faced death and had killed men with a face absolutely devoid of expression, and upon numerous occasions his nerve—the consummate *sang-froid* of him—had alone thrown off the suspicion that would have meant arrest upon charges which would have taken more than a lifetime to expiate. And as he sat at the little table beside Chloe Elliston, his eyes met unflinchingly the flashing, accusing gaze of the black eyes of the girl from the Northland—the girl who was his wife.

For a long moment their glances held, while the atmosphere of the little room became surcharged with the terrible portent of this silent battle of eyes. Harriet Penny gasped audibly; and as Chloe stared from one to the other of the white, tense faces before her, her brain seemed suddenly to numb, and the breath came short and quick between her parted lips to the rapid heaving of her bosom. The Louchoux girl's eyes seemed fairly to blaze with hate. The fingers of her hand dug into the wooden back of her chair until the knuckles whitened. She leaned far forward and, pointing directly into the face of the man, opened her lips to speak. It was then Lapierre's gaze wavered, for in that moment he realized that for him the game was lost.

With a half-smothered curse he leaped to his feet, overturning his chair, which banged sharply upon the plank floor. He glanced wildly about the little room as if seeking means of escape, and his eyes encountered the form of Big Lena, who stood stolidly in the doorway, blocking the exit. In a flash he noted the huge, bared forearm; noted, too, that one thick hand gripped tightly the helve of a chopping ax, with which she toyed lightly as if it were a little thing, while the thumb of her other hand played smoothly, but with a certain terrible significance, along the keen edge of its blade. Lapierre's glance flashed to her face and encountered the fishlike stare of the china-blue eyes, as he had encountered it once before. The eyes, as before, were expressionless upon their surface, but deep down—far into their depths—Lapierre caught a cold gleam of mockery. And then the Louchoux girl was speaking, and he turned upon her with a snarl.

CHAPTER XXII

CHLOE WRITES A LETTER

When Bob MacNair, exasperated beyond all patience by Chloe Elliston's foolish accusation, stamped angrily from the cottage, after depositing the wounded Ripley upon the bed, he proceeded at once to the barracks, where he sought out Wee Johnnie Tamarack, who informed him that Lapierre was up on Snare Lake, at the head of a band of men who had already succeeded in dotting the snow of the barren grounds with the black dumps of many shafts. Whereupon he ordered Wee Johnnie Tamarack to assemble the Indians at once at the storehouse.

No sooner had the old Indian departed upon his mission than the door of the barracks was pushed violently open and Big Lena entered, dragging by the arm the thoroughly cowed figure of LeFroy. At sight of the man who, under Lapierre's orders, had wrought the destruction of his post at Snare Lake, MacNair leaped forward with a snarl of anger. But before he could reach the trembling man the form of Big Lena interposed, and MacNair found himself swamped by a jargon of broken English that taxed to the utmost his power of comprehension.

"Ju yoost vait vun meenit. Ay tal ju som'ting gude. Dis damn LeFroy, he bane bad man. He vork by Lapierre, and he tak' de vhiskey to jour Injuns, but he don't vork no more by Lapierre; he vork by me. Ay goin' to marry him, and ju bet Ay keep him gude, or Ay bust de stove chunk 'crost his head. He vork by Mees Chloe now, and he lak ju gif him chance to show he ain't no bad man no more."

Big Lena shook the man roughly by way of emphasis, and MacNair smiled as he noted the foolish grin with which LeFroy submitted to the inevitable. For years he had known LeFroy as a bad man, second only to Lapierre in cunning and brutal cruelty; and to see him now, cowering under the domination of his future spouse, was to MacNair the height of the ridiculous—but MacNair was unmarried.

"All right," he growled, and LeFroy's relief at the happy termination of the interview was plainly written upon his features, for this meeting had not been of his own seeking. The memory of the shots which had taken off two of his companions that night on Snare Lake, was still fresh, and in his desire to avoid a meeting with MacNair he had sought refuge in the kitchen. Whereupon Big Lena had taken matters into her own hands and literally dragged him into MacNair's presence, replying to his terrified protest that if MacNair was going to kill him, he was going to kill and he might as well have it over with.

Thus it was that the relieved LeFroy leaped with alacrity to obey when, a moment later, MacNair ordered him to the storehouse to break out the necessary provisions for a ten-days' journey for all his Indians. So well did the half-breed execute the order that upon MacNair's arrival at the storehouse he found LeFroy not only supplying provisions with a lavish hand, but taking huge delight in passing out to the waiting Indians Lapierre's Mauser rifles and ammunition.

When MacNair, with his Indians, reached Snare Lake, it was to find that Pierre Lapierre had taken himself and his outlaws to the Lac du Mort rendezvous. Whereupon he immediately despatched thirty Indians back to LeFroy for the supplies necessary to follow Lapierre to his stronghold. Awaiting the return of the supply train, MacNair employed his remaining Indians in getting out logs for the rebuilding of his fort, and he smiled grimly as his eyes roved over the dumps—the rich dumps which represented two months' well-directed labour of a gang of a hundred men.

As Chloe Elliston sat in the little living-room and listened to the impassioned words of Lapierre, the man's chance of winning her was far better than at any time in the whole course of their acquaintance. Without in the least realizing it, the girl had all along held a certain regard for MacNair—a regard that was hard to explain, and that the girl herself would have been the first to disavow. She hated him! And yet—she was forced to admit even to herself, the man fascinated her. But never until the moment of the realization of his true character, as forced upon her by the action and words of the Louchoux girl, had she entertained the slightest suspicion that she loved him. And with the discovery had come a sense of shame and humiliation that had all but broken her spirit.

Her hatred for MacNair was real enough now. That hatred, the shame and humility, and the fact that Lapierre was pleading with her as he had never pled before, were going far to convince the girl that her previous estimate of the quarter-breed had been a mistaken estimate, and that he was in truth the fine, clean, educated man of the North which on the surface he appeared to be. A man whose aim it was to deal fairly and honourably with the Indians, and who in reality had the best interests of his people at heart.

No one but Chloe herself will ever know how near she came upon that afternoon to yielding to his pleading, and laying her soul bare to him. But something interposed—fate?

Destiny? The materialist smiles "supper." Be that as it may, had she yielded to Lapierre's plans, they would have stolen from the school that very night and proceeded to Fort Rae, to be married by the priest at the Mission. For Lapierre, fully alive to the danger of delay, had eloquently pleaded his cause.

Not only was MacNair upon his trail—MacNair the relentless, the indomitable—but also the word had passed in the North, and the men of the Mounted—those inscrutable sentinels of the silence whose watchword is "get the man"—were aroused to avenge a comrade. And Lapierre realized with a chill in his heart that he was "the man"! His one chance lay in a timely marriage with Chloe Elliston, and a quick dash for the States. If the dash succeeded, he had nothing to fear. Even if it failed, and he fell into the hands of the Mounted—with the Elliston millions behind him, he felt he could snap his fingers in the face of the law. Men of millions do not serve time.

For the men who awaited him in the Bastile du Mort, Lapierre gave no thought. He would stand by them as long as it furthered his own ends to stand by them. When they ceased to be a factor in his own safety, they could shift for themselves, even as he, Lapierre, was shifting for himself. Someone has said every man has his price. It is certain that every man has his limit beyond which he may not go.

Lapierre, a man of consummate nerve, had put forth a final effort to save himself. Had put forth the best effort that was in him to induce Chloe Elliston to marry him. He had found the girl kinder, more receptive than he had dared hope. His spirits arose to a point they had never before attained. Success seemed within his grasp. Then, suddenly, just as his fingers were about to close upon the prize—the prize that meant to him life and plenty, instead of death—the Louchoux girl, a passing folly of a bygone day, had suddenly risen up and confronted him—and he knew that his cause was lost.

Lapierre had reached his limit of control, and when he turned at the sound of the Indian girl's voice, his hand instinctively flew to his belt. In his rage at the sudden turn of events, he became for the instant a madman, whose one thought was to destroy her who had wrought the harm. The next instant the snarl died upon his lips and his hand dropped limply to his side. In two strides Big Lena was upon him and her thick fingers bit deep into his shoulder as she spun him to face her—to face the polished bit of the keen-edged ax which the huge woman flourished carelessly within an inch of his nose.

The fingers released their grip, Lapierre's gun was jerked from its holster, and a moment later thumped heavily upon the floor of the kitchen fifteen feet away, while the woman pointed grimly toward the overturned chair. Lapierre righted the chair, and as he sank into it, Chloe, who had stared dumbfounded upon the scene, saw that little beads of sweat stood out sharply against the pallor of his bloodless brow. As from a great distance the words of the Louchoux girl fell upon her ears. She was speaking rapidly, and the finger which she pointed at Lapierre trembled violently.

"You lied!" cried the girl. "You have always lied! You lied when you told me we were married. You lied when you said you would return! Since coming to this school I have learned much. Many things have I learned that I never knew before. When you said you would return, I believed you—even as my mother believed my father when he went away in the ship many years ago, and left me a babe in arms to live or to die among the teepees of the Louchoux, the people of my mother, who was the mother of his child. My mother has not been to the school, and she believes some day my father will return. For many years she has waited, has starved, and has suffered—always watching for my father's return. And the factors have laughed, and the rivermen taunted her with being the mother of a fatherless child! Ah, she has paid! Always the Indian women must pay! And I have paid also. All my life have I been hungry, and in the winter I have always been cold.

"Then you came with your laughing lips and your words of love and I went with you, and you took me to distant rivers. All through the summer there was plenty to eat in our teepee. I was happy, and for the first time in my life my heart was glad—for I loved you! And then came the winter, and the freezing up of the rivers, and the day you told me you must return to the southward—to the land of the white men—without me. And I believed you even when they told me you would not return. I was brave—for that is the way of love, to believe, and to hope, and to be brave."

The girl's voice faltered, and the trembling hand gripped the back of the chair upon which she leaned heavily for support.

"All my life have I paid," she continued, bitterly. "Yet, it was not enough. Years, when the children of the trappers had at times plenty to eat I was always hungry and cold.

"When you came into my life I thought at last I had paid in full—that my mother and I both had paid for her belief in the white man's word. Ah, if I had known! I should have known, for well I remember, it was upon the day before—before I went away with you—that I told you of my father, and of how we always went North in the winter, knowing that again his ship would winter in the ice of the Bufort Sea. And you heard the story and laughed, and you said that my father would not return—that the white men never return. And when I grew afraid, you told me that you were part Indian. That your people were my people. I was a fool! I listened to your words!"

The girl dropped heavily into her chair and buried her face in her arms.

"And now I know," she sobbed, "that I have not even begun to pay!"

Suddenly she leaped to her feet and, dashing around the table placed herself between Lapierre and Chloe, who had listened white-lipped to her words. Once more the voice of the Louchoux girl rang through the room—high-pitched and thin with anger now—and the eyes that glared into the eyes of Lapierre blazed black with fury.

"You have lied to her! But you cannot harm her! With my own ears I heard your words! The same words I heard from your lips before, upon the banks of the far-off rivers, and the words are lies—lies—lies!"—the voice rose to a shriek—"the white woman is good! She is my friend! She has taught me much, and now, I will save her."

With a swift movement she caught the carving-knife from the table and sprang toward the defenceless Lapierre. "I will cut your heart in little bits and feed it to the dogs!"

Once more the hand of Big Lena wrenched the knife from the girl's grasp. And once more the huge Swedish woman fixed Lapierre with her vacuous stare. Then slowly she raised her arm and pointed toward the door: "Ju git! And never ju don't come back no more. Ay don't lat ju go 'cause Ay lak' ju, but Ay bane 'fraid dis leetle girl she cut ju up and feed ju to de dogs, and Ay no lak' for git dem dogs poison!"

And Lapierre tarried not for further orders. Pausing only to recover his hat from its peg on the wall, he opened the outer door and with one sidewise malevolent glance toward the little group at the table, slunk hurriedly from the room.

Hardly had the door closed behind him than Chloe, who had sat as one stunned during the girl's accusation and her later outburst of fury, leaped to her feet and seized her arm in a convulsive grip. "Tell me!" she cried; "what do you mean? Speak! Speak, can't you? What is this you have said? What is it all about?"

"Why it is he, Pierre Lapierre. He is the free-trader of whom I told you. The man who—who deceived me into believing I was his wife."

"But," cried Chloe, staring at her in astonishment. "I thought—I thought MacNair was the man!"

"No! No! No!" cried the girl. "Not MacNair! Pierre Lapierre, he is the man! He who sat in that chair, and whose heart I would cut into tiny bits that you shall not be made to pay, even as I have paid, for listening to the words of his lips."

"But," faltered Chloe, "I don't—I don't understand. Surely, you, fear MacNair. Surely, that night when he came into the room, carrying the wounded policeman, you fled from him in terror."

"MacNair is a white man—"

"But why should you fear him?"

"I fear him," she answered, "because among the Indians—among the Louchoux—the people of my mother, and among the Eskimoes, he is called 'The Bad Man of the North.' I hated him because Lapierre taught me to hate him. I do not hate him now, nor do I fear him. But among the Indians and among the free-traders he is both hated and feared. He chases the free-traders from the rivers, and he kills them and destroys their whiskey. For he has said, like the men of the soldier-police, that the red man shall drink no whiskey. But the red men like the whiskey. Their life is hard and they do not have much happiness, and the whiskey of the white man makes them happy. And in the days before MacNair they could get much whiskey, but now the free-traders fear him, and only sometimes do they dare to bring whiskey to the land of the far-off rivers.

"At the posts my people may trade for food and for guns and for clothing, but they may not buy whiskey. But the free-traders sell whiskey. Also they will trade for the women. But MacNair has said they shall not trade for the women. At times, when men think he is far away, he comes swooping through the North with his Snare Lake Indians at his heels, and they chase the free-traders from the rivers. And on the shores of the frozen sea he chases the whalemen from the Eskimo villages even to their ships which lie far out from the coast, locked in the grip of the ice-pack.

"For these things I have hated and feared him. Since I have been here at the school I have learned much. Both from your teachings, and from talking with the women of MacNair's Indians. I know now that MacNair is good, and that the factors and the soldier-police and the priest spoke words of truth, and that Lapierre and the free-traders lied!"

As the Indian girl poured forth her story, Chloe Elliston listened as one in a dream. What was this she was saying, that it was Lapierre who sold whiskey to the Indians, and MacNair who stood firm, and struck mighty blows for the right of things? Surely, this girl's mind was unhinged—or, had something gone wrong with her own brain? Was it possible she had heard aright?

Suddenly she remembered the words of Corporal Ripley, when he asked her to withdraw the charge of murder against MacNair: "In the North we know something of MacNair's work." And again: "We know the North needs men like MacNair."

Could it be possible that after all—with the thought there flashed into the girl's mind the scene on Snare Lake. Had she not seen with her own eyes the evidence of this man's work among the Indians! With a gesture of appeal she turned to Big Lena.

"Surely, Lena, you remember that night on Snare Lake? You saw MacNair's Indians, drunk as fiends—and the buildings all on fire? You saw MacNair kicking and knocking them about? And you saw him fire the shots that killed two men? Speak, can't you? Did you see these things? Did I see them? Was I dreaming? Or am I dreaming now?"

Big Lena shifted her weight ponderously, and the stare of the china-blue eyes met steadily the half-startled eyes of the girl. "Yah, Ay seen das all right. Dem Injuns dey awful drunk das night and MacNair he come 'long and schlap dem and kick dem 'round. But das gude for dem. Dey got it comin'. Dey should not ought to drink Lapierre's vhiskey."

"Lapierre's whiskey!" cried the girl. "Are you crazy?"

"Naw, Ay tank Ay ain't so crazy. Lapierre he fool ju long tam'."

"What do you mean," asked Chloe.

"Ah, das a'right," answered the woman. "He fool ju gude, but he ain't fool Big Lena. Ay know all about him for a jear."

"But," pursued the girl, "Lapierre was with us that night!"

Lena shrugged. "Yah, Lapierre very smart. He send LeFroy

'long wit' das vhiskey. Den v'en he know MacNair's Injuns git awful drunk, he tak' ju 'long for see it."

"LeFroy!" cried Chloe. "Why, LeFroy was off to the eastward trying to run down some whiskey-runners."

Big Lena laughed derisively. "How ju fin' out?" she asked.

Chloe hesitated. "Why—why, Lapierre told me."

Again Big Lena laughed. "Yah, Lapierre tal ju, but, LeFroy, he don't know nuthin' 'bout no vhiskey-runners. Only him and Lapierre dos all de vhiskey-running in dis country. LeFroy, he tal me all 'bout das. He tak' das vhiskey up dere and he sell it to MacNair's Injuns, and MacNair shoot after him and kill two LeFroy's men. Ay goin' marry LeFroy, and he tal me de trut'. He 'fraid to lie to me, or Ay break him in two. LeFroy, he bane gude man now, he quit Lapierre. Ju bet ju if he don't bane gude Ay gif him haal. Ay tal him it bane gude t'ing if MacNair kill him das night.

"Den MacNair come on de school and brung de policeman, LeFroy he 'fraid for scart, and he goin' hide in de kitchen, and Ay drag him out and brung him 'long to see MacNair. LeFroy, he 'fraid lak' haal. He squeal MacNair goin' kill him. But Ay tal him das ain't much loss annyhow. If he goin' kill him it's besser he kill him now, den Ay ain't got to bodder wit' him no more. But MacNair, he don't kill him. Ay tal him LeFroy goin' to be gude man now, and den MacNair he laugh, and tal LeFroy to go 'long and git out de grub."

"But," cried Chloe, "you say you have known all about Lapierre for a year, and you knew all the time that MacNair was right, and Lapierre was wrong, and you let me go blindly on thinking Lapierre was my friend, and treating MacNair as I did! Why didn't you tell me?"

"Ju got yoost so manny eyes lak' me!" retorted the woman. "Ju neffer ask me vat Ay tank 'bout MacNair and 'bout Lapierre. And Ay neffer tal ju das 'cause Ay tank it besser ju fin' out yourself. Ay know ju got to fin' das out sometam'. Den ju believe it. Ju know lot 'bout vat stands in de books, but das mos' lak' MacNair say: 'bout lot t'ing, you damn fool!"

Chloe gasped. It was the longest speech Big Lena had ever made. And the girl learned that when the big woman chose she could speak straight from the shoulder.

Harriet Penny gasped also. She pushed back her chair, and shook an outraged finger at Big Lena. "Go into the kitchen where you belong!" she cried. "I really cannot permit such language in my presence. You are unspeakably coarse!"

Chloe whirled on the little woman like a flash. "You shut up, Hat Penny!" she snapped savagely. "You don't happen to do the permitting around here. If your ears are too delicate to listen to *the truth* you better go into your own room and shut the door." And then crossing swiftly to her own room, she opened the door, but before entering she turned to Big Lena, "Make a pot of strong coffee," she ordered, "and bring it to me here."

A few minutes later when the woman entered and deposited the tray containing coffee-pot, cream-pitcher, and sugar-bowl upon the table, she found Chloe striding up and down the room. There was a new light in the girl's eyes, and, very much to Big Lena's surprise, she turned suddenly upon her and throwing her arms about the massive shoulders, planted a kiss squarely upon the wide, flat mouth.

"Ah, Lena," she cried, happily, "you—you are a dear!" And the Swedish woman, with unexpected gentleness, patted the girl's shoulder, and as she passed out of the door smiled broadly.

For an hour Chloe paced up and down the little room. At first she could scarcely bring herself to realize that the two men, MacNair and Lapierre, had changed places. She remembered that in that very room she had more than once pictured that very thing. As the conviction grew upon her, her pulse quickened. Never before had she been so supremely—so wildly happy. There was a strange barbaric singing in her heart, as for the first time she saw MacNair—the real MacNair at his true worth. MacNair, the big man, the really great man, strong and brave, alone in the North fighting, night and day, against the snarling wolves of the world-waste. Fighting for the good of his Indians and the right of things as they should be.

Her mind dwelt upon the fine courage and the patience of him. She recalled the hurt look in his eyes when she ordered his arrest. She remembered his words to the officer—words of kindly apology for her own blind folly. She penetrated the rough exterior, and read the real gentleness of his soul. And then, with a shame and mortification that almost overwhelmed her, she saw herself as she must appear to him. She recollected how she had accused him, had sneered at him, had called him a liar and a thief, a murderer, and worse.

Tears streamed unheeded from her eyes as she recalled the unconscious pathos of his words as he stood beside his mother's grave. And the look of reproach with which he sank, to the ground when Lapierre's bullet laid him low. Her heart thrilled at the memory of the blazing wrath of him, the cold gleam of his eyes, the wicked snap of his iron jaw, as he said, "I have taken the man-trail!" She remembered the words he had once spoken: "When you have learned the North, we shall be friends." She wondered now if possibly this thing could ever be? Had she learned the

North? Could she ever atone in his eyes for her cocksureness, her blind egotism?

Chloe quickened her pace, as if to walk away and leave these things behind. How she hated herself! It seemed to her, in her shame and mortification, that she could never look into this man's eyes again. Her glance strayed to the portrait of Tiger Elliston that stared down at her from its bullet-shattered frame upon the wall. The eyes of the portrait seemed to bore deep into her own, and the words of MacNair flashed through her brain—the words he had used as he gazed into the eyes of that selfsame portrait.

Unconsciously—fiercely she repeated those words aloud: "By God! Yon is the face of a *man*!" She started at the sound of her own voice. And then, like liquid flame, it seemed to the girl the blood of Tiger Elliston seethed and boiled in her veins—spurring her on to *do*!

"Do what?" she questioned. "What was there left to *do*, for one who had blundered so miserably?"

Like a flash came the answer. She had done MacNair a great wrong. She must right that wrong, or at least admit it. She must own her error and offer an apology.

Seating herself at the table, she seized a pen and wrote rapidly for a long, long time. And then for a long time more she sat buried in thought, and at the end of an hour she arose and tore up the pages she had written, and sat down again and penned another letter which she placed in an envelope addressed with the name of MacNair. This done she took the letter, tiptoed across the living-room, and pushing open the Louchoux girl's door entered and seated herself upon the edge of the bed. The Indian girl was wide awake. A brown hand stole from beneath the covers and clasped reassuringly about Chloe's fingers.

She handed the girl the letter.

"I can trust you," she said, "to place this in MacNair's hands. Go to sleep now, I will talk further with you tomorrow." And with a hurried good-night, Chloe returned to her own room.

She blew out the lamp and threw herself fully dressed upon the bed. Sleep would not come. She stared long at the little patch of moonlight that showed upon the bare floor. She tried to think, but her heart was filled with a strange restlessness. Arising from the bed, she crossed to the window and stared out across the moonlit clearing toward the dark edge of the forest—the mysterious forest whose depths seemed black with sinister mystery—whose trees bed-coned, stretching out their branches like arms.

A strange restlessness came over her. The confines of the little room seemed smothering—crushing her. Crossing to the row of pegs she drew on her *parka* and heavy mittens, and tiptoeing to the outer door, passed out into the night, crossed the moonlit clearing, and stepped half-fearfully into the deep shadow of the forest—to the call of the beckoning arms.

As her form was swallowed up in the blackness, another form—a gigantic figure that bore clutched in the grasp of a capable hand the helve of an ax, upon the polished steel of whose double-bitted blade the moonbeams gleamed cruelly—slipped from the door of the kitchen and followed swiftly in the wake of the girl. Big Lena was taking no chances.

CHAPTER XXIII

THE WOLF-CRY!

So sudden and unexpected had been Lapierre's *denouement* at the hands of the Indian girl and Big Lena, that when he quitted Chloe Elliston's living-room the one thought in his mind was to return to his stronghold on Lac du Mort. For the first time the real seriousness of his situation forced itself upon him. He knew that no accident had brought the officer of the Mounted to the Lac du Mort stronghold in company with Bob MacNair, and he realized the utter futility of attempting an escape to the outside, since the shooting of the officer at the very walls of the stockade.

As the husband of Chloe Elliston, the thing might have been accomplished. But alone or in company with the half-dozen outlaws who had accompanied him to the school, never. There was but one course open to him: To return to Lac du Mort and make a stand against the authorities and against MacNair. And the fact that the man realized in all probability it would be his last stand, was borne to the understanding of the men who accompanied him.

These men knew nothing of the reason for Lapierre's trip to the school, but they were not slow to perceive that whatever the reason was, Lapierre had failed in its accomplishment. For they knew Lapierre as a man who rarely lost his temper.

They knew him as one equal to any emergency—one who would shoot a man down in cold blood for disobeying an order or relaxing vigilance, but who would shoot with a smile rather than a frown.

Thus when Lapierre joined them in their camp at the edge of the clearing, and with a torrent of unreasoning curses ordered the dogs harnessed and the outfit got under way for Lac du Mort, they knew their cause was at best a forlorn hope.

Darkness overtook them and they camped to await the rising of the late moon. While the men prepared the supper, Lapierre glowered upon his sled by the fire, occasionally leaping to his feet to stamp impatiently up and down upon the snow. The leader spoke no word and none ventured to address him. The meal was eaten in silence. At its conclusion the men took heart and sprang eagerly to obey an order—the order puzzled them not a little, but no man questioned it. For the command came crisp and sharp, and without profanity, in a voice they well knew. Lapierre was himself again, and his black eyes gleamed wickedly as he rolled a cigarette by the light of the rising moon.

The dogs were whirled upon the back-trail, and once more the outfit headed for the school upon the bank of the Yellow Knife. It was well toward midnight when Lapierre called a halt. They were close to the edge of the clearing. Leaving one man with the dogs and motioning the others to follow, he stole noiselessly from tree to tree until the dull square of light that glowed from the window of Chloe Elliston's room showed distinctly through the interlacing branches. The quarters of the Indians were shrouded in darkness. For a long time Lapierre stood staring at the little square of light, while his men, motionless as statues, blended into the shadows of the trees. The light was extinguished. The quarter-breed moved to the edge of the clearing and, seating himself upon the root of a gnarled banskian, rapidly outlined his plan.

Suddenly his form stiffened and he drew close against the trunk of his tree, motioning the others to do likewise. The door of the cottage had opened. A parka-clad figure stepped from the little veranda, paused uncertainly in the moonlight, and then, with light, swinging strides, moved directly toward the banskian. Lapierre's pulse quickened, and his lips twisted into an evil smile. That the figure was none other than Chloe Elliston was easily discernible in the bright moonlight, and with fiendish satisfaction the quarter-breed realized that the girl was playing directly into his hands. For, as he sat upon the sled beside the little camp-fire, his active brain had evolved a new scheme. If Chloe Elliston could not be made to accompany him willingly, why not unwillingly?

Lapierre believed that once safely entrenched behind the barriers of the Bastile du Mort, he could hold out for a matter of six months against any forces which were likely to attack him. He realized that his most serious danger was from MacNair and his Indians. For Lapierre knew MacNair. He knew that once upon his trail, MacNair would relentlessly stick to that trail—the trail that must end at a grave—many graves, in fact. For as the forces stood, Lapierre knew that many men must die, and bitterly he cursed LeFroy for disclosing to MacNair the whereabouts of the Mausers concealed in the storehouse.

The inevitable attack of the Mounted he knew would come later. For the man knew their methods. He knew that a small detachment, one officer, or perhaps two, would appear before the barricade and demand his surrender, and when surrender was refused, a report would go in to headquarters, and after that—Lapierre shrugged—well, that was a problem of tomorrow. In the meantime, if he held Chloe Elliston prisoner under threat of death, it was highly probable that he could deal to advantage with MacNair, and, at the proper time, with the Mounted. If not—*Voila*! It was a fight to the death, anyway. And again Lapierre shrugged.

Nearer and nearer drew the unsuspecting figure of the girl. The man noted the haughty, almost arrogant beauty of her, as the moonlight played upon the firm resolute features, framed by the oval of her *parka*-hood. The next instant she paused in the shadow of his banskian, almost at his side. Lapierre sprang to his feet and stood facing her there in the snow. The smile of the thin lips hardened as he noted the sudden pallor of her face and the look of wild terror that flashed for a moment from her eyes. And then, almost on the instant, the girl's eyes narrowed, the firm white chin thrust forward, and the red lips curled into a sneer of infinite loathing and contempt. Instinctively, Lapierre knew that the hands within the heavy mittens had clenched into fighting fists. For an instant she faced him, and then, drawing away as if he were some grizzly, loathsome thing poisoning the air he breathed, she spoke. Her voice trembled with the fury of her words, and Lapierre winced to the lash of a woman's scorn.

"You—you *dog*!" she cried. "You dirty, low-lived *cur*! How *dare* you stand there grinning? How *dare* you show your face? Oh, if I were a man I would—I would strangle the life from your vile, sneaking body with my two hands!"

The words ended in a stifled cry. With a snarl, Lapierre sprang upon her, pinning her arms to her side. The next instant before his eyes loomed the form of Big Lena, who leaped toward him with upraised ax swung high. In the excitement of the moment, the man had not noted her approach. With a swift movement he succeeded in forcing the body of the girl between himself and the up-raised blade.

With a shrill cry of rage Lena dropped the ax and rushed to a grip. Sounded then a sickening thud, and the huge woman pitched face downward into the snow, while behind her one of Lapierre's outlaws tossed a heavy club into the bush and rushed to the assistance of his chief. The others came, and with incredible rapidity Chloe Elliston was gagged and bound hand and foot, and the men were carrying her to the waiting sled.

For a moment Lapierre hesitated, gazing longingly toward the cottage as he debated in his mind the advisability of rushing across the clearing and settling his score with Mary, the Louchoux girl, whose unexpected appearance had turned the tide so strongly against him.

"Better let well enough alone!" he growled savagely. "I must reach Lac du Mort ahead of MacNair." And he turned with a curse from the clearing to see an outlaw, with knife unsheathed, stooping over the unconscious form of Big Lena. The quarter-breed kicked the knife from the man's hand.

"Bring her along!" he ordered gruffly. "I will attend to her later." And, despite the hurt of his bruised fingers, the man grinned as he noted the venomous gleam in the leader's eye. For not only was Lapierre thinking of the proselyting of LeFroy, who had been his most trusted lieutenant, but of his own disarming, and the meaning stare of the fishlike eyes that had prompted him to abandon his attempt to poison MacNair when wounded in Chloe Elusion's room.

It was yet early when, as had become her custom, the Louchoux girl dressed hurriedly and made her way to the kitchen to help Lena in the preparation of breakfast. To her surprise she found that the fire had not been lighted nor was Big Lena in the little room which had been built for her adjoining the kitchen.

The quick eyes of the girl noted that the bed had not been disturbed, and with a sudden fear in her heart she dashed to the door of Chloe's room, where, receiving no answer to her frantic knocking, she pushed open the door and entered. Chloe's bed had not been slept in, and her *parka* was missing from its peg upon the wall.

As the Indian girl turned from the room, Harriet Penny's door opened, and she caught a glimpse of a night-capped head as the little spinster glanced timidly out to inquire into the unusual disturbance.

"Where have they gone?" cried the girl.

"Gone? Gone?" asked Miss Penny. "What do you mean? Who has gone?"

"She's gone—Miss Elliston—and Big Lena, too. They have not slept in their beds."

It took a half-minute for this bit of information to percolate Miss Penny's understanding, and when it did she uttered a shrill scream, banged her door, turned the key, and shot the bolt upon the inside.

Alone in the living-room, the last words Chloe had spoken to her flashed through the Indian girl's mind: "I can trust you to place this in MacNair's hands."

Without a second thought for Miss Penny, she rushed into her room, recovered the letter from its hiding-place beneath the pillow, thrust it into the bosom of her gown, and hastily prepared for the trail.

In the kitchen she made up a light pack of provisions, and, with no other thought than to find MacNair, opened the door and stepped out into the keen, frosty air. The girl knew only that Snare Lake lay somewhere up the river, but this gave her little concern, as no snow had fallen since MacNair had departed with his Indians a week before, and she knew his trail would be plain.

From her window Harriet Penny watched the departure of the girl, and before she was half-way across the clearing the little woman appeared in the doorway, commanding, begging, pleading in shrill falsetto, not to be left alone. Hearing the cries, the girl quickened her pace, and without so much as a backward glance passed swiftly down the steep slope to the river.

Born to the snow-trail, the Louchoux girl made good time. During the month she had spent at Chloe's school she had for the first time in her life been sufficiently clothed and fed, and now with the young muscles of her body well nourished and in the pink of condition she fairly flew over the trail.

Hour after hour she kept up the pace without halting. She passed the mouth of the small tributary upon which she had first seen Chloe. The place conjured vivid memories of the white woman and all she had done for her and meant to her—memories that served as a continual spur to her flying feet. It was well toward noon when, upon rounding a sharp bend, she came suddenly face to face with the Indians and the dog-teams that MacNair had despatched for provisions.

She bounded among them like a flash, singled out Wee Johnnie Tamarack, and proceeded to deluge the old man with an avalanche of words. When finally she paused for sheer lack of breath, the old Indian, who had understood but the smallest fragment of what she had said, remained obviously unimpressed. Whereupon the girl produced the letter, which she waved before his face, accompanying the act with another tirade of words of which the Indian understood less than he had of the previous outburst.

Wee Johnnie Tamarack took his orders only from MacNair. MacNair had said, "Go to the school for provisions," and to the school he must go. Nevertheless, the sight of the letter impressed him. For in the Northland His Majesty's mail is held sacred and must be carried to its destination, though the heavens fall.

To the mind of Wee Johnnie Tamarack a letter was "mail," and the fact that its status might be altered by the absence of His Majesty's stamp upon its corner was an affair beyond the old man's comprehension.

Therefore he ordered the other Indians to continue their journey, and, motioning the girl to a place on the sled, headed his dogs northward and sent them skimming over the back-trail.

Wee Johnnie Tamarack was counted one of the best dog-mushers in the North, and as the girl had succeeded in implanting in the old man's mind an urgent need of haste, he exerted his talent to the utmost. Mile after mile, behind the flying feet of the tireless *malamutes*, the sled-runners slipped smoothly over the crust of the ice-hard snow.

And at midnight of the second day they dashed across the smooth surface of the lake and brought up with a rush before the door of MacNair's own cabin, which luckily had been spared by the flames.

It was a record drive, for a "two-man" load—that drive of Wee Johnnie Tamarack's, having clipped twelve hours from a thirty-six-hour trail.

MacNair's door flew open to their frantic pounding. The girl thrust the letter into his hand, and with a supreme effort told what she knew of the disappearance of Chloe and Big

Lena. Whereupon, she threw herself at full length upon the floor and immediately sank into a profound sleep.

MacNair fumbled upon the shelf for a candle and, lighting it, seated himself beside the table, and tore the envelope from the letter. Never in his life had the man read words penned by the hand of a woman. The fingers that held the letter trembled, and he wondered at the wild beating of his heart.

The story of the Louchoux girl had aroused in him a sudden fear. He wondered vaguely that the disappearance of Chloe Elliston could have caused the dull hurt in his breast. The pages in his hand were like no letter he had ever received. There was something personal—intimate—about them. His huge fingers gripped them lightly, and he turned them over and over in his hand, gazing almost in awe upon the bold, angular writing. Then, very slowly, he began to read the words.

Unconsciously, he read them aloud, and as he read a strange lump arose in his throat so that his voice became husky and the words faltered. He read the letter through to the end. He leaped to his feet and strode rapidly up and down the room, his fists clenched and his breath coming in great gasps.

Bob MacNair was fighting. Fighting against an irresistible impulse—an impulse as new and strange to him as though born of another world—an impulse to find Chloe Elliston, to take her in his arms, and to crush her close against his wildly pounding heart.

Minutes passed as the man strode up and down the length of the little room, and then once more he seated himself at the table and read the letter through.

"DEAR MR. MACNAIR:

"I cannot leave the North without this little word to you. I have learned many things since I last saw you—things I should have learned long ago. You were right about the Indians, about Lapierre, about *me*. I know now that I have been a fool. Lapierre always removed his hat in my presence, therefore he was a gentleman! Oh, what a fool I was!

"I will not attempt to apologize. I have been too *nasty*, and *hateful*, and *mean* for any apology. You said once that some day we should be friends. I am reminding you of this because I want you to think of me as a friend. Wherever I may be, I will think of you—always. Of the splendid courage of the man who, surrounded by treachery and intrigue and the vicious attacks of the powers that prey, dares to stand upon his convictions and to fight alone for the good of the North—for the cause of those who will never be able to fight for themselves.

"It will not be necessary to tell you that I shall go straight to the headquarters of the Mounted and withdraw my charge against you. I have heard of your lawless raids into the far North; I think they are *splendid*! Keep the good work up! Shoot as straight as you can—as straight as you shot that night on Snare Lake. I should love to stand at your side and shoot, too. But that can never be.

"Just a word more. Lena is going to marry LeFroy; and, knowing Lena as I do, I think his reformation is assured. I am leaving everything to them. The contents of the storehouse will set them up as independent traders.

"And now farewell. I want you to have my most valued possession, the portrait of my grandfather, Tiger Elliston, the man I have always admired more than any other until—"

Until what? wondered MacNair. The word had been crossed out, and he finished the letter still wondering.

"When you look at the picture in its splintered frame, think sometimes of the 'fool moose-calf,' who, having succeeded by the narrowest margin in eluding the fangs of 'the wolf' is returning, wiser, to its mountains.

"Yours very truly—and very, very repentantly,

"CHLOE ELLISTON."

Bob MacNair lost his fight. He arose once more, his great frame trembling in the grip of a new thrill. He stretched his great arms to the southward in a silent sign of surrender. He sought not to dodge the issue, strange and wonderful as it seemed to him. He loved this woman—loved her as he knew he could love no other—as he had never dreamed it was in the heart of man to love.

And then, with the force of a blow, came the realization that this woman—his woman—was at that very instant, in all probability, at the mercy of a fiend who would stop at nothing to gain his own ends.

He leaped to the door.

"By God, I'll tear his heart out!" he roared as he wrenched at the latch. And the next instant the shores of Snare Lake echoed to the wild weird sound of the wolf-cry—the call of MacNair to his clan! Other calls and other summons might be ignored upon provocation, but when the terrible wolf-cry shattered the silence of the forest MacNair's Indians rushed to his side.

Only death itself could deter them from fore-gathering at the sound of the wolf-cry. Before the echoes of MacNair's voice had died away dark forms were speeding through the moonlight. From all directions they came; from the cabins that yet remained standing, from the tents pitched close against the unburned walls of the stockade, from rude wickiups of skins and of brushwood.

Old men and young men they answered the call, and each in his hand bore a rifle. MacNair snapped a few quick orders. Men rushed to harness the dog-teams while others provisioned the sleds for the trail.

With one arm MacNair swung the Louchoux girl from the floor, and, picking up his rifle, dashed out into the night.

Wee Johnnie Tamarack, just in from a twenty-four-hour trail, stood at the head of MacNair's own dogs—the seven great Athabasca River dogs that had carried him into the North. With a cry to his Indians to follow and to bring the Louchoux girl, MacNair threw himself belly-wise onto his sled, gave voice to a weird cry as his dogs shot out across the white snow-level of Snare Lake, and headed south-ward toward the Yellow Knife.

He laughed aloud as he glanced over the back-trail and noted that half of his Indians were already following. He had chosen that last cry well. Never before had the Indians heard it from the white man's lips, and they thrilled at the sound to the marrow. The blood surged through the veins of the wild men as it had not surged in long decades. *It was the war-cry of the Yellow Knives*!

CHAPTER XXIV

THE BATTLE

Bob MacNair's sled seemed scarcely to touch the hard surface of the snow. The great *malemutes* ran low and true over the well-defined trail. He had selected the dogs with an eye to speed and endurance at the time he had headed northward with Corporal Ripley after his release from the Fort Saskatchewan jail.

The shouts of the following Indians died away. Familiar landmarks leaped past, and save for an occasional word of encouragement MacNair let the dogs set their own pace. For, consumed as he was by anxiety for what might lie at the end of the trail, he knew that the homing instinct of the wolf-dogs would carry them more miles and in better heart than the sting of his long gut-lash.

At daylight the man halted for a half-hour, fed his dogs, and boiled tea, which he drank in great gulps, hot and black, from the rim of the pot. At noon one of the dogs showed signs of distress, and MacNair cut him loose, leaving him to follow as best as he could. When darkness fell only three dogs remained in harness, and these showed plainly the effects of the long trail-strain. While behind, somewhere upon the wide stretch of the Yellow Knife, the other four limped painfully in the wake of their stronger team-mates.

An hour passed, during which the pace slackened perceptibly, and then with only ten miles to go, two more dogs laid down. Pausing only to cut them free from the harness, MacNair continued the trail on foot. The hard-packed surface of the snow made the rackets unnecessary, and the man struck into a long, swinging trot—the stride of an Indian runner.

Mile after mile slipped by as the huge muscles of him, tireless as bands of steel, flexed and sprung with the regularity of clockworks. The rising moon was just topping the eastern pines as he dashed up the steep bank of the clearing. For a moment he halted as his glance swept the familiar outlines of the log buildings, standing black and clean-cut and sombre in the light of the rising moon.

MacNair drew a deep breath, and the next moment the long wolf-cry boomed out over the silent snow. As if by magic, the clearing sprang into life. Lights shone from the barrack windows and from the windows of the cabins beyond; doors banged. The white snow of the clearing was dotted with swift-moving forms as men, women, and children answered the clan-call of MacNair, shouting to one another as they ran, in hoarse, deep gutturals.

In an instant MacNair singled out Old Elk from among the crowding forms.

"What's happened here?" he cried. "Where is the white *kloochman*?"

Old Elk had taken charge of the thirty Indians MacNair had despatched for provisions, and immediately upon learning from the lips of the Indian women of Chloe's disappearance he had left the loading of the sleds to the others while he worked out the signs in the snow. Thus at MacNair's question the old Indian motioned him to follow, and, starting at the door of the cottage, he traced Chloe's trail to the banskian, and there in a few words and much silent pantomime he explained without doubt or hesitation exactly what had taken place from the moment of Chloe's departure from the cottage until she was carried, bound and gagged and placed upon Lapierre's waiting sled.

As MacNair followed the old Indian's story his fists clenched, his eyes hardened to points, and the breath whistled through his nostrils in white plumes of frost-steam.

Old Elk finished and, pointing eloquently in the direction of Lac du Mort, asked eagerly:

"You follow de trail of Lapierre?"

MacNair nodded, and before he could reply the Indian stepped close to his side and placed a withered hand upon his arm.

"Me, I'm lak' y'u fadder," he said; "y'u lak' my own son. Y'u follow de trail of Lapierre. Y'u tak' de white *kloochman* away from Lapierre, an' den, by gar, when y'u got her y'u ke'p her. Dat *kloochman*, him damn fine 'oman!"

Realizing his worst fears were verified, MacNair immediately set about preparations for the attack on Lapierre's stronghold. All night he superintended the breaking out of supplies in the storehouse and the loading of sleds for the trail, and at the first streak of dawn the vanguard of Indians who had followed him from Snare Lake swarmed up the bank from the river.

MacNair selected the freshest and strongest of these, and with the thirty who were already at the school, struck into the timber with sleds loaded light for a quick dash, leaving the heavier impedimenta to follow in care of the women and those who were yet to arrive from Snare Lake.

The fact that MacNair had made use of the wolf-cry to call them together, his set face, and terse, quick commands told the Indians that this was no ordinary expedition, and the eyes of the men glowed with anticipation. The long-promised—the inevitable battle was at hand. The time had come for ridding the North of Lapierre. And the fight would be a fight to the death.

It took three days for MacNair's flying squadron to reach the fort at Lac du Mort. By the many columns of smoke that arose from the surface of the little plateau, he knew that the men of Lapierre waited the attack in force. MacNair led his Indians across the lake and into the black spruce swamp. A half-dozen scouts were sent out to surround the plateau, with orders to report immediately anything of importance.

Old Elk was detailed to follow the trail of Lapierre's sled to the very walls of the stockade. For well MacNair knew that the crafty quarter-breed was quite capable of side-stepping the obvious and carrying the girl to some rendezvous unknown to any one but himself. The remaining Indians he set to work felling trees for a small stockade which would serve as a defence against a surprise attack. Saplings were also felled for light ladders to be used in the scaling of Lapierre's walls.

Evening saw the completion of a substantial five-foot barricade, and soon after dark Old Elk appeared with the information that both Chloe and Big Lena, as well as Lapierre himself, were within the confines of the Bastile du Mort. The man also proudly displayed a bleeding scalp which he had ripped from the head of one of Lapierre's scouts who had blundered upon the old man as he lay concealed behind a snow-covered log. The sight of the grewsome trophy with its long black hair and blood-dripping flesh excited the Indians to a fever pitch. The scalp was placed upon a pole driven into the snow in the centre of the little stockade. And for hours the Indians danced about it, rendering the night hideous with the wild chants and wails of their weird incantations.

As the night advanced and the incantations increased in violence, MacNair arose from the robe he had spread beside his camp-fire, and drawing away from the wild savagery of the scene, stole alone out into the dense blackness of the swamp and detouring to the shore of the lake, seated himself upon an uprooted tree-butt.

An hour passed as he sat thinking—staring into the dark. The moon rose and illumined with soft radiance the indomitable land of the raw. MacNair's gaze roved from the forbidding blackness of the farther shore-line, across the dead, cold snow-level of the ice-locked lake, to the bold headlands that rose sheer upon his right and upon his left. The scene was one of unbending *hardness*—of nature's frowning defiance of man. The soft touch of the moonlight jarred upon his mood. Death lurked in the shadows—and death, and worse than death, awaited the dawning of the day. It was a *hard* land—the North—having naught to do with beauty and the soft brilliance of moonlight. He glanced toward the jutting rock-ribbed plateau that was Lapierre's stronghold. Out of the night—out of the intense blackness of the spruce-guarded dark came the wailing howl of the savage scalp-dance.

"The real spirit of the North," he murmured bitterly. He arose to his feet, and, with his eyes fixed upon the bold headland of the little plateau, stretched his great arms toward the spot that concealed the woman he loved—and then he turned and passed swiftly into the blackness of the forest.

But despite the frenzy of the blood-lust, at no time were the Indians out of MacNair's control, and when he ordered quiet, the incantations ceased at the word and they sought their blankets to dream eagerly of the morrow.

Morning came, and long before sunrise a thin line of men, women, and heavily laden dog-sleds put out from the farther shore of the lake and headed for the black spruce swamp. The clan of MacNair was gathering to the call of the wolf.

The newcomers were conducted to the log stockade where the women were left to store the provisions, while MacNair called a council of his fighting men and laid out his plan of attack. He glanced with pride into the eager faces of the men who would die for him. He counted eighty-seven men under arms, thirty of whom were armed with Lapierre's Mausers.

The position of the quarter-breed's fort admitted only one plan of attack—to rush the barricade that stretched across the neck of the little peninsula. MacNair longed for action. He chafed with impatience to strike the blow that would crush forever the power of Lapierre, yet he found himself wholly at the mercy of Lapierre. For somewhere behind that barrier of logs was the woman he loved. He shuddered at the thought. He knew Lapierre. Knew that the man's white blood and his education, instead of civilizing, had served to heighten and to refine the barbaric cruelty and savagery of his heart. He knew that Lapierre would stop at nothing to gain an end. His heart chilled at the possibilities. He dreaded to act—yet he knew that he must act.

He dismissed the idea of a siege. A quick, fierce assault—an attack that should have no lull, nor armistice until his Indians had scaled the stockade, was preferable to the heart-breaking delay of a siege. MacNair decided to launch his attack with so fierce an onslaught that Lapierre would have no time to think of the girl. But if worse came to worst, and he did think of her, what he would do he would be forced to do quickly.

Grimly, MacNair led his warriors to the attack, and as the lean-faced horde moved silently through the timbered aisles of the swamp, the sound of scattering shots was borne to their ears as the scouts exchanged bullets with Lapierre's sentries.

A cleared space, thirty yards in width, separated the forest from the barricade, and with this clearing in sight, in the shelter of the snow-laden spruces, MacNair called a halt, and in a brief address gave his Indians their final instructions. In their own tongue he addressed them, falling naturally into the oratorical swing of the council fire.

"The time has come, my people, as I have told you it must sometime come, for the final reckoning with Lapierre. Not because the man has sought my life, am I fighting him. I would not call upon you to risk your lives to protect mine; not to avenge the burning of my storehouse, nor yet, because he dug my gold. I am fighting him because he has struck at your homes, and the homes of your wives and your children. You are my people, and your interests are my interests.

"I have not preached to you, as do the good fathers at the Mission, of a life in a world to come. Of that I know nothing. It is this life—the daily life we are living now, with which I have to do. I have taught you to work with your hands, because he who works is better clothed, and better fed, and better housed than he who does not work. I have commanded you not to drink the white man's fire-water, not because it is wrong to be drunken. A man's life is his own. He may do with it as he pleases. But a man who is drunk is neither well nor happy. He will not work. He sees his women and his children suffering and in want, and he does not care. He beats them and drives them into the cold. He is no longer a man, but a brute, meaner and more to be despised than the wolf—for a wolf feeds his young. Therefore, I have commanded you to drink no fire-water.

"I have not made you learn from books; for books are things of the white men. In books men have written many things; but in no book is anything written that will put warmer clothes upon your backs, or more meat in your *caches*. The white *kloochman* came among you with books. Her heart is good and she is a friend of the Indians, but all her life has she lived in the land of the white men. And from books, the white men learn to gather their meat and their clothing. Therefore, she thought that the Indians also should learn from books.

"But the white *kloochman* has learned now the needs of the North. At first I feared she would not learn that it is the work of the hands that counts. When I knew she had learned I sent you to her, for there are many things she can teach you, and especially your women and children, of which I know nothing.

"The white *kloochman*, your good friend, has fallen into the hands of Lapierre. We are men, and we must take her from Lapierre. And now the time has come to fight! You are fighting men and the children of fighting men! When this fight is over there will be peace in the Northland! It will be the last fight for many of us—for many of us must die! Lapierre's men are well armed. They will fight hard, for they know it is their last stand. Kill them as long as they continue to fight, but *do not kill Lapierre*!"

His eyes flashed dangerously as he paused to glance into the faces of his fighters.

"No man shall kill Lapierre!" he repeated. "He is *mine*! With my own hands will I settle the score; and now listen well to the final word:

"Drag the ladders to the edge of the clearing, scatter along the whole front in the shelter of the trees, and at the call of the hoot-owl you shall commence firing. Shoot whenever one of Lapierre's men shows himself. But remain well concealed, for the men of Lapierre will be entrenched behind the loop-holes. At the call of the loon you shall cease firing."

MacNair rapidly tolled out twenty who were to man the ladders.

"At the call of the wolf, rush to the stockade with the ladders, and those who have guns shall follow. Then up the ladders and over the walls! After that, fight, every man for himself, but mind you well, that you take Lapierre alive, for Lapierre is mine!"

The laddermen stationed themselves at the edge of the timber, and the men who carried guns scattered along the whole width of the clearing. Then from the depths of the forest suddenly boomed the cry of the hoot-owl. Heads appeared over the edge of Lapierre's stockade, and from the shelter of the black spruce swamp came the crash of rifles. The heads disappeared, and of Lapierre's men many tumbled backward into the snow, while others crouched upon the firing ledge which Lapierre had constructed near the top of his log stockade and answered the volley, shooting at random into the timber. But only as a man's head appeared, or as his body showed between the spaces of the logs, were their shots returned. MacNair's Indians were biding their time.

For an hour this ineffectual and abortive sniping kept up,

and then from the walls of the stockade appeared that for which MacNair had been waiting—a white flag fluttering from the end of a sapling. Raising his head, MacNair imitated the call of the loon, and the firing ceased in the timber. Having no white rag, MacNair waved a spruce bough and stepped boldly out into the clearing.

The head and shoulders of Lapierre appeared above the wall of the barricade, and for several moments the two faced each other in silence. MacNair grim, determined, scowling—Lapierre defiant, crafty, with his thin lips twisted into a mocking smile. The quarter-breed was the first to speak.

"So," he drawled, "my good friend has come to visit his neighbour! Come right in, I assure you a hearty welcome, but you must come alone! Your retainers are too numerous and entirely too *bourgeois* to eat at a gentleman's table."

"But not to drink from his bottle," retorted MacNair. "I am coming in—but not alone!"

Lapierre laughed derisively. "O-ho, you would come by force—by force of arms, eh! Well, come along, but I warn you, you do so at your peril. My men are all armed, and the walls are thick and high. Rather, I choose to think you will listen to reason."

"Reason!" roared MacNair. "I will reason with you when we come to hands' grips!"

Lapierre shrugged. "As you please," he answered: "I was only thinking of your own welfare, and, perhaps, of the welfare of another, who will to a certainty fare badly in case your savages attack us. I myself am not of brutal nature, but among my men are some who—" He paused and glanced significantly into MacNair's eyes. Again he shrugged—"We will not dwell upon the possibilities, but here is the lady, let her speak for herself. She has begged for the chance to say a word in her own behalf. I will only add that you will find me amenable to reason. It is possible that our little differences may be settled in a manner satisfactory to all, and without bloodshed."

The man stepped aside upon the firing ledge, evidently in order to let someone pass up the ladder. The next instant the face of Chloe Elliston appeared above the logs of the stockade. At the sight of the girl MacNair felt the blood surge through his veins. He took a quick step toward and at a glance noted the unwonted pallor of her cheeks, the flashing eyes, and the curve of the out-thrust chin.

Then clear and firm her voice sounded in his ears. He strained forward to catch the words, and at that moment he knew in his heart that this woman meant more to him than life itself—more than revenge—more even than the welfare of his Indians.

"You received my letter?" asked the girl eagerly. "Can you forgive me? Do you understand?"

MacNair answered, controlling his voice with difficulty. "There is nothing to forgive. I have understood you all along."

"You will promise to grant one request—for my sake?"

Without hesitation came the man's answer; "Anything you ask."

"On your soul, will you promise, and will you keep that promise regardless of consequences?"

"I promise," answered the man, and his voice rang harsh. For revenge upon Lapierre with his own hands had been the dearest hope of his life. At the next words of the girl, an icy hand seemed clutching at his heart.

"Then fight!" she cried. "Fight! Fight! Fight! Shoot! And cut! And batter! And kill! Until you have ridded the North of this fiend!"

With a snarl, Lapierre leaped toward the girl with arm upraised. There was a chorus of hoarse cries from behind the walls. Before the uplifted arm could descend the figure of Lapierre disappeared with startling suddenness. The next instant the gigantic form of Big Lena appeared, head and shoulders above the walls of the stockade at the point where Lapierre had been. The huge shoulders stooped, the form of Chloe Elliston arose as on air, shot over the wall, and dropped into a crumpled heap upon the snow at its base. The face of Big Lena framed by flying strands of flaxen hair appeared for a moment above the wall, and then the sound of a shot rang sharp and clear. The face disappeared, and from beyond the wall came the muffled thud of a heavy body striking the snow.

A dark head appeared above the walls at the point near where the girl had fallen, and an arm was thrust over the logs. MacNair caught the glint of a blue-black barrel. Like a flash he drew his automatic and fired. The revolver dropped from the top of the wall to the snow, and the hand that held it gripped frantically at the logs and disappeared.

MacNair threw back his head, and loud and clear on the frosty air blared the call of the wolf. The whole line of the forest spit flame. The crash and roar of a hundred guns was in the air as the men from behind the barricade replied. Lithe forms carrying ladders dashed across the open space. Many pitched forward before the wall and lay doubled grotesquely upon the white strip of snow, while eager hands carried the ladders on.

Suddenly, above the crash of the guns sounded the war-cry of the Yellow Knives. The whole clearing sprang alive with men, yelling like fiends and firing as they ran. Dark forms swarmed up the ladders and over the walls. MacNair grabbed the rungs of a ladder and drew himself up. Above him climbed the Indian who had carried the ladder. He had no gun, but the grey blade of a long knife flashed wickedly between his teeth.

The Indian crashed backward, carrying MacNair with him into the snow. MacNair struggled to his feet. The Indian lay almost at the foot of the ladder, and, gurgling horribly, rose to his knees. MacNair glanced into his face. The man's eyes were rolled backward until only the whites showed. His lips moved, and he clung to the rungs of the ladder. Blood splashed down his front and reddened the trampled snow, then he fell heavily backward, and MacNair saw that his whole throat had been shot away by the close fired charge of a shotgun.

With a roar, MacNair scrambled up the ladder, automatic in hand. On the firing ledge's narrow rim a riverman snapped together the breech of his shotgun, and looked up—his face close to the face of MacNair. And as he looked his jaw sagged in terror. MacNair jammed the barrel of the automatic into the open mouth and fired.

CHAPTER XXV

THE GUN-BRAND

Chloe Elliston lay in the snow, partially stunned by her fall from the top of the stockade. She was not unconscious—her hearing and vision were unimpaired, but her numbed brain did not grasp the significance of the sights and sounds which her senses recorded. She wondered vaguely how it happened she was lying there in the snow when she distinctly remembered that she was standing upon the narrow firing ledge urging MacNair to fight. There was MacNair now! She could see him distinctly. Even as she looked the man drew his pistol and fired. Something struck the snow almost within reach of her hand. It was a revolver. Chloe glanced upward, but saw only the log wall of the stockade which seemed to tower upward until it touched the sky.

A blood-curdling cry rang out upon the air—a sound she had heard of nights echoing among rock-rimmed ridges—the pack-cry of the wolf-breed. She shuddered at the nearness of the sound and turned, expecting to encounter the red throat and slavering jaws of the fang-bared leader of the pack, and instead she saw only MacNair.

Then along the wall of the forest came thin grey puffs of smoke, and her ears rang with the crash of the rifle-volley.

She heard the wicked spit and thud of the bullets as they ripped at the logs above her, and tiny slivers of bark made black spots upon the snow. A piece fell upon her face, she brushed it away with her hand. The sounds of the shots increased ten fold. Answering spurts of grey smoke jutted from the walls above her. The loop-holes bristled with rifle-barrels!

In her nostrils was the rank smell of powder-smoke, and across the clearing, straight toward her, dashed many men with ladders. A man fell almost at her side, his ladder, tilting against the wall, slipped sidewise into the snow, crashing against one of the protruding rifle-barrels as it fell. Two other men came, and uprighting the ladder, climbed swiftly up the wall. Chloe saw that they were MacNair's Indians.

The scene changed with lightning rapidity. Men with rifles were in the clearing, now running and shooting, and falling down to remain motionless in the snow. Above the uproar of the guns a new sound rolled and swelled. An eery, blood-curdling sound that chilled the heart and caused the roots of her hair to prickle along the base of her skull. It was the war-cry of the Yellow Knives as they fired, and ran, and clambered up the ladders,

The sights and sounds were clean-cut, distinct, intensely thrilling—but impersonal, like the shifting scenes of a photo-play. She glanced about for MacNair. Her eyes travelled swiftly from face to swarthy face of the men who charged out of the timber. She directed her glance toward the wall, and there, not twenty feet away, she saw him reach for the rungs of the ladder. And the next moment two forms crashed backward into the snow. For an instant the girl closed her eyes, and in that instant her brain awoke with a start. About her the sounds leaped into terrible significance. She realized that she was outside the walls of the stockade. That the sights and sounds about her were intensely real.

The forces of MacNair and Lapierre had locked horns in the final struggle, and her fate, and the fate of the whole North, hung in the balance. All about her were the hideous sounds of battle. She was surprised that she was unafraid; instead, the blood seemed coursing through her veins with the heat of flame. Her heart seemed bursting with a wild, fierce joy. Something of which she had always been dimly conscious—some latent thing which she had always held in check—seemed suddenly to burst within her. A flood of fancies crowded her brain. The wicked crack of the rifles became the roar of cannon. Tall masts, to which clung shot-torn shrouds, reared high above a fog of powder-smoke, and beyond waved the tops of palm-trees. The spirit of Tiger Elliston had burst its bounds!

With a cry like the scream of a beast, the girl leaped to her feet. She tore the heavy mittens from her hands, and reached for the revolver which lay in the snow at her side. She leaped toward MacNair who had regained his feet, red with the life-blood of the Indian who lay upon his back in the snow, staring upward wide-eyed, unseeing, throatless. She called loudly, but her voice was lost in the mighty uproar, and MacNair sprang up the ladder.

Like a flash Chloe followed, holding her heavy revolver as he had held his. She glanced upward; MacNair had disappeared over the edge of the stockade. The next instant she, too, had reached the top. She paused, looking downward. MacNair was scrambling to his feet. Ten feet away a man levelled a gun at him. He fired from his knee, and the man pitched forward. Upon him, from behind, rushed two men swinging their rifles high. They had almost reached him when Chloe fired straight down. The nearest man dropped his rifle and staggered against the wall. The other paused and glanced upward. Chloe shot squarely into his face. The bullet ripped downward, splitting his jaw. The man rushed screaming over the snow, tearing with both hands at the wound.

MacNair was upon his feet now. Beyond him the fighting was hand to hand. With clubbed guns and axes, Lapierre's men were meeting the Indians who swarmed over the walls. Once more the wild wolf-cry rang in the girl's ears as MacNair leaped into the thick of the fight. The girl became conscious that someone was pounding at her feet. She glanced downward. Two Indians were upon the ladder waiting to get over the wall. Without hesitation she tightened her grip upon her revolver and leaped into the stockade. She sprawled awkwardly in the snow. She felt her shoulder seized viciously. Someone was jerking her to her feet. She looked up and encountered the gleaming eyes of Lapierre.

Chloe tried to raise her revolver, but Lapierre kicked it from her hand. There was the sound of a heavy impact. Lapierre's hand was jerked from her shoulder; he was hurled backward, cursing, into the snow. One of the Indians who had followed Chloe up the ladder had leaped squarely upon the quarter-breed's shoulders. Like a flash Lapierre drew his automatic, but the Indian threw himself upon the gun and tore it from his grasp. Then he scrambled to his feet. Lapierre, too, was upon his feet in an instant.

"Shoot, you fool! Kill him! Kill him!" cried Chloe.

But the Indian continued to stare stupidly, and Lapierre dashed to safety around the corner of his storehouse.

"MacNair say no kill," said the Indian gravely.

"Not kill!" cried the girl. "He is crazy! What is he thinking of?" But the Indian was already out of ear-shot. Chloe glanced about her for her revolver. An evil-faced half-breed, dragging his body from the hips, pulled himself toward it, hunching along with his bare hands digging into the crust of the snow. The girl reached it a second before him. The man cursed her shrilly and sank into the snow, crying aloud like a child.

Suddenly Chloe realized that the battle had surged beyond her. Shots and hoarse cries arose from the scrub beyond the storehouse, while all about her, in the trampled snow, wounded men cursed and prayed, and dead men froze in the slush of their own heart's blood. The girl followed into the scrub, and to her surprise came face to face with the Louchoux girl, who was carrying armfuls of dry brushwood, which she piled against the corner of the storehouse.

Chloe glanced into the black eyes that glowed like living coals. The Indian girl added her armful to the pile and, drawing matches from her pocket, dropped to her knees in the snow. She pointed toward the log storehouse.

"Lapierre ran inside," she said.

With a wild laugh Chloe passed on. The scrub thinned toward the point of the peninsula, where the rim-rocks rose sheer two hundred feet above the level of the lake. Chloe caught sight of MacNair's Indians leaping before her, and, beyond, the crowding knot of men who gave ground before the rush of the Yellow Knives. One by one the men dropped, writhing, into the snow. The others gave ground rapidly, shooting at their advancing enemies, cursing, crowding—but always giving ground.

At last they were upon the rim-rocks, huddled together like cattle. Chloe could see them outlined distinctly against the sky. They fired one last scattering volley, and then the ranks thinned suddenly; many were leaping over the edge, while others, throwing down their rifles, advanced with arms raised high above their heads. Some Indians fired, and two of these pitched forward. Then MacNair bellowed a hoarse order, and the firing ceased, and the Indians bound the prisoners with thongs of *babiche*.

The girl found herself close to the edge of the high plateau. She leaned far over and peered downward. Upon the white snow of the rocks, close to the foot of the cliff, lay several dark forms. She drew back and turned to MacNair, but he had gone. A puff of smoke arose into the air above the tops of the scrub-trees, and Chloe knew that the storehouse was burning. The smoke increased in volume and rolled heavily skyward upon the light breeze. She could hear the crackle of flames, and the smell of burning spruce was in the air.

She pushed forward into the cordon of Indians which surrounded the burning building, glancing hurriedly from face to face, searching for MacNair. Upon the edge of the little clearing which surrounded the storehouse she saw the Louchoux girl bending over a form that lay stretched in the snow. Swiftly she made her way to the girl's side. She was bending over the inert form of Big Lena. The big woman opened her eyes, and with a cry Chloe dropped to her knees by her side.

"Ay ain't hurt much," Lena muttered weakly. "Vun faller shoot me on de head, but de bullet yump off sidevays. Ju bet MacNair, he gif dem haal!"

At the mention of MacNair's name Chloe sprang to her feet and continued along the cordon.

One end of the storehouse and half the roof was ablaze, while thick, heavy smoke curled from beneath the full length of the eaves and through the chinkings of the logs. Chloe had almost completed the circle when suddenly she came to a halt, for there, pressed tight against the logs close beside the jamb of the closed door, stood MacNair. All about her the Indians stood in tense expectancy. Their eyes gleamed bright, and the breath hissed between parted lips—short, quick breaths of excitement. The flames had not yet reached the front of the storehouse, but tiny puffs of smoke found their way out above the door. As she looked the form of MacNair stiffened, and Chloe gasped as she saw that the man was unarmed.

Suddenly the door flew open, and Lapierre, clutching an automatic in either hand, leaped swiftly into the open. The next instant his arms were pinioned to his sides. A loud cry went up from the watching Indians, and from all quarters came the sound of rushing feet as those who had guarded the windows crowded about.

Lapierre was no weakling. He strained and writhed to free himself from the encircling arms. But the arms were bands of steel, clamping tighter and tighter about him. Slowly MacNair worked his hand downward to the other's wrist. There was a lightning-like jerk, and the automatic new into the air and dropped harmless into the snow. The same instant MacNair's grasp tightened about the other wrist. He released Lapierre's disarmed hand and, reaching swiftly, tore the other gun from the man's fingers.

Lapierre swung at his face, but MacNair leaned suddenly backward and outward, still grasping the wrist, Lapierre's body described a short half-circle, and he brought up with a thud against a nearby pile of stove-wood. Releasing his grip, MacNair crowded him close and closer against the wood-pile which rose waist high out of the snow. Slowly Lapierre bent backward, forced by the heavier body of MacNair. MacNair released his grip on the other's wrist, but his right hand still held Lapierre's gun. A huge forearm slid up the quarter-breed's chest and came to rest under the chin, while the man beat frantically with his two fists against MacNair's shoulders and ribs.

He stared wildly into MacNair's eyes—eyes that glowed with a greenish hate-glare like the night-eyes of the wolf. Backward and yet backward the man bent until it seemed that his spine must snap. His clenched fists ceased to beat futilely against the huge shoulders of his opponent, and he clawed frantically at the snow that hung in a miniature cornice along the edge of the wood-pile.

Chloe crowded close, shoving the Indians aside. There was a swift movement near her. The Louchoux girl forced past and leaped lightly to the top of the wood-pile, where she knelt close, staring downward with hard, burning eyes into the up-turned face of Lapierre.

The man could bend no farther now, his shoulders were imbedded in the snow and the back of his head was buried to the ears. His chest heaved spasmodically as he gasped for air, and the thin breath whined through his teeth. His lips turned greyish-blue and swelled thick, like strips of blistered rubber, and his eyes rolled upward until they looked like the sightless eyes of the blind. The blue-grey lips writhed spasmodically. He tried to cry out, but the sound died in a horrible throaty gurgle.

Slowly, MacNair raised his gun—Lapierre's own gun that he had wrenched, bare-handed from his grasp. Raised it until the muzzle reached the level of Lapierre's eyes. Chloe had stared wide-eyed throughout the whole proceeding. Gazing in fascination at the slow deliberateness of the terrible ordeal.

As the muzzle of the gun came to rest between Lapierre's eyes the girl sprang to MacNair's side. "Don't! Oh, don't kill him!" Her voice rose almost to a shriek. "Don't kill him—for my sake!"

The muzzle of the gun lowered and without releasing an

ounce of pressure upon the grip-locked body of the man, MacNair slowly turned his eyes to meet the eyes of the girl. Never in her life had she looked into eyes like that—eyes that gleamed and stabbed, and burned with a terrible pent-up emotion. The eyes of Tiger Elliston, intensified a hundredfold! And then MacNair's lips moved and his voice came low but distinctly and with terrible hardness.

"I am not going to kill him," he said, "but, by God! He will wish I had! I hope he will live to be an old, old man. To the day of his death he will carry my mark. Bone-deep he will carry the scar of the gun-brand! The cross of the curse of Cain!"

MacNair turned from the girl and again the gun crept slowly upward. The quarter-breed had heard the words. With a mighty effort he filled his lungs and from between the blue-grey lips sang a wild, shrill scream of abysmal soul-terror. Chloe Elliston's heart went sick at the cry, which rang in her ears as the very epitome of mortal agony. She felt her knees grow weak and she glanced at the Louchoux girl, who knelt close, still staring into the upturned face, the while her red lips smiled.

Closer, and closer crowded the Indians. MacNair deliberately reversed the gun, his huge fist still gripping the butt. The top of the barrel was turned downward, and the sight bit deep into the skin at the roots of the hair on Lapierre's temple. Deeper and deeper sank the sight. MacNair's fingers tightened their grip until the knuckles whitened and a huge shoulder hunched to throw its weight upon the arm.

Slowly, very slowly, the sight moved across the upturned brow, tearing the flesh, rolling up the skin before its dull, broad edge. The quarter-breed's muscles strained and his legs twined spasmodically about the legs of MacNair, while his fingers tore through the snow and clawed at the bark of the wood-pile. Deliberately, the gun-sight ripped and tore across the forehead—grooving the bone. The wide scar showed raw and red, and in spots the skull flashed white. The broad line lost itself in the hair upon the opposite temple.

Again MacNair buried the sight, this time among the hair roots of the median line. Once more the gun began its slow journey, travelling downward, crossing the lateral scar with a ragged tear. Once more the flesh and skin ripped and rolled before the unfaltering sight and gathered upon the edges of the wound in ragged, tight-rolled knots and shreds that would later heal into snaggy, rough excrescences, grey, like the unclean dregs of a slag-pot.

A thin trickle of blood followed slowly along the groove. The gun-sight was almost between the man's eyes, when, with a scream, Chloe sprang forward and clutched MacNair's arm in both her hands.

"You brute!" she cried. "You inhuman brute! *I hate you*!"

MacNair answered never a word. With a sweep of his arm he flung her from him. She spun dizzily and fell in a heap on the snow. Once more the gun-sight rested deep against the bone at the point of its interruption. Once more it began its inexorable advance, creeping down between the eyes and along the bridge of the nose. Cartilage split wide, the upper lip was cleft, and the steel clicked sharply against blood-dripping teeth.

Then MacNair stood erect and gazed with approval upon his handiwork. His glance swept the lake, and suddenly his shoulders stiffened as he scrutinized several moving figures that approached across the level surface of the snow. Striding swiftly to the edge of the plateau, he shaded his eyes with his hand and gazed long and earnestly toward the approaching figures. Then he returned to Lapierre. The man had stood the terrible ordeal without losing consciousness. Reaching down, MacNair seized him by the collar, and jerking him to his feet, half dragged him to the rim of the plateau.

"Look!" he cried savagely. "Yonder, comes LeFroy—and with him are the men of the Mounted."

Lapierre stared dumbly. His thin hand twitched nervously, and his fists clasped and unclasped as the palms grew wet with sweat.

MacNair gripped his shoulder and twisted him about his tracks. Slow seconds passed as the two men stood facing each other there in the snow, and then, slowly, MacNair raised his hand and pointed toward the forest—toward the depths of the black spruce swamp.

"Go!" he roared. "Damn you! Go hunt your kind! I did not brand you to delight the eyes of prison guards. Go, mingle with free men, that they may see—and be warned!"

With one last glance toward the approaching figures, Pierre Lapierre glided swiftly to the foot of the stockade, mounted the firing ledge, and swung himself over the wall.

Bob MacNair watched the form of the quarter-breed disappear from sight and then, tossing the gun into the snow, turned to Chloe Elliston. Straight toward the girl he advanced with long, swinging strides. There was no hesitancy, no indecision in the free swing of the shoulders, nor did his steps once falter, nor the eyes that bored deep into hers waver for a single instant. And as the girl faced him a sudden sense of helplessness overwhelmed her.

On he came—this big man of the North; this man who

trampled rough-shod the conventions, even the laws of men. The man who could fight, and kill, and maim, in defence of his principles. Whose hand was heavy upon the evil-doer. A man whose finer sensibilities, despite their rough environment, could rise to a complete mastery of him. Inherently a fighting man. A man whose great starved heart had never known a woman's love.

Instinctively, she drew back from him and closed her eyes. And then she knew that he was standing still before her—very close—for she could hear distinctly the sound of his breathing. Without seeing she knew that he was looking into her face with those piercing, boring, steel-grey eyes. She waited for what seemed ages for him to speak, but he stood before her—silent.

"He is rough and uncouth and brutal. He hurled you spinning into the snow," whispered an inner voice.

"Yes, strong and brutal and good!" answered her heart.

Chloe opened her eyes. MacNair stood before her in all his bigness. She gazed at him wide-eyed. He was fumbling his Stetson in his hand, and she noticed the long hair was pushed back from his broad brow. The blood rushed into the girl's face. Her fists clenched tight, and she took a swift step forward.

"Bob MacNair! *Put on your hat*!"

A puzzled look crept into the man's eyes, his face flushed like the face of a schoolboy who had been caught in a foolish prank, and he returned the hat awkwardly to his head.

"I thought—that is—you wrote in the letter, here—" he paused as his fingers groped at the pocket of his shirt.

Chloe interrupted him. "If any man ever takes his Stetson off to me again I'll—I'll *hate* him!"

Bob MacNair stared down upon the belligerent figure before him. He noticed the clenched fists, the defiant tilt of the shoulders, the unconscious out-thrust of the chin—and then his eyes met squarely the flashing eyes of the girl.

For a long, long time he gazed into the depths of the upturned eyes, and then, either the significance of her words dawned suddenly upon him, or he read in that long glance the wondrous message of her love. With a low, glad cry he sprang to her and gathered her into his great, strong arms and pressed her lithe, pliant body close against his pounding heart, while through his veins swept the wild, fierce joy of a mighty passion. Bob MacNair had come into his own!

There was a lively commotion among the Indians, and MacNair raised his head to meet the gaze of LeFroy and Constable Craig and two others of the men of the Mounted.

"Where is Lapierre?" asked the constable.

Chloe struggled in confusion to release herself from the encircling arms, but the arms closed the tighter, and with a final sigh of surrender the girl ceased her puny struggles.

Constable Craig's lips twitched in a suppressed smile. "Ripley was right," he muttered to himself as he awaited MacNair's reply. "They have found each other at last."

And then the answer came. MacNair stared straight into the officer's eyes, and his words rang with a terrible meaning.

"Lapierre," he said, "has gone away from here. If you see him again you shall never forget him." His eyes returned to the girl, close-held against his heart. Her two arms stole upward until the slender hands closed about his neck. Her lips moved, and he bent to catch the words.

"I love you," she faltered, and glancing shyly, almost timidly into his face, encountered there the look she had come to know so well—the suspicion of a smile upon the lips and just the shadow of a twinkle playing in the deep-set eyes. She repeated, softly, the words that rang through her brain: "I love you—*Brute MacNair*!"

Choose from Thousands of 1stWorldLibrary Classics By

A. M. Barnard
Ada Leverson
Adolphus William Ward
Aesop
Agatha Christie
Alexander Aaronsohn
Alexander Kielland
Alexandre Dumas
Alfred Gatty
Alfred Ollivant
Alice Duer Miller
Alice Turner Curtis
Alice Dunbar
Allen Chapman
Alleyne Ireland
Ambrose Bierce
Amelia E. Barr
Amory H. Bradford
Andrew Lang
Andrew McFarland Davis
Andy Adams
Angela Brazil
Anna Alice Chapin
Anna Sewell
Annie Besant
Annie Hamilton Donnell
Annie Payson Call
Annie Roe Carr
Annonaymous
Anton Chekhov
Archibald Lee Fletcher
Arnold Bennett
Arthur C. Benson
Arthur Conan Doyle
Arthur M. Winfield
Arthur Ransome
Arthur Schnitzler
Arthur Train
Atticus
B.H. Baden-Powell
B. M. Bower
B. C. Chatterjee
Baroness Emmuska Orczy
Baroness Orczy
Basil King
Bayard Taylor
Ben Macomber
Bertha Muzzy Bower
Bjornstjerne Bjornson
Booth Tarkington
Boyd Cable
Bram Stoker
C. Collodi
C. E. Orr
C. M. Ingleby
Carolyn Wells
Catherine Parr Traill
Charles A. Eastman
Charles Amory Beach
Charles Dickens
Charles Dudley Warner
Charles Farrar Browne
Charles Ives
Charles Kingsley
Charles Klein
Charles Hanson Towne
Charles Lathrop Pack
Charles Romyn Dake
Charles Whibley
Charles Willing Beale
Charlotte M. Braeme
Charlotte M. Yonge
Charlotte Perkins Stetson
Clair W. Hayes
Clarence Day Jr.
Clarence E. Mulford
Clemence Housman
Confucius
Coningsby Dawson
Cornelis DeWitt Wilcox
Cyril Burleigh
D. H. Lawrence
Daniel Defoe
David Garnett
Dinah Craik
Don Carlos Janes
Donald Keyhoe
Dorothy Kilner
Dougan Clark
Douglas Fairbanks
E. Nesbit
E. P. Roe
E. Phillips Oppenheim
E. S. Brooks
Earl Barnes
Edgar Rice Burroughs
Edith Van Dyne
Edith Wharton
Edward Everett Hale
Edward J. O'Biren
Edward S. Ellis
Edwin L. Arnold
Eleanor Atkins
Eleanor Hallowell Abbott
Eliot Gregory
Elizabeth Gaskell
Elizabeth McCracken
Elizabeth Von Arnim
Ellem Key
Emerson Hough
Emilie F. Carlen
Emily Bronte
Emily Dickinson
Enid Bagnold
Enilor Macartney Lane
Erasmus W. Jones
Ernie Howard Pie
Ethel May Dell
Ethel Turner
Ethel Watts Mumford
Eugene Sue
Eugenie Foa
Eugene Wood
Eustace Hale Ball
Evelyn Everett-green
Everard Cotes
F. H. Cheley
F. J. Cross
F. Marion Crawford
Fannie E. Newberry
Federick Austin Ogg
Ferdinand Ossendowski
Fergus Hume
Florence A. Kilpatrick
Fremont B. Deering
Francis Bacon
Francis Darwin
Frances Hodgson Burnett
Frances Parkinson Keyes
Frank Gee Patchin
Frank Harris
Frank Jewett Mather
Frank L. Packard
Frank V. Webster
Frederic Stewart Isham
Frederick Trevor Hill
Frederick Winslow Taylor

Friedrich Kerst
Friedrich Nietzsche
Fyodor Dostoyevsky
G.A. Henty
G.K. Chesterton
Gabrielle E. Jackson
Garrett P. Serviss
Gaston Leroux
George A. Warren
George Ade
Geroge Bernard Shaw
George Cary Eggleston
George Durston
George Ebers
George Eliot
George Gissing
George MacDonald
George Meredith
George Orwell
George Sylvester Viereck
George Tucker
George W. Cable
George Wharton James
Gertrude Atherton
Gordon Casserly
Grace E. King
Grace Gallatin
Grace Greenwood
Grant Allen
Guillermo A. Sherwell
Gulielma Zollinger
Gustav Flaubert
H. A. Cody
H. B. Irving
H.C. Bailey
H. G. Wells
H. H. Munro
H. Irving Hancock
H. R. Naylor
H. Rider Haggard
H. W. C. Davis
Haldeman Julius
Hall Caine
Hamilton Wright Mabie
Hans Christian Andersen
Harold Avery
Harold McGrath
Harriet Beecher Stowe
Harry Castlemon
Harry Coghill
Harry Houidini
Hayden Carruth
Helent Hunt Jackson
Helen Nicolay
Hendrik Conscience
Hendy David Thoreau
Henri Barbusse
Henrik Ibsen
Henry Adams
Henry Ford
Henry Frost
Henry James
Henry Jones Ford
Henry Seton Merriman
Henry W Longfellow
Herbert A. Giles
Herbert Carter
Herbert N. Casson
Herman Hesse
Hildegard G. Frey
Homer
Honore De Balzac
Horace B. Day
Horace Walpole
Horatio Alger Jr.
Howard Pyle
Howard R. Garis
Hugh Lofting
Hugh Walpole
Humphry Ward
Ian Maclaren
Inez Haynes Gillmore
Irving Bacheller
Isabel Cecilia Williams
Isabel Hornibrook
Israel Abrahams
Ivan Turgenev
J.G.Austin
J. Henri Fabre
J. M. Barrie
J. M. Walsh
J. Macdonald Oxley
J. R. Miller
J. S. Fletcher
J. S. Knowles
J. Storer Clouston
J. W. Duffield
Jack London
Jacob Abbott
James Allen
James Andrews
James Baldwin
James Branch Cabell
James DeMille
James Joyce
James Lane Allen
James Lane Allen
James Oliver Curwood
James Oppenheim
James Otis
James R. Driscoll
Jane Abbott
Jane Austen
Jane L. Stewart
Janet Aldridge
Jens Peter Jacobsen
Jerome K. Jerome
Jessie Graham Flower
John Buchan
John Burroughs
John Cournos
John F. Kennedy
John Gay
John Glasworthy
John Habberton
John Joy Bell
John Kendrick Bangs
John Milton
John Philip Sousa
John Taintor Foote
Jonas Lauritz Idemil Lie
Jonathan Swift
Joseph A. Altsheler
Joseph Carey
Joseph Conrad
Joseph E. Badger Jr
Joseph Hergesheimer
Joseph Jacobs
Jules Vernes
Julian Hawthrone
Julie A Lippmann
Justin Huntly McCarthy
Kakuzo Okakura
Karle Wilson Baker
Kate Chopin
Kenneth Grahame
Kenneth McGaffey
Kate Langley Bosher
Kate Langley Bosher
Katherine Cecil Thurston
Katherine Stokes
L. A. Abbot
L. T. Meade

L. Frank Baum
Latta Griswold
Laura Dent Crane
Laura Lee Hope
Laurence Housman
Lawrence Beasley
Leo Tolstoy
Leonid Andreyev
Lewis Carroll
Lewis Sperry Chafer
Lilian Bell
Lloyd Osbourne
Louis Hughes
Louis Joseph Vance
Louis Tracy
Louisa May Alcott
Lucy Fitch Perkins
Lucy Maud Montgomery
Luther Benson
Lydia Miller Middleton
Lyndon Orr
M. Corvus
M. H. Adams
Margaret E. Sangster
Margret Howth
Margaret Vandercook
Margaret W. Hungerford
Margret Penrose
Maria Edgeworth
Maria Thompson Daviess
Mariano Azuela
Marion Polk Angellotti
Mark Overton
Mark Twain
Mary Austin
Mary Catherine Crowley
Mary Cole
Mary Hastings Bradley
Mary Roberts Rinehart
Mary Rowlandson
M. Wollstonecraft Shelley
Maud Lindsay
Max Beerbohm
Myra Kelly
Nathaniel Hawthrone
Nicolo Machiavelli
O. F. Walton
Oscar Wilde
Owen Johnson
P.G. Wodehouse
Paul and Mabel Thorne
Paul G. Tomlinson
Paul Severing
Percy Brebner
Percy Keese Fitzhugh
Peter B. Kyne
Plato
Quincy Allen
R. Derby Holmes
R. L. Stevenson
R. S. Ball
Rabindranath Tagore
Rahul Alvares
Ralph Bonehill
Ralph Henry Barbour
Ralph Victor
Ralph Waldo Emmerson
Rene Descartes
Ray Cummings
Rex Beach
Rex E. Beach
Richard Harding Davis
Richard Jefferies
Richard Le Gallienne
Robert Barr
Robert Frost
Robert Gordon Anderson
Robert L. Drake
Robert Lansing
Robert Lynd
Robert Michael Ballantyne
Robert W. Chambers
Rosa Nouchette Carey
Rudyard Kipling
Saint Augustine
Samuel B. Allison
Samuel Hopkins Adams
Sarah Bernhardt
Sarah C. Hallowell
Selma Lagerlof
Sherwood Anderson
Sigmund Freud
Standish O'Grady
Stanley Weyman
Stella Benson
Stella M. Francis
Stephen Crane
Stewart Edward White
Stijn Streuvels
Swami Abhedananda
Swami Parmananda
T. S. Ackland
T. S. Arthur
The Princess Der Ling
Thomas A. Janvier
Thomas A Kempis
Thomas Anderton
Thomas Bailey Aldrich
Thomas Bulfinch
Thomas De Quincey
Thomas Dixon
Thomas H. Huxley
Thomas Hardy
Thomas More
Thornton W. Burgess
U. S. Grant
Upton Sinclair
Valentine Williams
Various Authors
Vaughan Kester
Victor Appleton
Victor G. Durham
Victoria Cross
Virginia Woolf
Wadsworth Camp
Walter Camp
Walter Scott
Washington Irving
Wilbur Lawton
Wilkie Collins
Willa Cather
Willard F. Baker
William Dean Howells
William le Queux
W. Makepeace Thackeray
William W. Walter
William Shakespeare
Winston Churchill
Yei Theodora Ozaki
Yogi Ramacharaka
Young E. Allison
Zane Grey

www.ingramcontent.com/pod-product-compliance
Ingram Content Group UK Ltd.
Pitfield, Milton Keynes, MK11 3LW, UK
UKHW041842190726
13854UKWH00002B/678